continued . . .

Also by Michelle Rowen

Immortality Bites Mysteries
BLOOD BATH & BEYOND
BLED & BREAKFAST

Berkley Sensation Titles
THE DEMON IN ME
SOMETHING WICKED
THAT OLD BLACK MAGIC
NIGHTSHADE
BLOODLUST

Anthologies
PRIMAL
(with Lora Leigh, Jory Strong, and Ava Gray)

FROM FEAR
TO ETERNITY

AN IMMORTALITY BITES MYSTERY

MICHELLE ROWEN

AN OBSIDIAN MYSTERY

OBSIDIAN
Published by the Penguin Group
Penguin Group (USA) LLC, 375 Hudson Street,
New York, New York 10014

USA | Canada | UK | Ireland | Australia | New Zealand | India | South Africa | China
penguin.com
A Penguin Random House Company

First published by Obsidian, an imprint of New American Library,
a division of Penguin Group (USA) LLC

First Printing, July 2014

ISBN 978-0-451-46613-6

Printed in the United States of America
10 9 8 7 6 5 4 3 2 1

PUBLISHER'S NOTE
This is a work of fiction. Names, characters, places, and incidents either are the
product of the author's imagination or are used fictitiously, and any resemblance to
actual persons, living or dead, business establishments, events, or locales is entirely
coincidental.

For my Mother,
who loves mysteries
(even the ones with fangs and wackiness).
I love you!

Acknowledgments

Sarah Dearly was the heroine of my very first published novel, and now she's the heroine of my latest. We've spent a decade together, both of us—author and character—growing and changing. (For the better, I'd like to think!) It's been a wonderful experience to write seven books that have starred Sarah, including three super-fun paranormal mysteries that have followed Sarah and Thierry after their initial "happily ever after." I had a gut feeling my sarcastic little fledgling vampire would embrace the challenge of solving mysteries. And she certainly has!

My deepest gratitude goes to my readers who have followed Sarah's adventures over the years and have remained enthusiastic to read more. *Fangs* very much to each and every one of you! You're *fangtastic*! I sincerely hope you enjoy *From Fear to Eternity*!

Chapter 1

Less than twenty-four hours ago, a mysterious invitation arrived in my husband's e-mail in-box from an anonymous sender.

> To Thierry de Bennicoeur,
>
> I have something you've wanted for more than three centuries.
>   Bid enough at my auction and it can finally be yours.
>
>   —An old friend

The invitation had a date—*today*; a time—*nine o'clock*; and a location—*Beverly Hills, California*.

And here we were.

With uneasiness, I eyed the massive mansion at the end of the long, winding driveway as our taxi drove off into the darkness.

"I don't feel good about this. We shouldn't have come here." My comment earned me the edge of a smile from Thierry. "What? Why is that funny?"

"It's only that you're suddenly the cautious one."

"I'm always cautious."

This earned a full-on look from him. "Always?"

"Look 'cautious' up in a dictionary and you'll see my picture. Also look up 'tentative' and 'wary.' It's a full photo spread. More of a collage, really."

"I think I must have left my real wife back in Hawaii. Who are you and what have you done with the delightfully reckless Sarah Dearly?"

When he got sarcastic, I knew I was in trouble. That was my specialty, not his.

"Sarah Dearly's been body-snatched by a much more paranoid alien. What is this place, Thierry? Who invited you? And, most importantly, when can we leave?"

"As soon as I get some answers."

But that wasn't nearly soon enough for me.

Until yesterday, I'd experienced the most amazing three weeks of my entire life in Maui on our honeymoon, which included beautiful beaches, shady cabanas (vampires don't burn up in the sun, but we will easily acquire nasty sunburns), all the fruity cocktails I could drink (I couldn't deal with solid food anymore, but alcoholic beverages were still a-okay), a luxurious private house overlooking the ocean, an overabundance of fabulous shops to explore, and spending one-on-one time with my gorgeous, if enigmatic, husband. I hadn't wanted it ever to end.

But, as the saying goes about all good things . . .

I honestly didn't think he would have been tempted to leave either if it hadn't been for that tantalizing personal message.

I have something you've wanted for more than three centuries.

Bid enough at my auction and it can finally be yours.

"You really think it's the amulet?" I whispered as we stood in front of the mansion. It wasn't the first time I'd said this to him since last night.

"There's only one way to find out."

He'd said I didn't have to come with him—that he would return as soon as he could. I hated flying. Being five miles up in the air, trapped inside a metal coffin of death was not fun times for me.

But I'd insisted. And here we were, all in pursuit of something that most believed had been destroyed centuries ago.

Back then, Thierry had grown bored with his already lengthy immortal life and had begun collecting expensive, magical, and sometimes deadly objects to pass the time. Enter the amulet. It allegedly contained a djinn—aka a genie. A djinn is a kind of demon that will grant the wishes of its master. And its master would be anyone who possessed the amulet.

I dug my nails into the sleeve of his black suit jacket as we approached the large red front door at the top of seven marble steps. Thierry wore a tailored Hugo Boss suit—as per his usual wardrobe. Tonight I'd chosen a red dress, which was cut low on the top and above the knee on the bottom, but it also had pockets—a perfect combo of style and comfort. The best of both worlds.

The full moon sat high in the night sky, the air even warmer than it had been in Hawaii.

"Why do you still want something like this?" I asked as I eyed the door with trepidation.

"It bothers you, doesn't it?"

"That you're so motivated by the possibility of getting your hands on something potentially dangerous and destructive? Maybe a little."

"Please try to give me the benefit of the doubt, Sarah. There is more to this evening than a shiny prize."

"If you say so." There wasn't time for prying, but if there *was* more to this evening, he'd neglected to fill me in on any other sordid details.

Knowing Thierry's tendency for secret keeping, I wasn't all that surprised. He didn't even do it on purpose; it had just become ingrained in him over time. At well over six hundred years old, he was the very definition of that old dog you just couldn't teach too many new tricks to—not that many old dogs would ever look as good as Thierry did. But I digress.

He had his secrets. Most of them I didn't need to know, so it didn't bother me that he kept them close to his chest. Well, it didn't bother me *too* much.

I hooked my arm through his as we entered the front doors and walked into the foyer of a house that looked like a cross between something out of the movie *Spartacus* and the Playboy Mansion. Expansive black marble floors. Thick Roman columns. A massive crystal chandelier hanging above our heads. On our right, twisting upward to the second floor, a winding staircase with gold railings that looked like something out of a big-budget movie.

I took it all in. "Wow. Welcome to *Lifestyles of the Rich and Snotty*."

"Yes, welcome," a handsome, dark-haired, tuxedoed man echoed. He made me jump since he seemingly appeared out of nowhere.

"Are you the host of this evening?" Thierry asked.

"No. I am Thomas, the butler. And you are?"

"Thierry de Bennicoeur. And this is my wife, Sarah."

Thomas nodded with approval, as if he had the guest list memorized. "Welcome. Your host will be joining you shortly, and the auction will begin soon after that. Please join the others in the parlor and enjoy some hors d'oeuvres and champagne until then."

Thierry's cool, appraising gaze swept the foyer. "And who might our host be?"

"Your questions will be answered in due time, sir. The parlor is just ahead through those doors." The butler gestured to our left with a white-gloved hand.

He moved away without another word.

"Mysterious host," I said. "Ominous mansion. Creepy butler who looks more like a male model than any butler I've ever seen before. An invitation with dubious intentions. But it is nice to know there's free champagne to look forward to."

"I knew you'd find the bright side to all of this."

There had to be a bright side, right? If so, then why was I so nervous about being here? "Promise me you're not going to do anything crazy tonight."

Thierry gave me a pointed look. "I don't do crazy, Sarah."

"Debatable. But okay."

If the foyer looked like Hugh Hefner visits Rome, the parlor was much more *Pride and Prejudice*. I swear, upon entering the room, I felt as if we'd stepped back in time.

There were at least twenty guests milling about and chatting with one another. As a pretty blond server in a chic black-and-white dress walked by, I snatched a flute of champagne off her tray and took a deep sip.

"Sir?" the server said to Thierry. "Would you like one as well?"

"I'd prefer a cranberry juice."

"Of course, sir. I'll be back in just a moment." She moved toward a door at the back of the room.

Thierry's gaze cut across the crowd, and his expression darkened. "I recognize several of the invited guests."

"You do?" At first glance, everyone was a stranger to me. But when you had been around as long as Thierry, your acquaintance list got a bit long in the fang. "Like who?"

His attention was fixed on a man on the other side of the room, thirtyish in appearance, who had black hair pulled back in a neat ponytail at the nape of his neck, dark brown eyes, and deeply tanned skin. His suit was black, like Thierry's, but the shirt beneath was light blue. Very expensive, though—the guy dripped money. If there was one talent I had, it was picking out designer threads at a distance.

"That is Atticus Kincade. He's the current head elder of the Ring."

A breath caught in my chest. "The *head* elder? I thought elders were all created equal."

"No. The others take direction from Atticus. Currently, he's the one with the power to make the ultimate decisions."

Which meant he was Thierry's boss—the leader of the vampire council known as the Ring. Thierry recently took a job with them as a consultant, a traveling investigator who looked into vampiric problems of all shapes and sizes as they arose; problems the council deemed dangerous or unsavory when it came to protecting the rest of the world from the secret that vampires existed and we very rarely sparkled.

I knew there was no love lost between Thierry and the vampire council. He hadn't exactly accepted this job because he relished the chance to sign fifty years of his life away—a standard employment contract of theirs—literally in blood.

They'd applied duress to get him to sign. He hadn't told me outright what they'd used as leverage to force a master vampire to agree to something he initially didn't want to do. But I knew. And he knew I knew.

For now, that was enough.

"They must have been right," Thierry said under his breath.

"Right about what?"

He shook his head. "It's nothing."

"Thierry . . . what's going on?"

His jaw tightened and he finally tore his gaze from Atticus to meet mine. "Remember what I said about the benefit of the doubt?"

"No questions?"

"Not yet."

"How about just one more? You're not surprised to see him here, are you?"

"No, I'm not surprised at all."

I took another sip of my champagne. "Benefit of the doubt invoked. But know this is a limited time offer. Got it?"

He nodded once. "Understood."

When it came right down to Thierry and his secrets, the thing was, I trusted him. And if it was something I needed to know, I knew he'd tell me.

But still. When he didn't disclose everything to me immediately, it was extremely unnerving. Especially since I knew that the elders were very unpleasant people who liked using intimidation and threats to get what they wanted. Another faction of the council were enforcers—the on-call assassins who the elders would use to take care of any pesky problem. Permanently. Judge, jury, executioners. It was a one-stop shop.

These were definitely not vampires I wanted to find myself on the bad side of. And one of them— apparently the most powerful one—was here tonight in the flesh.

Benefit of the doubt. Fine. I would try my best to be patient.

Another person who caught my eye was standing near Atticus, who was currently talking to a half dozen other guests. "Is that . . . No, it couldn't be. Wait. . . . Is that Tasha Evans?"

Thierry followed the direction of my gaze. "It is."

"Tasha Evans *here*?"

Color me starstruck. Tasha Evans was a stunningly gorgeous redheaded movie star infamous for her many tattoos, her two Academy Awards, and her long list of relationships with some of the hottest lead actors in Hollywood. Back when I wanted to be an actress, I aspired to be just like her.

I was a *total* fangirl.

"I'm not surprised she received an invitation to an auction like this," Thierry said. "I've heard rumors in the vampire community that she's an avid collector of supernatural items."

I tore my attention away from the actress to stare at Thierry. "Whoa. Are you saying that Tasha Evans is a *vampire*?"

He nodded. "She is indeed."

Come to think of it, she really hadn't aged a day in twenty years. All this time, I'd just assumed she had a fantastic plastic surgeon.

The tabloids would *love* this little piece of gossip.

"I see the Darks are here as well." Thierry's words

were now coated in a layer of disapproval. "Frederic and Anna Dark, the couple to your left in the corner looking deeply morose."

I glanced over where he gestured to see two people with impossibly pale skin, pitch-black hair, and black eyes. They wore black from head to toe to finish the monochromatic look.

"They're rather . . . dramatic." They were the physical representation of what most people expected when you said "vampire." Very Goth, very pale. And they were immersed in some deep conversation with each other as they ignored the rest of the cocktail party.

Thierry's gaze didn't shift from the couple. "They are part of a faction of vampires who consider themselves purified. They like to avoid the sunlight completely, they sleep in coffins, and they only go out at night. They would never consider drinking animal blood or the synthetic concoctions. In fact, to drink blood except from the vein is appalling to them. For them, vampirism is a religion and they'd prefer if all other vampires worshipped as they do."

I couldn't help but grimace at the picture he painted of the couple. "I'll pass, thanks."

The server returned with a tray of champagne and one highball glass filled with cranberry juice. Thierry thanked her as he took it off the tray and handed me a fresh flute of the bubbly.

"Should we make a toast?" he asked.

"Sure. Here's to having this night end without any unpleasantness."

"That's not a toast. That's wishful thinking."

"Wishful drinking, really. Cheers." I clinked my glass with his, and then something caught my eye—a woman who'd just walked into the room. For a moment, I forgot to breathe. "Thierry. You will not believe who's here."

His dark brows rose with curiosity, and he turned to look as I swallowed down the entire glass of champagne in one gulp.

"This is rather unexpected," Thierry said under his breath.

That was an understatement if ever I'd heard one.

"My dear Sarah! My darling Thierry!" She made a beeline toward us and clasped my face between her hands before kissing me noisily on both cheeks. Then she did the same to Thierry. "What a wonderful surprise to see you both. It's been much too long!"

She rivaled Tasha for being the most beautiful in the room. Where Tasha was fiery elegance, this woman was raven-haired, couture-styled, Louboutin-pumped, with the face of an angel and the body of a lingerie model. She wore a black dress that fit her like a second skin while still looking utterly and flawlessly elegant.

It was Thierry's ex-wife.

"Veronique." A smile—which looked more like a grimace—drew Thierry's upper lip back from his teeth. "You look as lovely as always."

"I do try." She flashed me a killer smile. "As does your darling little girlfriend."

"Wife," Thierry corrected. "Sarah and I were married almost a month ago."

"Married?" Veronique's look of shock at this announcement was very nearly comical.

Veronique and I were already well acquainted. We'd met back when Thierry was still married to her, though estranged. She was not only his ex-wife, but also his sire—the one who'd turned him into a vampire in the first place. They'd met during the Black Death plague in Europe six and a half centuries ago and had been together on and off ever since.

I still didn't think Veronique had gotten over her shock that her husband's brief "fling" (as she'd once called it) had turned into something way more than either of us could have predicted. Not that she really cared either way. If there had been any real love in their marriage, it had died around the same time as Shakespeare.

"Well," she said, clearly taken aback by this announcement. "Congratulations to both of you. How wonderful."

Thierry met my gaze and slid his arm around my waist to draw me closer to his side before returning his attention to her. "Thank you. We're very happy."

"Happy?" She raised a perfectly shaped eyebrow. "I had no idea you were capable of that particular emotion, Thierry."

"No. You wouldn't."

I decided to cut in with a smile. "It's really great to see you again, Veronique. I mean that. And it hasn't been *that* long. Only a few months."

"Long enough for major life-altering events to occur. Goodness, my dear. Married! To my husband!"

"*Ex*-husband."

"Of course." Her red-glossed lips curved. "Jacob, darling, please join us." She beckoned to a man in a gray pin-striped suit. "I must introduce you to a couple dear friends of mine."

The man's grin had a greasy quality to it, as if he'd had a few too many drinks already. He was in his fifties and had hair that was thinning enough that he'd attempted a comb-over to camouflage it. "Veronique, my sweet, any friends of yours are certainly friends of mine."

"This is Sarah Dearly and my former husband, Thierry de Bennicoeur. Sarah and Thierry, this is Jacob Nelson, my beau."

"Charmed, charmed. Yes, I definitely recognize the name. Very clever, Veronique!" Jacob enthusiastically clasped both of our hands in turn. "Are you looking forward to the auction?"

"I am," Thierry said. "Although I'm not yet clear about who sent the invitation."

"I have no idea who it might be, either," Veronique said. "Not that it really matters. We're here and it is set to be a lovely evening."

Debatable, I thought. *Definitely debatable.*

This evening would be lovely once we were finished here and on our way back to the hotel.

The guests talked and drank and nibbled at hors d'oeuvres delivered on trays by both the blond server and Thomas the butler. A grandfather clock in the far corner told me it was already quarter after nine. The auction was supposed to *start* at nine.

"Show them the book, my sweet," Jacob suggested with barely restrained glee.

"Oh, darling, I don't want to brag."

"You have every reason to brag. It's incredible. You're incredible, and everyone should know it."

I exchanged a wry look with Thierry. These were words Veronique would certainly appreciate, no matter who delivered them.

"What book?" I asked.

"Veronique's novel," Jacob said. "It came out yesterday, and with the pre-orders and Internet buzz I have every confidence that it will make a very strong showing on the *New York Times* list next week."

"You wrote a book?" Thierry asked, surprised. "I didn't even know you read books."

"There are many things you don't know about me, Thierry. Perhaps this is only one of them." Veronique shrugged an elegant bare shoulder. "What can I say? I was inspired to tell a fictional tale. It came out of me in a rush of creative magic, if you will. And before I knew it, I was finished. All I needed then was a publisher."

"And that's where I came in." Jacob's chest puffed out with pride. "Little did I know when I met Veronique that this beautiful woman had penned a page-turner that I had to get on the shelves in record time. And we succeeded, didn't we?"

"We certainly did. And I just happen to have a copy with me tonight." Veronique fished in her large Louis Vuitton bag and handed me a thick hardcover novel that had to be at least six hundred pages long. It weighed approximately the same as a phone book.

The cover featured an artfully photographed black silk scarf on a glossy red background. I stared at the title with disbelief. *"The Erotic Memoir of a Vampire."*

"Catchy, isn't it?" Jacob grinned. "Brilliant from cover to cover. And hot like you've never read before. My fingers are still singed from it! *Whew!* Thierry, you'll be pleased to know your name is utilized in many chapters. Quite an honor, don't you think?"

"Mmm. And this is a *novel*, you said?" Thierry gingerly took the book from me to glance at the back cover, which was a full-color photo of Veronique.

Jacob laughed. "Well, it's not a *real* memoir, of

course. After all, there are no such things as vampires."

Veronique patted his arm with the same affection she might offer a precocious toddler. "Of course there aren't, darling."

A seven-hundred-year-old vampire's new boyfriend didn't believe in vampires. *Okay.*

I took the book from Thierry and opened it to read the description on the cover flap. This "novel" was about a seven-centuries-old vampire and her many adventures, including those with her original sire, Marcellus, and also her equally ancient husband, Thierry.

You'd have thought she could have at least changed the names. But, no, of course not.

I grimaced. "Does this actually say 'tall, dark, and fangsome'?"

"You can have that copy, my dear," Veronique said. "I'll sign it for you later. Happy reading."

My very own copy of my husband's gorgeous first wife's erotic memoir, thinly disguised as fiction. Just what I'd always wanted.

I suddenly felt an intense desire to clear my head. "I think I need some ice for my drink. Very, very badly."

"Ice for champagne?" Thierry glanced at me with concern. "Are you all right?"

"Fine. Great. Um, if you'll excuse me. I'll be back in a minute."

I pulled away from him, tucked the book under my arm, and departed stage left.

"Excuse me!" I called after the blond server, but she slipped around a corner up ahead. Following her through another set of doors, I found myself in a huge, stainless-steel sea of a kitchen. Nobody was in there, and the blonde had already vanished.

At least I was away from the party.

I pressed my back against the wall and stared at the cover of the book again with dismay.

Was I crazy to let this bother me?

Yes.

Did it bother me anyway?

Uh-huh.

This book was concrete proof that Thierry had had a whole other life before he'd met me. And he kept his secrets close to his chest probably for a very good reason—because learning too many of them too quickly would mess me up, especially when they involved a long-term relationship with a beautiful woman who'd just given me a whole volume of proof that she had more in common with him than I ever would.

But that was then, and this was now. Despite our differences, what we had was real, and I knew it. I didn't question it anymore. Veronique didn't threaten my relationship with Thierry, and I wasn't jealous of her.

So why exactly was I freaking out?

It was a silly knee-jerk reaction. That was all. And it was passing as quickly as it had arrived, which was a major relief.

After a few more minutes, my head had cleared, and I felt way better. Since I'd come here to get some ice, I decided to follow through with that plan. I moved toward a large refrigerator and opened the top freezer section.

However, instead of ice cubes, the severed head of a man looked out at me.

My empty champagne glass fell from my grip, shattering against the ceramic tiles, and I clamped my hand over my mouth to keep from screaming at the sight before me.

A severed head. In the freezer.

And that wasn't even the freakiest thing about it.

A second later his eyes popped open.

"You!" he blurted. "You have to help me! I've been murdered!"

Chapter 2

Doing an uncanny impression of a bat out of Hell, I ran out of the kitchen and back to the party, scanning frantically to find someone to help—to find Thierry and tell him what I'd just seen.

A severed head.

A *talking* severed head!

"Darling," Veronique said as I zipped past her, "we really must catch up."

"Absolutely," I assured her. "Soon. Very soon."

Soon wasn't now. I didn't want to panic anyone about what I'd seen, but I knew Thierry would know what to do, what to say.

However, it was the strangest thing. With every step I took, the memory of what had happened in the kitchen faded. Faded.

Faded.

Until by the time I spotted Thierry it was like a wisp of smoke that had dissipated in the air. Gone.

Why had I felt the driving need to talk to him?

I had absolutely no idea.

Still, after setting Veronique's book down on the nearest table so I wouldn't have to keep carrying it, I followed him as he moved through an archway and out of the parlor, into the hall. He was with Atticus and they walked until they turned a corner and were out of sight, but I could still hear them.

"Why are you here, de Bennicoeur?" Atticus asked.

"I received an invitation which intrigued me. I assume the same happened for you."

They were calm questions and answers, but there was something in both of their tones that stopped me from marching right up to them. I stayed where I was, behind the corner, and considered going back to the parlor.

For some strange reason, my heart was pounding hard and fast like I'd just run a marathon. Maybe Veronique's book had upset me more than I thought it had.

"How long has it been since I last saw you?" Atticus asked Thierry. "Has it been a century already since you stepped down from your position with the council?"

"Approximately."

Small talk between two people who hadn't seen each other in ages. I wasn't going to eavesdrop any longer. I wasn't that rude.

Atticus's words held a light Mediterranean accent. Thierry had once spoken French, as well as many other languages over the years, but there wasn't a trace of an accent anymore when he spoke.

"How incredible that so much time has passed in the blink of an eye," Atticus said. "So much that I even forget why you stepped down as leader."

"I find it hard to believe that you don't remember."

"Ah, yes." There was now a smile in Atticus's voice. "Your very dangerous addiction is no longer as troublesome to you as it once was, I hope?"

"I have it under control."

"That's good to hear. I wouldn't want to have to mark you down as a danger."

"No, wouldn't want that."

"I'm sure you're rather angry with me," Atticus said when silence fell. "But I felt I had no choice in what I did."

"I disagree. There were plenty of other choices."

"You wouldn't have agreed to join our ranks again if pressure hadn't been applied."

So, the rude eavesdropping thing I wanted to stop? Scratch that. I was officially eavesdropping. The wall was cool against my palms as I pressed against it, straining to hear more of this enticing exchange.

"I didn't appreciate it, Atticus. I knew it came from you and not the others. And it wasn't even necessary. I was ready to return to the Ring without any ultimatums issued. I'd become extremely disenchanted with civilian life and needed a change, something to occupy my time for the indeterminate future."

"I'm so pleased it's all worked out for the best."

"Threatening Sarah, though, was excessive. Even for you."

I could barely believe what I was hearing. It had been a threat leveled specifically toward me that I knew had forced Thierry's hand in taking the position as consultant. He'd just refused to admit it to me in so many words.

Proof. Finally some proof!

Which didn't make me feel much better about the whole situation. But now I knew Atticus was the one directly to blame for it. I surely wouldn't underestimate him, but anger ignited in my chest at the thought that he would threaten me to try to control Thierry. This jerk didn't even know me.

"Unfortunately," Atticus said, "*excessive* is often what's required. I've heard that you're deeply smitten by your new bride." He chuckled softly. "Which, I have to admit, stuns me greatly. Thierry de Bennicoeur, enamored of a mere fledgling. I never would have guessed it. You fooled me."

"I fool many."

"She is a pretty little thing, I'll admit, but when I heard the news that you'd become seriously involved with her, I didn't believe it. I mean, knowing your previous views on romance."

"I didn't have any views on it at all."

"Exactly. You've changed."

"Perhaps not nearly as much as you might think." Thierry was now the one to laugh, but it was a sound that held very little humor. "Atticus, there was a time when you knew me very well. Do you honestly believe I could be so wholly taken in by a fledgling a fraction of my age with a temperament so completely different from my own?"

"You've changed your life for her. You've brought her along on two assignments so far. You married her."

"Sarah has certainly proven to be an amusement to me. But I've lived long enough to know that such amusements have short shelf lives. I choose to keep her nearby for as long as she entertains me with her starry-eyed views of the same world I've grown so jaded about. After that, I will move on. Which is why your threat against her was so ridiculous to me. Did you really think someone like her could mean enough to me that it would truly make any difference?"

"I wasn't sure."

"Had I not wanted to return to the fold, I would

have denied your request and not cared about the consequences. As it was, it amused me to make you believe you had that sort of power over me."

"I must say, it's an excellent charade."

"Thank you."

I didn't think I'd taken a breath in three whole minutes. My face had to be blue by now.

An entertaining, starry-eyed charade?

I moved closer to the corner and peeked around. Thierry's back was to me, with Atticus facing him, his expression impassive. No one else was in the hallway.

Thierry finally spoke again just as I began relearning how to breathe. "Are you enjoying your reign as head elder, Atticus?"

"Very much so." Atticus absently brushed his left sleeve, as if he'd noticed a microscopic piece of lint on it.

"You've heard what happened to the others."

Atticus looked up and narrowed his eyes. "Of course. However, I am surprised that news of this has reached you."

"I have my sources."

"As do we all."

"Are you concerned?" Thierry asked.

"For myself? Not particularly. You?"

"I have weathered many difficulties over the centuries. This threat—if that is what this is—is meaningless. Anyone with ill intentions would be wise to stay far away from me if they value their life."

Atticus smiled at this, a strangely cold expression. "Incredible, de Bennicoeur. If I hadn't seen you, I would have believed the rumors that you've softened. But you're every bit as ruthless as you ever were." There was admiration in his voice. "I think you shouldn't remain a consultant for long. Perhaps I want you back as an official elder, especially now that two positions have become available. How do you feel about that?"

Thierry was silent for a moment. "It's certainly worth further discussion."

"We'll speak again very soon."

"I look forward to it."

Atticus left Thierry and moved back toward the parlor. I retreated into the shadows and flattened myself against the wall. He didn't even notice me as he walked by. Atticus was a man who was so self-assured that it dripped from him like a waterfall of confidence.

I didn't like him in the slightest. For all his good looks, nice clothes, polished shoes, and shiny words, the man was a serious creep.

I turned to my right to check on Thierry, only to find him now leaning against the wall directly next to me.

I let out an involuntary yelp.

"Eavesdropping?" he asked.

"Maybe."

"Hear anything interesting?" He still held his highball glass loosely in his right hand.

My stomach was tied up in knots. I studied him for a moment, all the horrible things he'd said churning through my brain. "The benefit of the doubt we discussed earlier? The meter has officially expired."

"Yes, I'm sure that it has." He took my elbow and guided me farther down the hallway to put more distance between us and the parlor. We didn't pass any more servants; in fact the only ones I'd seen so far had been the butler and the blond woman serving drinks.

Thierry ushered me into a large room with a high ceiling, a long oak table in the center, and walls lined with bookshelves. The library. I eyed the books, not ready to give my full attention to Thierry quite yet.

"I already got my next reading material from Veronique," I said, my chest tight. "Although I think I'm going to wait for the movie."

"Sarah . . . look at me."

I turned to face him, my fists clenched at my sides so my nails bit into my palms. "What the hell is going on, Thierry?"

"You heard what I said to Atticus."

"About me being an amusement, one you fully anticipate will become less amusing in the near future. Kind of like a juggling monkey in a cute little red dress and high heels."

He regarded me with a familiar blank expression, so I continued. "That Atticus was the one responsible for threatening my life, making you agree to work for the Ring again. But that it wouldn't really matter, since fledglings like me are a dime a dozen and you're a coldhearted snake, which is totally cool with Atticus, and he's glad you aren't really taken by someone as naive and ridiculous as me."

"I don't believe I used the word 'naive' or 'ridiculous.' Nor did I compare you to a juggling monkey in any form of attire."

"It was implied."

Thierry glanced out the door as if checking for additional eavesdroppers, then closed it with a click. He turned to me, his expression completely unreadable.

"What I said to Atticus about you—" he began.

"Was a lie," I finished.

He regarded me with surprise. "You believe I was lying?"

"Of course I do."

His gray eyes, before so blank, now held deep relief. "Considering how dismayed you looked a moment ago, you sound so certain of this."

"It wasn't fun to hear, no matter why you said it. I'm assuming you were playing him for some reason, but please let me know if I'm wrong about that. I'd really like a heads-up."

A smile had grown on his face during my little speech. "Do you have any idea how much I adore you?"

I just glared at him. "Prove it."

He gently grasped my chin and bent forward to brush his lips against mine. When I didn't kiss him in return, he leaned back and raised an eyebrow.

"Prove it," I repeated, "by telling me the truth. Right here, and right now. Benefit of the doubt, Thierry. Tick-tock."

"Very well." His expression finally sobered as he placed his empty glass on a nearby shelf. "We are here tonight because I received an invitation to this auction from an anonymous sender, but also because Atticus Kincade received an identical invitation. I wasn't absolutely certain he would be in attendance, which is why I hesitated in sharing this information with you."

"Go on."

"If you were listening closely, you would have heard me mention a recent development within the council. Two elders who held positions just below Atticus were murdered in the past two months. They were part of the original group who founded the Ring."

"They were murdered?" I blinked, alarmed by his words. "You're the one who founded the Ring in the first place—you must have chosen them."

"Yes, that's right."

"Does that mean you might be at risk, too?"

"It's possible," he allowed. His gaze scanned the shelves nearby before returning to me. "I was contacted by lower-ranking elders yesterday who wanted me to come here, to reacquaint myself with Atticus so I could acquire more information which could help in their investigation."

Something horrible occurred to me. "They think Atticus is the murderer, don't they?"

He hesitated for only a second. "Yes."

My heart started pounding harder. "So it's possible that you're currently under the same roof as somebody who wants to kill you next."

"I'm not convinced I'm on his list of potential victims. I no longer hold any true power within the council. As consultant, I'm not a threat to him."

"But you founded the Ring and you left it of your own free will. If you really wanted to, you could challenge him for his position as leader, couldn't you?"

His lips thinned, which was enough of a confirmation for me.

I'd known since we arrived that this was a bad place to be. Call it vampire intuition—paranoia now with evidence to back it up. "We need to leave."

"We can't do that. Not yet."

"Why?"

"The others believe Atticus wants the amulet. If it is here tonight they want me to acquire it using council funds to do so, to keep it out of his possession."

We didn't even know for sure if it this specific amulet was up for grabs tonight. We'd been guessing until now. But I could understand why keeping something that contained a powerful genie away from an accused murderer might be an excellent idea. Here I'd thought Thierry had been jonesing for it himself.

And he'd never given me any clue there was another reason for us being here.

"You could have told me that much, you know."

"I'm telling you now." Again, that smile played at his lips. "Better late than never?"

Thierry didn't want this dangerous amulet after all. He wanted to prevent someone nasty from getting their hands on it. The tight knot that had formed in my gut last night when he'd first told me about this auction finally eased.

A little, anyway.

One question continued to nag at me. "I'm still not sure why you told Atticus what you did about us."

His expression shadowed. "To gain his trust, he must believe I'm the same man I was in the past. He might confide in me then and confess his crimes and what his ultimate agenda is. If he knew you were more to me than I let on, it would give him more leverage than I want him to have, especially given the threats he's made in the recent past."

"Honor among thieves, as the saying goes."

"Essentially."

Thierry knew this guy and how to deal with him. I had to put my faith in that. "But, in truth, you're madly and passionately in love with me and I helped change your life completely for the better."

The smile returned to his lips. "A feat I never thought possible."

"I juggle really well."

"You do."

When he kissed me this time, I returned it with

great enthusiasm, sliding my hands up his chest and over his shoulders. His hands tightened at my waist as the kiss grew more passionate and he pressed me against the shelf of hardcover books behind me.

Once, I would have doubted his words, but I didn't anymore. We might be opposites in so many ways, and he was so vastly older than me that his life experience eclipsed mine like a cruise ship next to a rubber dinghy, but there was something about us. We worked.

He drove me crazy a lot of the time with his secrets, but I was crazy about him. That definitely helped to balance the scales.

And, I'd admit it, he was an amazing kisser.

"When's the auction supposed to start?" I breathed. While I didn't really want to interrupt, this I had to know. "It's already well after nine."

"I've been told it's been delayed an hour. We have time."

Even though I didn't want to be stuck here longer than necessary, at the moment I was fine with this news.

His breath was hot on my skin as he traced his mouth down and over my throat. Nobody would notice a hickey back at the cocktail party, would they? And, really, who cared if they did?

This room was nice and private. Since the auction had been pushed back, nobody would miss us for quite some time, so maybe—

I froze as his sharp fangs sank into my neck.

Panic seized me. "Thierry, what are you doing?"

Yes, vampires drank blood—even one another's— but this particular situation was not a good thing. At all. No, his drinking my blood after an incredibly hot kiss was a very *bad* thing.

As Atticus had alluded to in their conversation, Thierry de Bennicoeur suffered from an addiction—a *blood* addiction. Vampires, as a whole, did not have this. Sure, they were driven by their need for blood, but it didn't control them unless they were dying of thirst.

As a master vampire—in simpler terms, an *old* vampire—Thierry did not need to drink blood very often. He could go for long stretches—I didn't even know how long. Months, years, decades, maybe, without a drop. Which was a very good thing, because in the past if Thierry had even a taste of blood, he could lose his mind. And when a master vampire with Superman-level strength lost his mind he might kill someone.

And that someone might be me.

"Thierry, stop it!" I shoved him as hard as I could. He reared back from me, his lips peeled away from his fangs, his eyes the pitch-black of a hungry vampire instead of their usual pale gray shade.

I loved him with all my heart, but sometimes he scared the hell out of me.

"I need more," he growled.

When he lunged for my throat again I slapped him as hard as I could. His eyes widened slightly before his brow furrowed.

"Sarah, why did I—?" Clarity entered his gaze, swiftly followed by concern. "Are you hurt? Did I hurt you?"

I pressed my hand against the puncture wounds on my throat, trying very hard to stay calm and not get upset. That would only make matters worse. "I'll be fine."

An expression of complete devastation crossed his

face, but before he could turn away from me, I grabbed hold of his arm with my free hand.

"I'm okay, really. But what's wrong with you?" I asked him very seriously.

"I don't know." He grimaced. "Please be careful, Sarah. The need hasn't left me yet."

"Okay." I took him at his word and put some space between us.

"I can't remember being this thirsty without it first being triggered by the taste of blood," he managed. "And it's not abating."

"Did it come on just like that? Like zero to sixty?"

"The thirst began shortly after we arrived, but I thought I could handle it. I don't know what triggered it." His pained gaze met mine. "Wait. My drink."

I didn't understand what he meant for a moment. "What about it?"

"Someone must have tampered with it."

I gasped. "Someone spiked your drink with blood."

I grabbed the empty glass off the bookshelf and held it under my nose. One whiff told me that it had contained more than cranberry juice.

"How many did you have?"

"That was my second."

"You didn't taste the blood?"

His jaw tensed. "No, I didn't."

I gave him a look of disbelief. "Really? Because it smells like it was loaded."

He hissed out a breath, confusion now sliding through his eyes. "I smelled nothing but what I expected. I don't know why."

It made no sense to me. "So is this a bonus shot of blood for the vampires here tonight, or does some-body know your secret?"

"An excellent question."

"Could it have been Atticus?"

"If he found evidence that this is still a problem for me after so many years, he could label me a threat to the security of the Ring and order my immediate execution."

I felt the blood drain from my face. "So if Atticus is a killer, what better way to get rid of the next person on his hit list, right?"

Thierry shook his head. "No, I don't believe Atticus would choose a method like this. He would prefer a much more direct attack."

I put the glass down and gave Thierry every ounce of my attention. "Then who was it?"

When he didn't answer, I drew close enough to touch his arm. He flinched away from me. "Please, Sarah. You need to keep your distance from me until I fully regain my control. I might not be able to stop next time."

Before I could say anything in reply to that chilling warning, he turned and left the library, headed back toward the parlor. I followed after him, trying not to get too close. For now.

Thomas, the butler, walked past us and Thierry stopped him.

"Yes, sir?"

"I need to know the identity of the host of this party."

"That will be revealed very shortly, sir, I assure you."

Thierry scanned the room. "Suddenly I'm not all that patient. I need to know who the host is, and I insist on knowing right now." He raised his voice enough to catch the attention of the others in the room. Conversation hushed. Atticus Kincade watched us curiously from his position next to Tasha Evans.

"I suppose it is finally time we get this party started." A deep voice cut through the silence. A man in a black tuxedo entered the room and moved toward us. He had light brown hair and green eyes. A smile curled the corners of his mouth.

Thierry stared at him with shock on his normally hard-to-read face.

"You—" he began.

"Long time no see," the man said. "Hi, Dad."

Chapter 3

Maybe it was all in my imagination, but I swear the entire room went deathly silent as that word echoed all around, bouncing off the walls covered in tasteful paintings with gilded frames and threading through the crowd of invited guests.

Dad?

Excuse me?

"Sarah," Thierry said. All expression had left his face. All tone or emotion had left his voice. He'd suddenly become the Thierry who wore an impenetrable mask of icy composure, rather than the passionate yet dangerous Thierry I'd just been alone with. "This is Sebastien Lavelle."

"Sarah Dearly." Sebastien turned to me and thrust out his hand. I shook it automatically. "I've heard all about you."

I just stared at him. "Sorry I can't say the same. Did you call Thierry *Dad?*"

"I did. Thierry and I go way back."

"He's your . . . father?"

"No," Thierry said. "I'm his sire."

Sebastien smiled. "Same difference."

"No, it isn't."

I tried to rein myself in and appear as calm as

Thierry did. I was still busy processing the information about Atticus, as well as the disturbing idea that someone had spiked Thierry's drink with blood, so I had to shuffle both troublesome subjects off to the side in my mind to make space for this. My brain was getting as crowded as this room.

I needed time to deal with this. Unfortunately, calling a time-out wasn't exactly an option right now.

And I felt like there was something else, too. Wasn't there? Something important that I'd managed to forget . . .

Whatever. If I'd forgotten it, it couldn't have been all that important.

Sebastien crossed his arms over his chest. "Thierry didn't sire enough fledglings to warrant a full-scale reunion. I think we could be counted on one hand. A few fingers, actually. He didn't care for the responsibility a good sire is required to take for a fledgling. He preferred to—how would you put it, Thierry?— forget about us?"

There was more than an edge of contempt in that statement.

Call me crazy, but I thought I had a good idea who might have spiked Thierry's drinks. The waves of animosity rolling off this guy were nearly surfable.

"*Mon dieu!* Sebastien, my darling!" Veronique made her way through the swell of guests now elbow to elbow in the parlor, her Louboutins clicking noisily against the floor.

"Veronique," he said warmly.

She beamed at him before kissing him on both cheeks. "Where have you been all this time? I had believed you were lost to us forever. All these years— why haven't you been in touch?"

"Come." Sebastien took her hand. "Let's talk in private. We still have a little time left before the auction will begin. Thierry, you and your lovely wife are welcome to join us if you wish."

Without another word, he turned and led Veronique out of the room.

This stupid auction was never going to start, was it?

I eyed Thierry. "Want to give me a quick overview?"

His gaze moved toward Atticus, who was still with Tasha. The actress didn't seem intimidated by the boss of the Ring at all—she had a big smile on her face at whatever he was saying to her.

"Sebastien was a human who supplied information for me when I needed it in Paris in the second half of the seventeenth century. One night I found him after he'd been attacked by enemies and left for dead, his throat cut. He had previously requested that I sire him, but I'd refused. When I found him so near death, I finally gave in and turned him into something like me. But I did much too good a job, since Sebastien inherited my thirst."

A shiver went through me and I lowered my voice. "Is he one of the bad guys—like Atticus?"

Thierry considered this for a moment. "Despite his struggle as a fledgling, I never found Sebastien to be malicious in his actions. But he is an unexpected complication tonight, since I don't know what his intentions are."

"When was the last time you saw him?" I asked.

"Over three hundred years ago. There must be a reason he's taken so long to contact us again."

"What do you think it is?"

"I wish I knew."

"Okay. So let's go find out."

We left the crowded parlor to follow Sebastien and Veronique out to the hall, where they were speaking in an alcove close to the library. Thomas nodded as he moved past us with a fresh tray of champagne.

"It is so unexpectedly wonderful to see you again, my darling," Veronique purred, still touching Sebastien like a cherished lost pet that had finally come home.

"You too, Veronique. You're every bit as beautiful as I remember."

She nodded. "Of course I am. But tell me, have you been so busy that you couldn't even send word that you were well? I've been worried about you."

Sebastien had his hands clasped behind him. "I was unavoidably detained until recently. But one of the first items on my list was to make contact with old friends again. And here we are."

Thierry watched the other man carefully. "Making contact with old friends by sending out cryptic invitations to an auction? What is this, Sebastien?"

"It's fun, Thierry. That's what it is. At least, it's fun for those able to have fun." Sebastien's gaze landed on me. "I've tried to amass as much information as I could about what I've missed, but I don't know everything about recent developments. There must be quite a story about how the two of you met."

"Five volumes worth," I said. "Give or take."

"That is our Sarah." Veronique laughed. "Always so amusing. The great love story is worth retelling, isn't it? I mean, it must be. It was only recently that Thierry chose to officially end things between us."

"Things had been ended between us for centuries, Veronique," Thierry reminded her.

"That is certainly debatable."

Thierry's expression held weary patience. "Not debatable. Truth."

Veronique sighed. "What can I say, Sebastien? Thierry is a difficult man to please. But it seems as if Sarah has managed to please him thus far."

I wasn't sure if that was supposed to be a compliment. It didn't really feel like one.

"I aim to please," I said. "And I have very good aim."

"What's this all about, Sebastien?" Thierry asked in an attempt to shift the subject back to the burning question. "Why tonight? And why not identify yourself in the invitation?"

Sebastien shook his head. "You were never one to appreciate a little fun."

"Is that what you think this is? Fun?"

"I do indeed. Look at us here, in my mansion—"

"This is your mansion?" Veronique asked. "It's very impressive, darling."

He slid his hand along a carved detail on the wall behind him. "Borrowed from a friend, I'll admit. But certainly more than sufficient for the evening I have planned."

Personally, I wasn't sure why borrowing a massive mansion from someone in Beverly Hills was necessary to host an auction. To me, it seemed as if Sebastien was just trying to impress his guests.

All I knew for sure was that we were here for a very specific reason. And given the unpleasantness of the evening so far, I was tired of waiting.

"How did you get the amulet?" I asked, then shrugged at Thierry's look. "Why should we let the elephant dance around the room a moment longer?"

Sebastien's gaze tracked to me and his smile widened. "Straight and to the point. I think I like you, Sarah."

"Gee, thanks." But I wasn't sure if it was a good thing to be liked by this guy. Even with the shiny smile and the suave and well-dressed exterior, there was something incredibly unpleasant bubbling just beneath the surface of Sebastien Lavelle.

He was up to something. And I was willing to bet it was nothing good.

Sebastien cocked his head. "Can you be more specific, Sarah? What amulet do you mean?"

"Don't play games," Thierry growled.

Sebastien grinned, but it was more the baring of teeth than a genuinely pleasant expression. I recognized it, since Thierry had a predator's smile just like that when the situation called for it. "Why not? Games are fun. I've always liked having fun."

"You never took anything seriously."

His eyes narrowed. "And you, my dearest daddy, took everything far *too* seriously. Believe me, the last three hundred years have increased my need for fun and I'll get it wherever and however I can." Sebastien raked a hand through his hair, which struck me as a nervous gesture. He began moving along the hallway, gazing up at the oil paintings of cherubs and Greek goddesses. "I have several items up for auction tonight that I've acquired in the past and safely stored away until now. Perhaps I just want to make a little money from them. Immortals need to think about their retirement plans, after all."

"So that's where you've been," Veronique said. "Scouring the earth from corner to corner for new trinkets, having adventures, getting into trouble. You always did enjoy traveling."

"Adored it," he agreed. "I mean to travel again extensively. I have an uncontrollable urge to stretch my legs."

"The amulet, Sebastien?" Thierry prompted. "I searched for years for that piece. Only recently did I learn that it was destroyed centuries ago."

The edge of ease that had been in Sebastien's expression fell away as he returned his attention to his sire. "I heard that rumor, too, but I'm not sure who started it."

"The council thought Thierry had it hidden somewhere," I said.

Yet now they wanted Thierry to acquire it so Atticus wouldn't. Funny how a few weeks could change things.

And by "funny," I meant not the least bit funny. At all.

Sebastien moved past me, again studying the paintings as if they were much more interesting than this conversation. Veronique watched him, her expression guarded, but I could see some confusion there.

"Thierry was once the one most interested in acquiring it," Sebastien said, "so I'm not all that surprised that he would be the one most would assume to possess it. I acquired it back when he was obsessing over it. I'd planned on giving it to him as a surprise gift, to prove my worth to him, so he wouldn't continue to think I was 'a pathetic waste of breath.'" He gave Thierry a tight smile that missed the mark if he was aiming for friendliness. "But I never got the chance to give it to him. Perhaps it's better that I never did. You taught me that, Thierry."

Thierry's mouth was a thin line. "What did I teach you?"

"That power corrupts." He shrugged. "After all, I saw your corruption whenever you had an extra ounce of power."

I glared at him. "Hey. Watch it, Junior."

Sebastien laughed, a short, almost nervous bark of a sound. "She comes to your defense like a vicious Chihuahua, Thierry. Isn't that adorable?"

I did come to Thierry's defense, whenever the situation called for it. I couldn't help myself. "You might not think my bite is adorable. I leave marks."

"I'm sure you do." He regarded me with curiosity in the shadows of the alcove. "So different from what I'm used to when it comes to your choices, Thierry. This is quite a revelation."

Thierry stepped forward, his hands clenched at his sides. "Enough, Sebastien. You always liked to cause trouble, didn't you? Are you certain you want to go to such dark places with me tonight?"

"Oh, I think I can handle you."

I'd stopped breathing, sensing that something horrible was about to happen. Something violent. As I shared a tense look with Veronique, she slipped between them and put a hand on each man's chest to keep them apart.

"We were once good friends, the three of us. We had many enjoyable years together and it can certainly be like that now. Let us be friends once again. Sebastien, I will get you a copy of my memoir to remind you of more pleasant days. You, among many others, helped inspire my story. And remember that girlfriend of yours? The plain one you insisted was your one great love? What was her name—Bettina?"

The fury faded from his gaze. "I remember her."

"What ever happened to her?"

"We parted ways. Not everything can last forever." His expression grew haunted. "And Bettina wasn't plain. She was beautiful."

"Reminiscing isn't his goal tonight. It's something else entirely." Thierry hadn't relaxed a fraction. "What is it, Sebastien?"

"I guess you'll just have to wait and see," Sebastien said smugly.

"Can we put an actual time on that?" I asked. "I mean, ten? Ten thirty?"

"Soon."

Great.

There were plenty of people who had an uneasy history with Thierry, but this one felt . . . I wasn't sure. More *personal* in his distaste. This kind of tension came only from those you were closest to—at least at one time.

However, just because someone was family didn't make them any less dangerous if they had an ax to grind. Sometimes those axes were literal ones.

Veronique hooked her arm through Thierry's. "Come. Let's go back to the parlor. You barely got the chance to become properly acquainted with my new lover."

I couldn't help but notice that she looked worried. That made two of us. With Atticus and Sebastien both under this roof, I wasn't sure how smoothly the rest of the evening would go.

"Sarah?" Thierry cast a tense glance over his shoulder at me and our eyes locked.

Why did I want to protect him so badly when I knew he could take care of himself?

"I'll be right behind you," I assured him.

He nodded, then allowed Veronique to lead him back toward the cocktail party.

I stayed right where I was, since Sebastien hadn't yet made a move to follow them. I needed to know what his problem was and what level of threat he might be tonight.

The best approach would be to keep things light. "Did Veronique always try to push Thierry around?"

"She tried her best." Sebastien watched me curiously, assessing me from head to toe without attempting to hide it.

It was making me extremely self-conscious. "What?"

He shook his head. "Don't take this the wrong way, but you're the last woman I'd ever expect Thierry de Bennicoeur to end up with."

"Why's that?"

"Because you seem very nice. It's not a word I would ever associate with that man."

I tended to make a first impression on people that got them to either like me or hate me. There wasn't usually a lot of indifference. Maybe I could use this to break through Sebastien's guard and get to the truth. "That just goes to show that you don't know me at all. I used to be nice. Then someone bit my neck and made me a vampire against my will, with hunters lying in wait, wanting to end my life. That can shake the nice out of anybody."

Thomas walked past us in the hallway with a tray of drinks. He nodded at Sebastien, but didn't slow his steps. No cranberry juices on the tray. No whiff of blood. Just more champagne.

"It certainly can. But it is a good test of one's personal will to see how driven she is to survive."

I couldn't figure this guy out. Was he an old acquaintance with a strange sense of humor or was he up to something nasty? Unfortunately, my gut instinct was gesturing wildly toward door number two. "Why haven't you stayed in touch with Veronique or Thierry? Three hundred years is a very long time."

"You have no idea how long three centuries can feel."

"True." The ice in his words made a chill run down my spine. "So why now? Why after all this time have you made the decision to reconnect?"

Sebastien paced to the other side of the room, his face in shadows, his jaw tight. For a moment, he reminded me so much of Thierry that I thought they could very well be blood relatives after all.

"He never told you about me?" he said.

"Sorry, no."

His expression darkened. "How easy it must have been for him to forget."

"Forget what?"

"What he did to me."

I thought I was finally starting to get the hang of this. Sebastien Lavelle was not much better than a fanged college kid with a long list of separation issues when it came to his parents. He was having a temper tantrum because enough attention hadn't been paid to him over the years. Well, too bad, Junior.

I was going to try for patience to deal with him. Maybe it didn't have to get any more unpleasant than it already had. Our number one priority tonight was dealing with the Atticus situation. Anything else wasn't worth our time and attention.

Still, this guy was obviously in pain about his past with Thierry, a sire who hadn't really been as attentive

as he could have been. In that regard, I felt bad for
Sebastien.

"Whatever your deal is with Thierry," I said gently, "you need to let it go. You don't have to have a
relationship with him, but I'm sensing some serious
anger issues here. However, having his drink spiked
with blood when apparently you have the very same
blood addiction isn't cool. You'd know very well what
kind of torture that is for him."

"Spiking his drink?" Now a smile played at his
lips. "What do you mean?"

I narrowed my eyes, my sympathy waning in
record time. "Yeah. Don't try to tell me it wasn't you
who told the blonde to put blood in Thierry's drinks.
You know his problems and you wanted to make him
lose his composure tonight."

"That would be a cruel trick."

"Yes, it would."

"He seems fine." His attention moved to my neck,
mostly covered by my hair. "But perhaps that's only
an act. Is it?"

"You need to back off."

"Do I?" His gaze grew glacial again in seconds.
"Do you know what he did to me? This man you proclaim to love with all your heart?"

I didn't flinch from his furious glare; I met it full on.
"Go ahead. Tell me. It's obvious that you're dying to."

He raked a hand through his hair, turning to pace
a few feet down the hall before he swiveled to face me
again. "Up until three months ago I was locked in a
tomb no bigger than a closet. Trapped. Abandoned.
Starving and wasting away to nothing but skin and
bones. Your darling new husband did that to me,
Sarah. He locked me up and threw away the key."

I stared at him in shock. "You're lying."

"I'm not lying." There was not even a glint of humor in Sebastien's eyes anymore. "Spiking his drink to bring out his dark side is the very least I wish to do to dearest Daddy this evening. And if you're smart, I'd suggest you stay out of my way."

Chapter 4

Sebastien walked off without another word, and all I could do was watch him go since I was busy picking my jaw up from the floor where it had fallen.

Thierry had described him as a complication, taking attention away from his assignment regarding Atticus.

A complication was definitely an understatement.

No way this could be true. Not a chance. I knew Thierry had done some shady things in his life, but locking a fledgling in a tomb and forgetting about him for three centuries? No way.

Sebastien had to be lying . . . although, he sure hadn't looked like it. No, he'd looked as serious as a heart attack.

There had to be another explanation for this and I was going to find out what it was.

I quickened my steps as I moved back toward the parlor to find Thierry. At the very least, I knew Sebastien was responsible for spiking Thierry's drinks with blood tonight. What exactly had he expected would happen? That Thierry would have killed me?

He hadn't. He'd stopped.

One day he might not be able to stop, a little voice said quietly inside of me.

I liked to call her my "sliver of doubt." She was

small but insistent, especially when I had fresh fang marks on my neck.

When I spotted the blond server approaching just outside the parlor doors, I stopped her.

"Can I help you?" she asked.

I eyed her with more attention this time. She wore a strong perfume that smelled pleasantly of vanilla. She was medium height with a shapely body—pretty, but not overly Hollywood-looking, despite our current location. "What's your name?"

"Melanie."

"Can you do me a favor, Melanie?"

"Of course, ma'am. What is it?"

I tried very hard not to raise my voice. "Stop putting blood in my husband's drinks."

Her eyes widened. "But I—I—"

"Sebastien told you to do that, didn't he?"

Confusion crossed her face. "Yes, but . . . your husband is a vampire. Didn't he appreciate the addition to his drink?"

She knew we were vampires and didn't seem remotely fazed by it. To me that indicated nonhuman. "Are you a vampire, too?"

"No, I'm a . . ." She hesitated. "A werewolf."

Huh. I wouldn't have guessed that at all, but I hadn't met very many werewolves before. "Okay. Then let's put it this way. If you spike Thierry's drinks again tonight I'll have you permanently leashed. *Capiche?*"

"Yes, ma'am." She didn't say it with attitude or snark; she said it as if she legitimately felt bad about what she'd done. Maybe I'd scared her. It would be hard to scare a werewolf, so I felt rather accomplished. And maybe a little guilty.

"Good," I said. "Thank you."

She nodded and turned to move away from me, balancing her full tray of drinks as she entered the parlor. I gave her a moment before I followed and scanned the busy room for any sign of Thierry.

Who, of course, was nowhere to be seen right when I needed to talk to him the most.

I groaned with frustration. This was turning into the longest cocktail party ever. Seriously.

Still searching, I threaded through the throng of auction guests, nodding and smiling until my face felt strained as I made my way toward an unoccupied corner where I could catch my breath.

But then someone stepped right in front of me to block my path.

"Finally, we have a chance to meet," he said. "I'm Atticus Kincade, an associate of your husband's with the council."

My heart and stomach sank in unison like a pair of synchronized swimmers.

Be cool, Sarah, I told myself.

"Sarah Dearly." I took his hand and he squeezed mine rather than shaking it. "A pleasure."

"The pleasure is mine." He bent his head and brushed his lips against the back of my hand.

I pulled it back without looking too anxious and swept my gaze over the cocktail party, trying again to pinpoint Thierry's location.

Hello? Evil boss man front and center. Where are you?

Atticus leaned in a little. "I'm surprised your husband has left your side. If you were with me I wouldn't let you out of my sight for fear that another man might sweep in and steal you."

Since Thierry had left him with the impression earlier that our relationship had as much depth to it as a sheet of paper, I wasn't too surprised at his care-less flirtation. Maybe he even thought it might work.

For the record, it really didn't. Atticus was attractive, but I got a very unpleasant vibe from him—and not only because of what he'd been accused of. This man had threatened my life before. He was dangerous. And seriously creepy.

But . . . wild guess here. Maybe he had a thing for brunette fledglings allegedly in unhappy marriages.

Could I use this unexpected friendliness to my advantage? It made me uneasy to be this close to someone like Atticus, but I wanted to be helpful in Thierry's investigations. And his current assignment was to investigate the man who'd just kissed my hand.

"Thierry is . . ." I searched for an adequate word. "Easily distracted. At least, it seems that way when he's with me."

"If Thierry doesn't appreciate what he has with you"—he shook his head—"then he's a fool."

"I couldn't agree more."

Melanie moved past us and Atticus grabbed two glasses of champagne from her tray, handing one to me.

"Has there been something specific on his mind lately to distract him?" he asked.

I took a quick sip of the bubbly. "Oh, I don't know. I just figured it's how he is. I suppose anyone would be the same at his age." I forced a smile. "I'm assuming you're much younger."

"Not as much as you might think. It's true, once one has seen centuries pass them by, life appears differently than it would to a younger man. It can change us—some for the better, many for the worse. Time is one thing that brings out our truest selves."

"Kind of like having too much champagne."

"Quite." He clinked glasses with me. "I want you to feel comfortable with me, Sarah. If there are any specific problems you're having with your husband, anything that might be troubling you, I encourage you to come straight to me."

Somehow, the direction of this conversation felt increasingly odd. "Problems? Other than feeling ignored?"

His grip on his champagne glass tightened. "Thierry de Bennicoeur has always been a dangerous man, no matter what current goals he claims. I don't think time has changed this."

"I'm not sure I know what you mean."

"If that's so, then I'm glad to hear it." He swirled his untouched champagne, looking down into the crystal flute as if it might give him some answers. "Let me ask you this, Sarah. Do you know what piece Thierry is interested in acquiring at the auction tonight?"

I tried my best to look confused. By now it wasn't all that difficult. "I don't know, really. Something shiny and expensive, I'm sure. He doesn't share info like that with me."

"Fair enough." Atticus nodded, then reached into the inner pocket of his suit jacket, pulled out a business card, and pressed it into my hand. "I would like you to call me if you need anything, either now or in the future."

I looked at the card, which had his name and a phone number printed on it. "Anything?"

"Advice. Assistance. Anything you like." He leaned closer so no one else could hear. "It would be best if Thierry not know I've made you this offer. He might not understand I'm only trying to be helpful."

"Of course. I understand."

With a nod, Atticus moved away from me and joined another nearby group who were toasting something and wanted the leader of the Ring to be a part of it. I was left standing there in the corner of the parlor trying to decipher my short conversation with him. Was Atticus Kincade a devious murderer who'd paved his road to success with the bodies of dead elders? Or was he a flirtatious centuries-old vampire who was legitimately concerned for my well-being after knowing me all of five minutes?

My gut instinct was not helping me at the moment. Not at all.

"Looks like you just got an earful," a female voice said.

I glanced to my left to see that Tasha Evans now stood next to me.

The Tasha Evans, my favorite movie star ever, looking every bit as flawless two feet away as she did on the big screen, with her long red hair—I didn't think they were extensions—tight designer halter-style black dress, black pashmina draped over her right arm, sky-high silver heels, and visible (but tasteful!) tattoos adorning her left shoulder blade and encircling her upper left arm. Apparently the writing on that one was some old language and it translated to "always believe in yourself."

Or something like that. I didn't really care what it meant; it just looked seriously cool.

I finally found my voice. "An earful?"

"From Atticus." She grinned. "He's a notorious womanizer, you should know."

"I kind of gathered that."

"We dated once. He's . . ." She flicked a look in his direction. "Certainly interesting enough."

"Faint praise."

"Oh, no. It's actually full praise. It didn't work out, but there were no hard feelings between us. Just not a love to span the centuries." She extended her hand. "I'm Tasha."

As if I even needed the intro!

"I'm Sarah." I shook her hand, trying to compose myself. "Great to meet you."

"You too." Her gaze swept the room again. "So when is this auction supposed to start? The invite said nine o'clock and it's nearly ten. I have to be on set bright and early."

References to movie sets seriously made me swoon. And it nearly made me forget my need to find Thierry and talk about Sebastien—and now more Atticus—with him.

"It's been pushed to ten and I hope it won't be delayed any longer than that," I told her. "Do you know Sebastien?"

"Sebastien?"

"The host, Sebastien Lavelle."

Her brows drew together slightly. "Hmm, I don't think so. My invitation was sent anonymously. Call me crazy, but I was intrigued enough to show up to see what might be available. Auctions like this typically have secretive hosts."

"I wouldn't know. This is my first one."

Thomas and Melanie now circulated through the room with more drinks and hors d'oeuvres. There was no sign of either Sebastien or Thierry. Or, for that matter, Veronique. I did spot Veronique's publisher boyfriend, Jacob, in the corner, laughing boisterously at a joke someone had just made.

My gut churned. *Thierry, why do you always disappear on me?*

"What do you do, Sarah?" Tasha asked.

"I assist my husband with his job with the vampire council. He's their newest consultant."

"Oh, very nice. Thierry de Bennicoeur, right? He's an interesting man."

"That's how I like my husbands. Very interesting."

She laughed at this. "Well, I wish you the best of luck. The Ring isn't the easiest organization to deal with. Personally, I think it's the fault of the current leader—no offense toward Atticus intended."

"I'm sure he'd be open to the criticism," I said dryly.

"Definitely. All vampires of that advanced age are open to criticism and not set in their ways at all." She raised an eyebrow when I didn't reply. "I suppose you're wondering how old *I* am."

"I'm going to go with a solid twenty-seven."

Her smile widened. "Eternally, thankfully. Although the latest gossip is that I've just hit forty."

"You look great for forty." I couldn't keep it inside any longer. Despite my commitment to being professional—although, when had I made that particular commitment?—I had to get this off my chest. "I have to say it, Tasha—I'm a huge fan of yours. I'm so thrilled to meet you. Sorry . . . I'm gushing. I don't want to make you uncomfortable."

"Not at all." She laughed. "Gushing is good—I don't mind. It means I've done something right in my life."

I was glad she was taking it as a compliment and not running in the opposite direction. "I wanted to be an actress after college. It didn't work out, but you were my idol. I mean, two Oscars, doing everything from comedy to thrillers . . . so amazing."

"Thank you so much." Tasha reached down to squeeze my hand. "That means a lot to me."

Frederic Dark and his wife, Anna, brushed past me and gave me a disapproving look from their black eyes—but maybe that was how they looked at everyone who hadn't embraced the Purist vampire lifestyle like they had. I swear the air around them was even a few degrees cooler. I shivered.

Someone else caught my eye. Veronique entered the parlor and moved directly toward Jacob, who was still speaking animatedly to his new friends. I couldn't help but notice that Tasha's expression grew chilly at the sight of her.

"Do you know Veronique?" I asked.

"I've had the displeasure."

An interesting response. "Is there bad blood between you two?"

"Nothing worth mentioning." Her attention returned to me, her expression relaxed and filled with nothing but good humor. "Listen. If you're in town for a few days, why don't you come by the set for a visit? It's a remake of *Dracula*."

"I read about that in *Entertainment Weekly*." My heart started pounding very hard. "You're playing Dracula."

"How's that for a twist? A female Dracula. If only they knew the truth." She finished her champagne and set the glass on a nearby table. "I'm sure I can get you on camera as an extra if you're interested."

"You would—really? Wow, that would be fantastic! Thank you!"

"You're very welcome." She glanced across the room. "Your husband seems to be looking for you."

I turned to see that Thierry was now in the parlor again, scanning it until his gray eyes landed on me. I babbled some more thanks to Tasha and started to make my way over to him, feeling like I'd drunk a thousand glasses of champagne.

And I'd thought this night would only be filled with difficulties. Wrong! Tasha Evans wanted me to be an extra in her new movie. So much awesome!

But I knew I couldn't let my conversation with Tasha distract me from the most important problems tonight. Atticus's weird offer of help. And Sebastien's vendetta against the sire he believed had locked him up for centuries. I couldn't lose my head over all this talk of movies and acting and . . .

Wait. *Lose my head.*

Why did I feel like I was forgetting something really important?

"You've been keeping very busy," Thierry said as I reached his side. "I couldn't find you."

"We need to talk. Stat."

"Stat?"

"Yes, stat. It's very important."

A bell rang and conversation halted. Thomas the butler was holding a . . . well, a bell. That he'd just rung.

"If I may have your attention, please," Thomas said. "Your host, Sebastien Lavelle, wishes for you all to enter the main salon, where the auction is about to begin."

As the guests filed out of the parlor, Thierry slid his hand into mine. "I promise we'll talk after I have what we came here for. All right?"

An auction wouldn't take that long. And then Thierry would have the amulet and Atticus wouldn't. One problem would be crossed off the list and then I could focus on our host's accusations and his current agenda against Thierry.

It sounded fair enough.

I squeezed his hand. "All right."

Chapter 5

The salon was a large room with a twenty-foot ceiling. Its shiny floor was set in an intricate crisscross pattern of dark and light hardwood. Gigantic oil paintings of landscapes that looked like they were each worth a small fortune adorned the walls. It was a room that felt as if important people like senators, presidents, and kings had spent time in it. I'd never been intimidated by crown molding before, but there was a first time for everything.

There was a podium set up at the far end, right in front of stained-glass windows that took up the entire wall.

Thirty chairs were arranged in several neat rows, and Thierry and I took a seat in the second row from the front. Veronique and Jacob sat in front of us. Atticus sat across the aisle in the first row, Tasha next to him.

Both Melanie and Thomas were present, standing dutifully at the back of the room in case they were needed. I had yet to see any hired help for the evening other than the two of them.

Ten minutes after the announcement by Thomas, Sebastien moved behind the podium.

"Thank you all for coming this evening and for

your patience. I know my invitation was a bit mysterious. Mystery piques the interest of those who enjoy a bit of adventure, and I hope this evening will hold all the adventure you've been wishing for." He didn't look at me and Thierry, but his gaze swept the rest of the audience and his smile was firmly fixed. If I hadn't known better, I never would have guessed that he wasn't nearly as cheery and welcoming as he appeared to be.

There was so much I needed to know about what had happened to him. Had he really been trapped for all that time?

Apparently if vampires went without blood long enough, they would fall into a deep sleep I'd heard described as a "corpselike state." I assumed that would have happened to Sebastien. And if that was true, how had he woken up enough to manage a prison break?

Also, just how long would a vampire have to go without blood to fall into that deep sleep? A day? No, I'd gone longer than a day without blood.

A week? A month?

As a master vampire, Thierry rarely needed any blood at all. If he were trapped, it would take a very long time for him to fall asleep—if ever.

Just the thought of it made me shudder.

"Thomas will be kind enough to handle the financials for me later," Sebastien said, nodding to the butler at the back of the room, "and I will be your auctioneer this evening."

Thierry was entirely focused on Sebastien. I put a hand on his arm to feel how tense he was.

"You've got this," I assured him. "Everything's okay."

His eyes met mine and held long enough for me to

see that he was definitely worried. "It will be okay once I've acquired the amulet."

"You'll get it."

"I hope you're right."

My words of encouragement seemed to be working, since he relaxed a fraction.

Like, a fraction of a fraction.

Low conversation moved through the gathered guests before Sebastien spoke again. "The first item up for bid this evening is one I acquired in the early sixteenth century, a painting of a duchess said to be haunted by her spirit to this very day." He gestured to an easel that held a painting of a stern-looking woman with her chin raised, eyes straight forward. She reminded me of a teacher I had in public school who scolded me for my hilarious one-liners during her classes. Some teachers didn't appreciate funny students.

"Did he say he acquired the painting in the sixteenth century?" Jacob whispered to Veronique. "How is that possible?"

"You must have heard him wrong, darling," she replied.

I had no idea how long she thought she could keep this up. Bringing a human to a vampire function didn't seem like the brightest idea in the universe.

Humans might like the notion of vampires in theory. But faced with an actual vampire with fangs and a thirst for blood, they inevitably freaked out.

"We'll start the bidding at ten thousand dollars," Sebastien said.

People raised their hands, and he acknowledged their bids, which escalated until—

"Going . . . going . . . gone!" He struck the gavel

against the podium. "Sold to Ms. Peterman for thirty-two thousand dollars."

Ms. Peterman, who was seated in the back row, seemed very pleased to now own the creepy-haunted-teacher painting.

Thomas moved the easel to the side and brought out the next item, unwrapping it from shimmery blue fabric and holding it up for everyone to see. It was a knife about seven inches in length with a wavy golden blade and sapphires set into the hilt. The blade itself was carved with small swirling symbols.

"The Amaranthian Dagger. There are rumors that to drink the blood from a wound made by this dagger will substantially lengthen a mortal's life. Legend has it that if the blood is consumed by an vampire, they will never need to fear death, for they will be truly and wholly immortal, without any fear of wooden stakes or other means used to end their existences."

"More strange talk of vampires," Jacob mused. "Quite a coincidence, don't you think, my sweet?"

"Yes, quite," Veronique agreed.

After a heated battle that drove the price up to nearly two hundred thousand dollars, Frederic Dark was the victor. I couldn't tell if he or his wife, Anna, was pleased by the win. Their pale, morose expressions didn't shift for even a moment into anything cheerier.

"I'm not surprised he won," Thierry said under his breath. "Frederic is said to possess a wide collection of supernatural weaponry."

"He sounds like a really fun guy."

"And Anna likely would be interested in such an item, too. She was once a vampire hunter."

I stared at him. "You're kidding."

"No, I'm not."

"How long have they been married?"

"Twenty years, I believe. He is also her sire."

I glanced toward the Purist couple with much more interest now, and a large helping of caution. A vampire hunter and a vamp who liked things old-school.

Talk about opposites attracting.

The auction continued and I lost track after a full hour passed. My mind began to wander to other subjects beyond that of what creepy object was being highlighted at the podium. I kept a close eye on Atticus, who hadn't bid on anything yet. However, he did seem every bit as focused on the proceedings as Thierry.

Was he really a murderer? And if so, how far would someone like him be willing to go to achieve a higher level of power? Had it all been to become the sole elder in charge of the Ring?

Yet he'd spoken to me about Thierry as if he was the real danger.

It made no sense. All I knew for sure was that I trusted Thierry and I didn't trust Atticus.

That made things very simple. If Thierry was at risk from his current vampire boss, then I would do anything I could to protect him.

By the time the auction had nearly reached its end, we were well past eleven and moving closer to midnight.

"Our last item," Sebastien said, taking a black velvet box the size of his hand from Thomas, "is the most infamous by far. Please, if you have questions, don't hesitate to ask. I will answer them the best I can."

He opened the box and walked down the aisle so everyone could get a look at what lay inside.

It appeared to be a small emerald bottle about two inches in height. Thin gold bands wrapped around it, holding it in place like a large pendant. On the gold bands were lines of engraved symbols. A thick gold chain was attached to two golden loops on either side of it.

As he passed my chair, I could have sworn I felt something coming off the object. A hum. A vibration. It *felt* magical even from a distance.

"This is the Jacquerra Amulet," Sebastien said as he turned around to walk back to the front. "Created in the sixth century by a coven of witches who possessed a spell to summon and trap a djinn. Djinn—sometimes referred to as genies—are real, but they are not exactly what one might expect. Inside this amulet is a djinn, imprisoned by that original coven's spell, which is etched into the amulet itself. Once summoned, the djinn will be bound to its master, the current owner of the amulet, and will be at that master's command."

A woman in the front row raised her hand. "Will the djinn grant wishes?"

"Yes," Sebastien replied, his voice grave. "But be cautioned that you must ask very specifically for what you want, and there should be no room for interpretation—just in case the djinn wants to cause trouble. And the legends you may have heard are true. A djinn's master will be allowed precisely three spoken wishes before the djinn will be able to fight the compulsion to obey."

Another man spoke up. "If the djinn was trapped so long ago, would it even understand English?"

"The djinn will understand the language of its master. And it's said that it will also naturally have a firm grasp of current customs and knowledge."

I raised my hand and Thierry eyed me curiously.

"Yes, Sarah?" Sebastien said. "You have a question?"

It was something that had been bothering me ever since I'd found out about the amulet's existence. "If the djinn is angry about being imprisoned, wouldn't it try to seek revenge the moment it's released?"

His jaw tightened. "It doesn't work that way."

"How do you know? Have you tried it?"

"No, never."

"Why not? Because you know how dangerous it is?"

"Since I've been detained for quite some time, I haven't had the chance."

I wasn't buying that. He'd been out of the tomb for a while. If he wanted revenge on Thierry so badly, why wouldn't he have released the djinn and made a trio of malevolent wishes?

What exactly was he up to?

Sebastien turned from me to answer another question and I grabbed hold of Thierry's hand.

"I really don't like this," I told him, worry churning inside of me. "I'm feeling a great need to get out of this place as soon as possible."

He leaned closer to whisper in my ear. "As soon as I acquire the amulet we can leave, I promise. But I have to do this first."

I didn't like this at all, but I nodded. The alternative was to let Atticus have it. And if he was as bad as the other elders thought he was, he couldn't be allowed that kind of power.

Jacob raised his hand to ask a question. "When you say there's a genie inside that object, you're speaking metaphorically, aren't you? Genies don't actually exist."

Sebastien blinked. "Are there any other questions?"

"I have a question," Thierry said, loud enough for all to hear. "When and from whom did you acquire this piece? And where have you hidden it all these years?"

The look Sebastien gave him was sharp enough to cut glass.

"A long time ago in a land far away from here," Sebastien replied, his words clipped. "And I have my hiding spots, Thierry—places I could hide anything and it would not be discovered for, oh, centuries. If I tell you where those hiding places are, they wouldn't be much good to me, would they? I'm sure you also have hiding places like that, don't you?" His tone held absolutely no warmth at all now. "So, let's begin. We'll be starting the bidding at one million dollars."

My mouth fell open at that.

The other objects had gone for tons of money, but the most expensive one up until now had been the dagger Frederic Dark acquired for two hundred grand.

One million was the *opening* bid?

"Be calm, Sarah," Thierry murmured again, watching me nervously twist my hands on my lap.

"I'm calm. Totally, totally calm. But that is a lot of money."

"It certainly is." He actually had the audacity to smile at my financial anxiety attack. "But just wait."

"Wait? Wait for what?"

He didn't have to answer. I knew what he meant as the bidding swiftly escalated.

All I could do was watch and listen as, in increments of a quarter million, one million became two. Two became three. I couldn't see the faces of the participating men in the back row without turning and staring, but I heard the greed in their voices as they called out their bids.

I looked at Thierry, expecting him to join in.

"Not yet," he said under his breath.

This was stressful.

At the five-million-dollar mark, Atticus finally showed his hand. Literally. He raised his arm to signal his bid.

"Five million from Atticus Kincade," Sebastien acknowledged. "Do I hear five and a quarter?"

I realized I was holding my breath. This was way more exciting than the auctions I was used to, which admittedly had only been on eBay.

I had to remind myself that Thierry was using Ring money to help acquire the amulet and keep it out of Atticus's greedy mitts.

The men in the back row helped to raise the bidding to eight million, but Atticus still looked confident. Smug, really.

I glanced over my shoulder to see the other bidders. With an annoyed groan of disdain, one of the men slumped back in his chair.

He was out.

Several bids later, the other man joined him in his defeat.

Atticus practically glowed. He was going to get his prize for the bargain-basement price of ten million dollars.

Was it hot in here, or was it just me?

"Going once," Sebastien said, "going twice . . ."

"Eleven million." Thierry finally spoke up, jumping the bid by a full million.

Like it was no big deal. *Sure, eleven million. Just let me check my wallet.*

The room went completely silent for a few heavy moments.

"We have a bid for eleven million dollars from Thierry de Bennicoeur." Sebastien said his name like it tasted rotten.

Atticus turned in his seat and fixed Thierry with what I could only describe of as a look of death.

Hadn't he expected that Thierry would be bidding on this? He knew Thierry's previous interest in the amulet, so what was up with the nasty glare?

"He's not happy with you right now," I said very quietly.

"I'm sure he's not. Likely, he believed I would step aside for him in order to maintain our working relationship."

Before I could say another word, Atticus spoke up, his tone dark. "Eleven point five."

"Do I hear twelve?" Sebastien asked.

"Twelve," Thierry said.

Veronique turned fully around in her seat to look at Thierry with shock. "*Mon dieu*! What on earth are you doing?"

"Let him bid on the trinket, my sweet," Jacob said. "He obviously has the money to spare."

She ignored him. "After all this time, you're still desperate to acquire that horrible object?"

Thierry's expression tensed. "It's none of your business, Veronique. It never was."

Her gaze flicked to me. "This is not good, my dear. He was obsessed by this piece at one time."

"A little obsession is good for the soul?" I offered.

She frowned. "You are much less help than I would have expected."

Veronique turned back around, but there was a

tension in her shoulders that indicated that she was angry with the both of us. For what it was worth, I thought her little outburst showed that she cared for Thierry's well-being.

For now, and for her own good, she couldn't know the truth.

Look at me—I was getting to be just as secretive as Thierry.

"Twelve and a half!" Atticus, who now favored fractions, practically shouted.

"Thirteen," Thierry countered.

Another glare that could crush diamonds hurtled from the lead elder in our direction. His gaze fixed on me, and I tried to look shocked by anything Thierry said. Shocked and slightly embarrassed, as if I was sorry Thierry was making Atticus's life difficult.

I wondered if Tasha might be impressed by my acting skills.

"Hello?" someone said, loud and clear in my ear.

I turned around to look, but saw only the bland expressions of the people sitting behind me.

Thierry and Atticus continued to battle back and forth. The bidding reached fifteen million, which only helped the big knot in my stomach get bigger and knottier.

"Helloooo?" the voice said again, a bit more urgently. "Can anyone hear me?"

"Who's saying that?" I whispered.

"You can hear me!" There was a note of triumph in the voice now, as well as a large helping of desperation. "Oh, please, you have to help me. I don't know what's going on. This has been a very bad night! I think. But I don't really remember! I don't even know where I am. Where am I? What is this place?"

Again, I turned in my seat, trying to pinpoint the owner of the voice. He sounded vaguely familiar. "Who is that?"

Thierry eyed me with concern. "What's wrong?"

Good question. What was wrong? I didn't know for sure, but something was.

"I'm hearing something," I said. "Something . . . strange. Somebody's talking to me."

"You seem so familiar to me," the voice said.

"Who are you?" I said louder, feeling breathless and tense. I'd gained the attention of many people, who now looked at me with growing alarm.

"Wait. I know you! You're the one I spoke to earlier! I recognize your voice!"

I'd spoken to him earlier? Wouldn't I remember something like that?

Just then the realization hit me like a bucket of cold water right in my face.

I shot straight up from my chair, which clattered backward, hitting the gentleman behind me in his knees. Everyone in the room stared at me with shock.

"Holy crap!" I exclaimed, making a jabby gesture in the general direction of the kitchen. "The head! There was a talking head!"

The gavel slammed down, its crack echoing through the room.

Sebastien pointed at me. "Sold to Sarah Dearly for seventeen million dollars."

Chapter 6

"**W**ait! That's not fair!" Atticus leapt to his feet, his face red with outrage. "You didn't even give me a chance to counterbid!"

"Sorry. My auction, my rules." Sebastien turned to the rest of the audience. "Thank you all for coming. For those of you with the winning bids, please see Thomas to arrange payment and claim your item."

I couldn't process what he was saying. I was too busy trying to scoot out of my row, blocked by all of the other guests who now wanted to leave the salon.

"Sarah, what is going on?" Thierry asked, his hands firmly on my shoulders. "What do you mean by a talking head?"

My thoughts were a jumble, but at least my memories were working properly again. "I saw it, and then . . . then what? I just forgot? Why did I forget?" I felt ill. The voice I'd heard had disappeared, but the memory was now scorched into my brain. "I need to get to the kitchen."

"Sarah, are you all right?" Tasha asked as I slipped past her toward the exit.

"Nope! Not really!"

Thierry kept pace with me, turning his back on the

amulet to follow me out of the room. I made a beeline to the kitchen, where I'd gone earlier to get ice.

I'd seen him, and then I'd forgotten him—like, it had just vanished from my head. Even still, all evening it was as if there was something on the tip of my tongue. Something just out of reach.

He'd asked for my help and I'd forgotten he even existed. Now I could hear him without seeing him.

What in the world was going on here tonight?

"I know it sounds hard to believe, Thierry," I said, not taking my eyes off my target. "But there's a severed head in the freezer. One that spoke to me, told me he'd been *murdered*. I don't know why I forgot about him, but something very strange is going on here. Stranger than . . . well, the strangeness this evening already had."

He raised his eyebrows. "A talking severed head."

"You must think I'm nuts, but just wait." My heels clicked as I pushed open the door to the kitchen. Melanie the server trailed after us.

"Can I help you find something?" she asked.

"I can't believe you didn't notice anything strange." I looked at her with accusation. "You're the only server on duty tonight other than Thomas."

She placed a hand on her chest as if taken aback by my words. "I don't know what you mean. Strange in what way?"

"My dear, what on earth is happening?" Veronique also joined us in the kitchen, and Tasha was right behind her.

"Here's what's happening." I took a position directly in front of the freezer. "Take a look at this!"

I swung open the freezer door expecting to hear gasps of horror from those gathered in front of me.

Instead, I got blank looks.

I turned to see that the freezer was empty, apart from several ice cube trays. Peering closer at the inside, I could confirm that nothing else was in there. No bloodstains, no drool, no messages scratched by a desperate tooth. Nothing at all that would show that there had been a head in there.

But there *was* a head in there.

Wasn't there?

"Sarah . . ." Thierry's voice was as gentle and supportive as I'd ever heard it, which wasn't necessarily a good sign. "Do you see a severed head in the freezer right now?"

Great. He really did think I was crazy.

"No, there is no head."

"But there was before."

"Yes."

"Are you absolutely certain about that?"

"Yes! I'm absolutely certain!"

"You said you forgot about it until just a little while ago when you heard . . . a voice." At my bleak look, he spread his hands. "I'm not doubting you. I'm simply trying to understand."

I racked my brain for answers. "Maybe it was a ghost. A ghost head."

"You are able to see ghosts?" Veronique asked, brightening. "Vampiric clairvoyance is a skill I've always envied."

I shot her a look. "Don't envy it. It hasn't been a lot of fun so far."

"I suppose it's all in how you look at it, isn't it? Thierry, you've had that ability as well from time to time. You didn't see anything? Hear anything?"

"No." His jaw tensed. "However, I have discovered

recently that Sarah's skills at clairvoyance may be superior to my own. In the recent past, she's seen things that I have not."

"Great. Just what I always want to excel at." I sighed, and then looked in the freezer again as if I might have missed a human head sitting in there. "I don't know what's going on."

Had I imagined it? That would explain the first sighting, but not the talking in my head. I'd been known to have long conversations with myself sometimes, but not usually with an imaginary friend.

"What did this . . . head . . . say to you?" Thierry asked.

"Not much. He sounded confused, but he was certain he'd been murdered. Which isn't much of a stretch. There aren't too many decapitated heads walking around from self-inflicted wounds."

"Or walking around at all," Veronique added unhelpfully. "Since it would have no legs."

"Maybe something was put in Sarah's drink that might make her hallucinate," Tasha suggested. "Recreational drugs are everywhere and if you're not used to them they can pack a punch, even for a vampire."

"Drugs might affect Sarah more than the rest of us," Veronique agreed. "She is, after all, a mere fledgling."

"It wasn't drugs," I said, choosing to ignore the "mere fledgling" remark. "I—I don't know what happened, but he's gone now."

"What did he look like?" Tasha asked. "Any discerning features?"

"He looked . . . normal, I guess. Nothing weird. Just a guy. Brown hair, brown eyes."

"A ghost," Thierry said, nodding. "It must be. Many

of these old mansions are rumored to be haunted. I think this would be the most likely explanation."

"Perhaps he was murdered decades ago," Tasha said. "And he's been haunting this place every day since."

"I don't know." After the initial shock at remembering the head, I'd started to calm down and think a bit more rationally. Emphasis on *a bit*. "I guess that's possible. And if so, I don't think there's much I can do to help him."

"We should leave," Thierry said.

Even though that was all I'd wanted to do since we first arrived, the thought of leaving now felt wrong. Maybe the ghost head had been here for ages, but the fact that he'd directly asked for my help and I couldn't do anything to help him bothered me deeply.

I did know that the average, run-of-the-mill ghost was not a threat to the living. They were more like watching something on a TV screen. They could be seen (by those with that ability), they could be heard, but they couldn't harm the living. They couldn't kill. They were just super-creepy. Especially when they weren't all in one piece.

"Sorry, ghost guy," I said under my breath as I allowed Thierry to guide me out of the kitchen and back toward the foyer, where there was a mass exodus going on of guests leaving through the front doors.

Atticus stepped in front of me and offered me a patient smile.

"Sarah, we need to talk about the amulet."

Thierry nudged me aside. "You need to do no such thing."

"I believe I was talking to your wife, not to you."

His eyes flashed. "Had I known for sure that you would challenge me for that piece—"

"What would you have done?" Thierry asked. "Please tell me. I'm fascinated."

Atticus stepped closer to Thierry, all pretense of friendliness gone. "Don't push me, de Bennicoeur."

"I haven't even touched you. Yet."

"I wanted the amulet."

"I know. That message has come through loud and clear. Unfortunately, you were not the winner of the auction."

"Nor were you."

"No. But the results are the same."

Atticus spoke to me over Thierry's shoulder. "I will pay you twice the winning bid. I need that amulet."

Thirty-four million dollars? "Why do you want it so badly?" I asked.

"I have my reasons."

"Reasons to possess a powerful djinn with the ability to grant your wishes," Thierry said coldly. "Interesting that you'd *need* something like that."

"Don't even go there, de Bennicoeur. You were the one who wanted it first. What reasons did you have to exploit its powers?"

"None worth sharing in present company."

"It's fascinating to witness how many you've fooled. But, as they say, a tiger doesn't change its stripes."

"Are you speaking about me or yourself?"

"We were friends once."

"Friends don't push friends into agreements under threat."

"I thought we'd dealt with this."

"Perhaps to your satisfaction, but not to mine."

I hooked my arm through Thierry's and pulled

him back a couple of steps. "Okay, let's break this up. No reason why things have to get nasty."

"Your wife has much more sense than you do," Atticus observed. "For all her youth, she surprises me with her ability to see potential difficulties."

Thierry's arm was like steel beneath my grip. "She will not sell you the amulet."

"Be careful with this one, Sarah," Atticus cautioned. "Get away from him while you still can."

"This is ridiculous," I said, nervously tucking a lock of hair behind my ear. "We should get going."

Atticus's gaze moved to my throat. "Just as I suspected. Thierry, have you again given in to your thirst tonight?"

Crap. I'd just flashed him the bite marks.

Thierry's silence spoke very dangerous volumes before he uttered a word. "We're done here, Atticus."

"You think it's that easy? You disappointed me. I thought we were starting out as friends anew, after all this time apart. I guess I was wrong."

"You've been wrong about many things over the years."

"Not that you cared. You disappeared a hundred years ago and left Silas, Michael, and me with all the bulk of the responsibility. The others never forgave you for abandoning the Ring."

"Silas and Michael are dead now, aren't they? They won't be forgiving anyone anymore."

Anna and Frederic stood nearby, speaking to each other, but it was clear to me that they were also listening in on this argument. Tasha lingered by the entrance to the hallway leading back toward the parlor, and she shared a tense look with me.

"Your thirst puts those around you in danger. It

always has," Atticus continued. "This is only more evidence. Perhaps I should call in an enforcer to deal with these difficulties."

"Oh, Atticus." Veronique spoke up. She'd been observing till now, her arms crossed over her chest. "You always did overreact to the silliest things."

His gaze flicked to me before returning to Thierry. "I wasn't going to tell you, but I've given my card to Sarah. If she has any issues with you, she's to call me immediately."

"Issues?" Thierry's brows shot up as his tone turned darker. "Let me repeat myself, Atticus. We're done here. Sarah, let's arrange payment for the amulet and be on our way."

By far the best idea he'd had all evening. Possibly all year.

Atticus was deadly silent as Thierry put his hand on the small of my back and guided me across the foyer in the direction of the salon.

"I'm sorry he saw the marks," I said.

"Don't be." His jaw clenched and his expression grew pained. "I'm sorry I bit you. Devastated, actually."

I shook my head. "I'm fine. Really, I am. Are you feeling better now?"

His gray eyes flicked to mine, the ice that had been in them before while dealing with Atticus only a chilly memory now. "I wish I could say I was, but I'm not. I'm afraid it's still dangerous to be around me right now."

"You have it under control."

"I do give that impression, but don't buy into it completely, Sarah. If I ever really harmed you . . ." He hissed out a breath. "I don't think I could live with myself."

I pulled him off to the side of the hallway and cupped his face between my hands. "Stop it. That's not going to happen because you've got this. A little blood doesn't make or break you. You hear me?"

His expression remained tense, but he nodded. "I hear you."

"Good." I couldn't let this swirl around my mind a moment longer. I had to get it out. "Before we get the amulet, I have to tell you something about Sebastien."

I told him about the blood in the glass being Sebastien's doing. About his being trapped in the tomb for centuries. About his assumption that it had been Thierry's fault.

Thierry's eyes widened. "What?"

It was a good reaction. I liked the shock. Thierry didn't do shock unless he was really, well, shocked.

"He's simmering with a lot of anger toward you. I mean, rightfully so, really. If somebody locked me in a closet for hundreds of years, I'd be really pissed off, too."

He gaped at me. Again, Thierry did not gape. I didn't think gaping was an expression I'd ever seen on his face before, actually.

"I'm assuming that he's wrong," I said when he didn't reply. "That you didn't do it."

"Of course I didn't."

Relief flowed over me. "I can't tell you how happy I am to have a little confirmation."

"Did you believe him?"

"No." It was a tiny lie. I'd hoped really, really hard he hadn't done it. I absently slid my hand over a golden frame on the wall in the dimly lit hallway. "But I knew you were a little more . . . well, ruthless, back in the day. For the record, I do separate that Thierry from you in my mind."

He had his arms crossed over his chest. "I'm the exact same man."

I flicked a look at him. "You're not helping."

"I didn't trap Sebastien as he claims."

"You said he had your thirst. If he was harming people . . ."

"If I had a serious issue with him, locking him away would not have been my solution. I would have chosen something much more permanent."

"Again, not really helping, especially spoken so casually." I grimaced at the thought. "So basically we have a little problem that what he thinks happened did not actually happen."

"He always hated me. Now, believing this to be true, he'll feel justified in trying to seek revenge."

"All the more reason for us to get out of here ASAP. But first we need that amulet."

"Agreed."

In the parlor, the last of the winning guests were finishing up with Thomas, gold and platinum credit cards sparkling under the light from several chandeliers hanging from the high ceiling.

Sebastien watched us approach. "Problems?"

"Numerous," Thierry replied.

Please don't say anything, I pleaded internally. I just wanted to get out of there and deal with the fallout tomorrow. Or never. Never would be good.

Don't get me wrong, I actually felt horrible for Sebastien. I couldn't imagine what he'd been through. And for him to believe it was someone he'd looked up to as a father figure who'd betrayed him so horribly . . .

A simple explanation or a flat denial wasn't going

to do a thing to change his mind right now. I knew it wouldn't for me.

"Did I hear something about a head?" Sebastien asked.

"Yes." I tried to sound casual, though I felt anything but. "I'm seeing severed heads floating around tonight. Either it's a ghost on the loose or I'm finally going insane. It's fifty-fifty, really."

"Who does this mansion belong to?" Thierry asked. "Perhaps the owner would know if it's haunted."

Why was he asking questions and prolonging this? I glanced at the clock. We were getting closer to midnight. Time to make like a pumpkin and scram before I lost my glass slipper.

Sebastien shrugged a shoulder. "I don't know them personally."

"Earlier you said it was a friend."

"I was exaggerating. Many multimillionaires will rent out their houses to movie producers or those who wish to throw elegant parties to impress their friends."

"Did you think it would impress everyone to be here?"

"I've recently felt the intense need to surround myself with luxury."

Do not say anything, Thierry, I thought. *Just don't.*

"It's time we wrap this up," Thierry said. "I'd like to arrange payment for the amulet."

"Excellent."

Thierry handed over an American Express card, which Sebastien gave to Thomas. Thomas dialed a number on a phone and held it to his ear, stepping a few feet away from us.

"Both a butler and a bookkeeper," I said. "Handy."

Sebastien's gaze flicked to me. "We're short-staffed tonight."

"So I gathered. I spoke with your werewolf server earlier. Lovely girl. She takes direction well, doesn't she?"

"She certainly does."

He was definitely infuriating. And smug. And incredibly hard to read. It was only a reminder that we'd stayed long beyond when we should have gotten out of here.

"Is there anything further you wish to say to me, Sebastien?" Thierry asked.

My fingertips dug deep into his arm.

Sebastien swallowed and a shadow of pain crossed his eyes, which I hadn't expected. It wasn't outrage. It wasn't fury.

It was sadness.

"Nothing at all," he said, his voice hoarse.

He'd spiked Thierry's drink with blood to bring out his dark side, he'd been spouting angry words earlier and hinting at unpleasantness ahead, and yet now I had the sudden urge to give him a hug.

"It seems you've acquired a very powerful amulet, Sarah," he said, after getting a nod from Thomas as the butler ended his call.

"I'm not sure it'll go with any of my outfits."

"Be very careful with it."

"I'll try my best." I hesitated as something occurred to me that I'd pondered earlier. "You said you didn't have time to use it, but I know you did. You could have tested it out. Wished for a million dollars, or something."

He raised an eyebrow. "You really want to know why?"

"If I didn't I wouldn't ask."

"It's said that to own an amulet like this will curse you with bad luck."

My stomach sank. "Sure, now you tell me."

"I received the worst luck simply by owning it, not by using it. I decided not to press what little luck I had left. Now it's your choice if you will or not. Perhaps it'll work out better for you."

A cursed amulet with a troublemaking djinn trapped inside. All for seventeen million dollars. What a deal.

"We'll be putting it somewhere safe," Thierry said. "No one will be accessing its magic ever again."

Sebastien's jaw was a tight line. "I think that's a very good plan."

"Is that why you let me win?" I asked. "So Atticus wouldn't?"

"That sounds rather underhanded, doesn't it?" he replied after a moment.

"Is that a yes?"

"Atticus's reputation precedes him. I doubted his motives for wanting to add this piece to his collection."

"But you didn't doubt mine?" Thierry said.

"Perhaps. But you didn't win it. Sarah did."

"Does that really make a difference?" I asked. "I mean, it's Thierry's money"—or, the council's money—"that's paying for it."

"Intention is the most important thing, especially as a piece like this shifts from one owner to another. The amulet now belongs to you, Sarah, and you alone. It doesn't matter whose name is on the credit card."

Sebastien reached behind the podium to draw out the black velvet box.

"Here it is."

I tried not to cringe at the sight of it. "My very own cursed amulet. Hooray."

He glanced down at the box. "Whether or not you believe in the curse, I suggest you leave it in the box. Lock it up. And keep it out of the hands of people like Atticus Kincade."

"So responsible," Thierry said. "You've changed over the years."

"You have no idea how much I've changed." Sebastien hissed out a breath, then returned his attention to me. "Here you go, Sarah. The Jacquerra Amulet— it's all yours."

He opened the box.

"There's a problem," I said.

He looked down at the box and frowned.

Yes, definitely a problem.

The amulet was gone.

Chapter 7

Gone. Nothing was in the box but air.

By the shock on Sebastien's face, this was not something he'd expected.

"What are you playing at?" Thierry growled. "Where is it?"

"I'm not playing at anything. It was here. Nobody touched it."

"Obviously, somebody did. Somebody who wanted it badly and has since before this night began."

Without another word, Thierry turned and swiftly moved out of the salon. I had to run to keep up with him.

"Thierry—"

"Atticus stole it from right under our noses, Sarah. And then he made that scene in the foyer to divert attention, to establish his innocence once the discovery had been made."

"You don't know that."

"Wrong. I do."

Almost everyone had left by now, but Atticus was still here. He was halfway out the front door when Thierry grabbed his shoulder, pulled him back inside, and kicked the door shut.

Atticus looked stunned by this. "De Bennicoeur—"

"Where is the amulet?"

"I assume it's in the salon waiting for you to claim it."

"The box is there. The amulet is missing."

The odds of us getting out of here before something very unpleasant happened between the two of them seemed slim to none at this point, but I didn't know what I could do to help. And if Atticus had swiped the amulet, he had to come clean.

Another heated conversation drew my attention to the left of the foyer. The voices were lowered, but the argument was no less intense.

The Darks were in the corner, glaring at each other, which finally proved to me they could make facial expressions after all.

"Don't you dare lie to me," Anna snarled.

"I'm not lying."

"Do you think I'm stupid? I know exactly what's going on here."

"Really, Anna? If you do it would be the first time in two decades that you weren't totally ignorant to something important that's happening around you."

"How dare you speak to me like that after what you've done!"

"This conversation is over."

"And this marriage?"

"That is yet to be determined. I can think of others I'd much rather spend eternity with."

"Fine with me!"

Anna stomped away from him toward the other side of the foyer, meeting my gaze directly as she passed me. And, yikes, the glare she gave me was fiery enough to singe my eyebrows.

Frederic Dark shot me a tight smile. "Please ignore her."

I felt the need to respond to that. "Drama queen?"

"She's . . . unexpectedly temperamental this evening."

"Maybe it's a full moon. Although I hope not. There is a werewolf in the house." I sent a look toward Melanie, who lurked at the edges of the foyer.

"You're Thierry de Bennicoeur's new wife, aren't you?" Frederic asked.

"I am."

"Hmm." He swept his gaze down the front of me as if noticing me for the first time tonight. From his bland expression, I couldn't tell if he liked what he saw or if I completely disgusted him.

"It was really nice to meet you," I lied, and turned back to the standoff between Thierry and Atticus.

Atticus was turning his pockets out. "See? I have nothing on me but a wallet and a cell phone. Would you like to frisk me?"

"That won't be necessary," Sebastien said as he entered the foyer. "We will find the amulet."

"Someone stole it," Thierry said.

"So intelligent you are," Atticus said, sarcasm dripping. "Just what the council needs in our investigating consultants."

"So it's true, Thierry." Sebastien glanced between the two, his expression impossible to read. "You're working for the council."

"At the moment."

"I never thought I'd see the day where you took anyone else's orders but your own."

I stood there frozen in place, waiting for something horrible to happen, ready to spring into action to defend . . . well, whoever needed defending.

Veronique and Jacob stood over by the archway

near the staircase. Tasha had pulled her pashmina around her shoulders. The three looked on with interest but without comment as Sebastien drew closer to Thierry.

Thierry watched his approach. "I know what you believe I did, but it's not true."

Uh-oh. Not the time, Thierry. So not the time!

"Do you, now?" Sebastien clasped his hands together and flicked a glance at me, one that held either accusation or relief, I couldn't tell which. "Does everyone know about this? Shall we tell them?"

"Sebastien, darling, what is going on?" Veronique asked.

"You should know this already. You let me down. Unless you're the one who assisted him." He pointed at her with each sentence as if punctuating it. "He hated me. He did from the very beginning. I was a burden. I threated his sense of being the master of his world. He didn't want the responsibility of watching over a fledgling, especially one who reminded him so much of himself."

"It was never as bad as you thought it was, darling." Veronique drew closer to him, but finally faltered when he held up a hand to stop her. "We were a family. Families have difficulties, but nothing that can't be worked out with time and effort. If only you'd stayed close to us, I'm sure you and Thierry would have reconciled your differences."

"Wrong. He left me there in a tomb no bigger than a coffin. I suffered for weeks before I fell unconscious, wasting away to nothing but a flesh-covered skeleton. And nobody searched for me. Nobody found me. It took three centuries for me to gain my freedom."

Her eyes widened with shock. "And you believe Thierry was the one who did this to you?"

Sebastien nodded with a stiff jerk of his head. "I do."

I watched Thierry for his reaction to this, but his expression remained stoic and controlled.

Still, when he spoke, his voice was softer and didn't have any of the anger in it from before. "It wasn't me. Whatever you've been led to believe, and whoever led you to believe it, I did not do this to you."

Veronique now regarded Thierry with trepidation. "You said that he was trouble. . . ."

"It doesn't matter what I said. Even at my worst, I would not do such a thing to a living being, no matter who they were. He disappeared. We assumed he had moved on as he had threatened to do many times. How were we to know?"

"Oh, my darling." Veronique rushed toward Sebastien, her arms outstretched, but he backed away from her and shook his head.

"No. It's not that easy, Veronique."

"How long have you been freed?"

"Long enough to gather my treasures and plan this evening." Sebastien's jaw clenched. "I wanted to see your face when you saw me again, Thierry, knowing what you did to me."

"He said he didn't do it," I said, my throat tight. Everyone else remained completely silent. I could almost forget we had a sizable audience for this uncomfortable conversation.

Sebastien gave me a look of disgust. "Of course *you'd* believe that. He's your husband."

I shoved my hands deep into the convenient

pockets of my red dress. "I believe it because it's true. I'm sorry for what you had to go through, really I am, but if Thierry did do what you say he did, he'd own it. He wouldn't lie about it."

"Or perhaps he doesn't want his armor to be tarnished in the eyes of his new bride. Perhaps someone as experienced as Veronique could handle a truth like this, but a mere fledgling . . . that's a different thing."

There was that "mere fledgling" phrase again.

Sebastien had been through a lot, so I wanted to be understanding with this acting out, but he'd caused all this trouble based on what? An assumption?

"Are you feeling the effects of the blood from earlier, Thierry?" Sebastien said. "You should probably know by now that it wasn't normal blood."

Thierry looked at him, his brow lowered. "What are you talking about?"

Sebastien's eyes narrowed cruelly. "My revenge was contained in that glass. The blood has a powerful spell cast upon it, which will not loosen its hold on you anytime soon."

With growing dismay, I noticed for the first time that there was a thin sheen of perspiration on Thierry's forehead. How could I have missed this? If it was true, he had to have been masking the severity of his thirst. "Is it that bad? Do you feel it?" I asked.

"I'm fine." Thierry didn't look at me. His attention was fixed entirely on Sebastien. "You need to break this spell."

"No, I don't think I will." He glanced at me, at my throat. "He had to taste another's blood for the spell to fully take hold. Looks like he's tasted yours. Your shiny new husband now has an insatiable need to feed tonight. He won't be able to resist for long. And when Thierry let his thirst take hold of him in the past, very few of his victims survived it."

All of my sympathy for this guy went out the window in milliseconds. As well as the last remaining piece of my ability to see the good side in just about everyone. "Big mistake, Sebastien."

He just shrugged at me, which only infuriated me further.

"What witch do you associate with that would help with this horrible act?" Veronique said, shocked.

"As if I'd tell you anything," Sebastien replied. "I doubt if I've even crossed your mind more than once or twice in all these years."

Her shock dissipated, replaced by an anger that reflected my own. "How dare you say such a thing?"

"If I may interject," Atticus said flippantly. "I see Thierry has more difficulties than I believed. I'll call in an enforcer to deal with this. I can have one here in less than an hour."

No, big mistake. An enforcer would deal with a vampire bespelled with uncontrollable bloodlust in only one way—a stake through the heart.

That was *not* going to happen.

My mind reeled. I'd thought it was dangerous for Sebastien to spike Thierry's drink with blood, but I'd assumed that had been merely a mean-spirited act of mischief. But blood that contained a spell to drive him to feed . . .

To drive him to kill . . .

Let's not get ahead of ourselves.

He was fine and nothing bad had happened. I could handle a couple of minor bite marks.

But I knew I had to do something before this

escalated. My track record with witches and spells hadn't been stellar so far in my supernatural life. I definitely wouldn't underestimate one tonight.

To break a witch's spell, we'd likely need another witch. And we'd just happened to meet a couple of very powerful—and very friendly—witches recently who might be able to help. They were on the East Coast, but that was a minor inconvenience at this point.

My tension eased just a little at having a potential game plan in mind. For now, I'd keep it to myself.

"We need to get out of here," I told Thierry.

He regarded me with a tight jaw and a furrowed brow. "I can't leave. Not given how I'm feeling."

Atticus pulled his cell phone from his pocket and looked down at the screen. "Why is there no reception?"

"It will be fine." Veronique drew closer and linked arms with me. "Once Sebastien comes to his senses he'll realize what he's done is immature and petty and he will break this ridiculous spell."

"Three hundred years, Veronique," Sebastien reminded her. "He has to pay for that time he stole from me."

She gave him a sharp look. "When you come to your senses and realize what you've done," she repeated, every word crisp, "you will remember that Thierry gave you the gift of immortality when you were moments from death. You owe him for that."

Silence fell between them.

"What the hell is going on here?" Jacob had been silent until now, but he roared this like a cornered lion. "I've been thinking I was a part of some sort of amusing role-playing party all night, but what is this? Who the hell are you people?"

Veronique winced. "Role-playing. Yes, that's it. That's all it is, darling. Aren't you having fun?"

The rich publisher marched over to a side table by the front door, where I saw that someone had placed Veronique's book that she'd given me earlier. He hoisted it up so the cover could be seen by everyone.

"This," he hissed, "is supposed to be fiction."

"It is," Veronique replied. "Yes, it is."

"This is your *actual* memoir, isn't it?"

"Fictional memoir. Darling." She cleared her throat.

Jacob jabbed his index finger at her accusingly. "You have fangs. Actual fangs. I thought they were specialty veneers owned by one who enjoys vampire lore a bit too much. But . . . but they're real, aren't they?"

Atticus rolled his eyes. "This human should not have been invited here this evening. Do you know what an inconvenience this is, Veronique?"

Jacob reared back, his eyes wide. "You're *all* vampires, aren't you? You all have fangs!"

Finally, he noticed. Better late than never. Or, really, *never* would have been much better.

"Not me." Tasha said this to me directly. "I have mine ground down every other week to appear as human as possible. The tabloids would have a field day otherwise. They're such vultures."

"They totally are." Still starstruck. I seriously couldn't help it.

"I need to get out of here." Jacob made for the door.

"I'm afraid I can't let you leave yet." Atticus stepped in front of him to block his path. "Calm yourself. We mean you no harm." He cocked his head. "Although perhaps you should stay away from de Bennicoeur."

I watched most of this unfold from the corner of my eye as I studied Thierry closely. He'd been silent since the truth about the blood spell came out and, honestly, I had no idea how he was feeling right now. I had to admit, it worried me.

He dealt with his thirst on a daily basis, but I knew he normally had it well under control.

But a malicious spell could definitely change a lot.

"We're leaving, Thierry," I told him again, even firmer this time. "I'll keep my distance, I promise, but we're going to figure this out together."

"Loyal, isn't she?" Sebastien gave us a cold grin. "All the way to the bloody end."

"You will regret this," Thierry said, words as dark as ever I'd heard them. "You think three hundred years locked in a tomb was torture? Just you wait."

The grandfather clock in the center of the foyer near the stairs clicked to twelve o'clock and began to chime.

Midnight. I'd really hoped we'd be long gone by now.

"Veronique, you will have to restrain your human and keep him calm," Atticus said, pulling his phone from his pocket again. "I'll call in reinforcements as soon as I can get reception on my phone and they'll ensure that he forgets all of this."

"Very well," she said with a sigh.

"Veronique!" Jacob blustered.

"I'm sorry, darling. But it will be better soon, I promise. We can start over once you've forgotten what you've heard here tonight. It will all be fiction once again."

Fiction. Yeah, that was a good way to put it. If Atticus had an enforcer here . . . I knew they had a way—most likely through magical means—of erasing unpleasant memories. They usually used it on humans who'd seen a bit too much disturbing vampire activity. No memories, no threat of rumors spreading.

If there was an enforcer *already* in our midst, that would explain me forgetting the ghost head. But I honestly didn't think it was going to have that neat of an explanation.

However, the ghost head was the least of my problems at the moment.

"That's odd." Tasha had her phone out as well and was looking down at her screen. "I'm not getting any signal here either. Here in Beverly Hills? That's very strange, isn't it?"

"I don't have a phone," Frederic said, pursing his lips with distaste. "Modern inventions interfere with the pureness of a supernatural."

I rolled my eyes. *Whatever, Fred.*

"Something strange is going on here." Melanie stared around at all of us, her eyes widening. "I can feel it."

"Feel it?" Tasha said. "Can't you *see* the strangeness easily enough without feeling it, too?"

"Actually, I have some, um . . . *abilities*." Melanie twisted a finger nervously through her blond hair. "Abilities that make me very sensitive to the presence of magic."

A psychic werewolf.

Surprisingly, she wasn't the first one I'd ever met. Maybe it was a thing, like clairvoyant vampires.

But I didn't care about bad cellular reception, furry psychics, or anything else going on under this roof. All I cared about was getting Thierry to someone who could help break this spell before it got any worse.

"Did you sense the magic in the blood you slipped into Thierry's drink?" I asked Melanie, failing to keep the accusation out of my voice.

"Were anyone else's drinks tainted?" Tasha asked.

"No—no to both questions." Melanie frowned very hard, then touched her temples as if she'd gotten a terrible headache. "But I can feel something else. Something big. It's been growing in the last couple of minutes."

"What?" I asked. My skin also prickled now with something that didn't feel remotely natural. I shot Thierry a wary look. "Can you feel that, too?"

He nodded. "What is it?"

Melanie gasped. "Get out of here right now while you still can. It's coming."

"What's coming?" I asked, my chest tightening.

When she looked directly at me her eyes had gone a stark glowing white.

I stopped breathing. "She's been possessed!"

"By what?" Veronique demanded.

I shot her a look through my rising panic. "The correct response to 'she's been possessed' should always be 'let's get out of here.'"

Veronique nodded. "A point well made."

Atticus was at the door first, pulling at the handle. "It's locked."

Anxiety clawed at my chest like a vicious hell-kitten. "Unlock it!"

Thomas raced over and began fiddling with the door, yanking on the handle as well. "He's right. It's locked, and I can't unlock it."

"Break a window," Veronique suggested. Even her voice now held strain.

Sebastien grabbed a heavy metal sculpture from

the bottom of the staircase and without hesitation, hurled it at the large, curtained window to the left of the door.

It pinged back without causing even a single crack to appear.

Everyone in the foyer slowly turned to look at Melanie, who had moved up several steps on the staircase so she could look down at us over the ornate gold railing.

"That's correct. You're all trapped here until dawn." Her eyes continued to glow that eerie bright white. "And don't bother looking for an escape. There is none."

Chapter 8

Yes, the werewolf was definitely possessed. Apart from the glowing white eyeballs, she held herself oddly, her shoulders were stiff, her expression creepily calm. I'd witnessed both demonic and ghostly possessions before, but something about this felt different.

Different wasn't necessarily good—especially when it came with an announcement like that.

Thierry was the first to step forward, his fists clenched at his sides, while the others just gaped at the possessed girl on the stairs. "Who are you? And what do you want with us?"

Her white eyes tracked to him. "What question do you want answered first, vampire?"

"Who are you?"

She raised those bright eyes upward as if searching for the answer on the high ceiling of the foyer. "I am a warning. I am a word of caution. I am a moment of direction in the darkness that stretches before you."

Was she a fortune cookie, too? She sure sounded like one.

"Are you a ghost or a demon?" I asked.

"Neither."

"Are you the djinn from the Jacquerra Amulet?" Atticus asked.

"No. I am an echo of the coven of witches who imprisoned this djinn. We have been summoned here due to the amulet and what is contained within it."

"Which means what?" Thierry had drawn close enough to touch me, but he didn't take his attention away from Melanie. "The amulet's missing. Someone stole it and has escaped with it."

Melanie cocked her head as if considering his words. "Incorrect. The amulet is still in this location, hidden from sight. I am here because it has been damaged. Disrespected. Desecrated."

Damaged? What was she talking about? "Who damaged it? And how?" I asked.

She swiveled to regard me directly. "By one who wished to manipulate its power beyond what is allowed."

Huh? Definitely a fortune cookie. "Can you be a little less cryptic?"

She blinked slowly. "No."

There were eleven of us here in the foyer, including her. Thomas the butler, Sebastien, Atticus, Thierry and me, Veronique and Jacob, Tasha, Anna and Frederic. All standing quietly and as still as statues. Everyone else had left before midnight.

Lucky them.

Sebastien scanned the group of us gathered at the stairway before he stepped forward. "The amulet looked fine when I last saw it."

"The damage done is not visible to the untrained eye. But it was enough to summon this warning for you all."

"This warning"—I spoke up, since many of the others had been stunned into veritable silence—"that comes with a supernatural lockdown until dawn."

"Yes."

The amulet had been taken and hidden. But why wouldn't that person have just hightailed it out of here if they wanted to steal something like that? "Where is the amulet hidden?" I asked.

"Here. Somewhere."

I glared at her with growing frustration. "Helpful, thanks. And we need to find it, like some sort of hide-and-seek game?"

"All magic that has escaped must be returned to the safety of the amulet by dawn."

"How?"

"You must figure that out for yourself."

I exchanged a look with Thierry. To see worry in his gray eyes did nothing to ease my mind that all of this would be easily handled.

"Is the person who hid it still among us?" Thierry asked.

"I do not know."

"What *do* you know?" His voice turned sharp and impatient. "There must be some reason why you're here. Some message you must relate other than what is already obvious to us. We're trapped here. Till dawn, you say. What happens at dawn if we're unable to return the magic to the amulet if we don't even know how to do this? Tell us something that might help us."

"This location has been secured to protect what lies beyond," she replied. "We must find a way to better contain the escaped magic."

That wasn't exactly an answer, but it sure wasn't good news.

From the stunned looks on the others' faces, I'd be willing to bet this was their very first possession. I didn't think there was a suitable Hallmark card for that.

To me, information was the best way to stave off panic. Don't get me wrong—I had plenty of panic, growing by the second. I'd honestly thought dealing with Atticus's accusations and investigation, and then Sebastien's claims and threats, was bad enough.

This wasn't a fantastic third layer to this supernatural club sandwich.

"Escaped magic," I repeated. "What does that mean? Are we in danger?"

"We will find a way to contain a portion of this magic before we leave. That may help you." She said this as if discussing the weather. No tone, no emotion. Just flat words.

"What happens if we don't restore the amulet by dawn?" Thierry asked.

An excellent question.

Melanie regarded him for a moment in silence. "When the sun rises, if the amulet has not been restored, all the magic will have escaped from it. The mortal world will be at risk. The amulet will be destroyed and this location will cease to exist."

Anna let out a squeak of fear and clutched at her husband's arm.

"Cease to exist," I said slowly, trying to wrap my head around her casual announcement. "You mean, *we'll* cease to exist, too."

"Yes."

The single word clutched my heart and squeezed. "Then I guess we'd better find it and restore it."

Jacob had been silent until now, his eyes so wide they looked like they'd pop right out of his head. He clutched Veronique's book to his chest as if it was a shield. "Don't listen to this *thing*," he snarled. "It's a demon—a demon sent from Hell to devour us all!"

"Darling . . ." Veronique touched his arm. "Calm yourself."

He flinched away from her. "Calm myself? Just the opposite. I need to protect myself from this beast!"

With that, he hurled Veronique's heavy memoir right at the possessed werewolf's head.

He had an excellent arm and perfect aim.

However, the book froze three feet from her face, suspended in the air. She regarded it with interest.

"What is this?" The cover fell open and the pages flipped forward. "Oh, yes, very good."

"Why, thank you." Veronique smiled up at her. "I'm quite happy with how it turned out. If you'd like a signed copy, I'd be happy to provide one."

"We can use this to contain some of the magic. It will help, although not nearly enough."

The book flipped to the last page and closed. Then it exploded in a burst of bright white light that made me wince and shield my eyes.

Veronique blinked with dismay at the spot where her book had hovered before it had been destroyed. Had that been the equivalent of a bad review?

"We, the coven's echo, will not return," the possessed Melanie said. "For it will be too late. At dawn, the outcome will either be positive or negative. Either way, the mortal world will be safe from harm. The only lives at risk are your own."

My stomach lurched and I grabbed Thierry's arm.

"What now?" I mouthed to him.

His gaze moved to Sebastien, who stepped forward, his face pale. "Wait! It's my fault the Jacquerra Amulet was here in the first place. I should have kept it under lock and key. I will stay and search for it, but let the others leave."

This guy was full of surprises. One moment he was Mr. Vengeance, the next he was selfless and self-sacrificing. Which was the real Sebastien Lavelle?

Melanie regarded him and shook her head. "It is too late for that now. It is after midnight and you are already wasting precious time. We suggest you use that time. Find the amulet. Restore it to its full power by returning to it all of its magic."

"How do we do that?" I asked.

"You will need to figure that out without our help. Farewell to you all."

"But wait—" I began, confused and frustrated, but it was too late.

Without another word, she closed her eyes, let out a sharp gasp, and fell forward. She would have fallen down the stairs, but Thomas was there to catch her.

"Are you all right?" he asked her.

Melanie smiled up at him. "What happened?"

"Nothing good, I'm afraid."

He was right about that. Everyone was silent for several long, uncomfortable moments.

"If whoever hid the amulet wants to step forward and admit it so we can fix this mess right now," I said when no one else spoke first, "that would really help. No judgment."

Atticus glared at each in the group turn. "No judgment other than that I will kill the guilty party where they stand for this inconvenience."

I shot him a withering look. "No, you won't. Can we all agree that if someone wants to admit what they've done, we're fine with it? Just speak up and tell us where you hid the amulet and all is forgiven. Whatever it takes to keep this from getting worse."

"Worse than this?" Anna said, her voice pinched.

"Actually, yes. By the sound of it, dawn will be much worse. Or did you miss the part where she basically said this location will be destroyed along with everyone in it?"

Her black eyes flashed. "I didn't miss it. I was standing right here."

"I agree with Sarah's plan," Veronique said. "Speak up and we will forgive the thief."

The others, including Atticus—but not including Jacob, who'd drawn back from us into a corner—mumbled their agreement, and we waited for someone to step forward and confess.

But, of course, nobody did.

That would have been way too easy. Besides, we had no confirmation that the guilty party was still among the eleven of us. They could have hightailed it out of here after the free champagne and hors d'oeuvres.

I could use another glass of that champagne right about now.

"Do you think my book was really destroyed?" Veronique asked glumly. "I don't understand why she would do that."

"The book is real," Jacob mumbled. "My God, the book is a real memoir."

"We're trapped here all night." Anna watched him, twisting a pale finger nervously through her long black hair. "I haven't fed today. I'll need blood before dawn."

"Unfortunately," Sebastien said, "the only blood I had on hand was bespelled and it's all been used."

Again, my desire to punch Sebastien in the nose returned in full force. He'd been all selfless a minute ago while bargaining for our escape, but now he was back to sounding like a jerk.

Anna hadn't taken her attention off Jacob. "It's fine. Luckily, we have a perfect food source among us."

Jacob's eyes widened further. "Do not look at me like that, creature of darkness."

She shrugged and her lips peeled back from her sharp fangs, her previous fear vanishing. "You're the lone human among us. How else should I look at you? Human blood has always my preference."

"Close your mouth, Anna." Frederic sounded disgusted with her. "You're scaring him."

She didn't close her mouth. I could have sworn that, if anything, her fangs got sharper and longer. "Any human surrounded by nine vampires who isn't scared would be a damn fool."

Jacob pressed back against the wall and let out a whimper. "Please don't hurt me."

"She will not come near you, I promise." Veronique went to stand near him, but he scrambled to get away from her.

"Don't touch me, you monster," he hissed. "None of you monsters dare touch me. Do you know who I am? I could buy and sell every one of you if I wanted to. You're disgusting! Come near me and I'll kill you!"

With that, he pushed past Veronique and ran up the stairs to the second-floor landing, quickly disappearing from sight.

I watched him flee. "Seems like a perfectly reasonable reaction to me."

Veronique sighed. "I should go after him and make him see reason."

Anna smiled broadly. "Or I should."

Veronique turned to face her, her own smile in place. "Darling, if you touch one hair on that human's head I will personally rip out your fangs and make pretty earrings from them. Do you understand me?"

Anna's smile disappeared. "Bitch."

"Yes. And please don't forget it." She glanced at the rest of us. "If you'll excuse me."

With that, she headed up the stairs to follow after her panicked, but no longer ignorant, human boyfriend.

Had to admit, I was more than a little impressed by how intimidating she could be when she wanted.

"We must start searching for the amulet," Thierry said with a glance at Sebastien. "Agreed?"

Sebastien nodded. "Let's get started."

I remembered something from earlier. "I felt the magic from the amulet when it was four feet away from me. Did anyone else?"

"I did," Thierry said.

"Not me." Frederic's words were tight and unhappy.

After a quick check, it seemed that only Thierry, Melanie, and I had sensed the magic. Since we were the ones who already had a few extrasensory chips in the cookie dough, I wasn't too surprised about that. But that meant that along with hide-and-seek, we could play hot potato, cold potato and maybe be able to sense the amulet before we saw it.

That could help.

"We should separate into groups." Atticus paced back and forth between the stairway and the locked front door. "We'll keep the search organized and structured."

"No," Frederic said with a sneer. "You do your thing; I'll do mine. I don't take orders from anyone associated with the council, especially not its current leader."

Atticus sighed with annoyance. "These aren't orders. They are firm suggestions."

"Anna, let's go." Frederic nodded to her. "We'll find the amulet ourselves without the help of these people."

"Fine." But she didn't sound excited to spend time with a husband she'd been publicly squabbling with a very short time ago.

The two headed down the hallway, back toward the parlor.

"There are six hours before dawn," Thierry said, crossing his arms over his chest. The strain on his face probably wasn't only because of the missing amulet. He was thirsty and trying very hard to deal with that. "Whether we search individually or in pairs, we should reconvene here in three hours and assess our progress."

I couldn't help but be impressed. Even while dealing with a bloodlust spell, Thierry was the epitome of organization.

"Agreed," Sebastien said. "Everyone, please be careful."

Before I could celebrate the fact that Sebastien had agreed with a plan made by the man he claimed to despise and wanted to destroy, he turned and disappeared down another hallway.

From the corner of my eye, I saw Thierry was already walking away from me in the opposite direction, his steps swift. Without a second thought, I followed him, leaving Melanie, Thomas, Atticus, and Tasha behind me.

"Where are you going?" I asked him.

He didn't turn. "The library." Finally, he glanced over his shoulder. "And you shouldn't come with me."

I'd had a funny feeling he'd say something like that. "And yet, here I am."

"Don't take this the wrong way, but you some-times make extremely unwise decisions."

Well, that was a rather nice way of saying it.

I followed him into the library, where we'd been earlier, fighting the urge to touch my tender neck. "I'm officially keeping an eye on you, but I promise not to get too close."

His jaw was tense as he scanned the shelves of books. "Your decision. I know how futile it is to argue with you."

"Eight months together and you finally got the memo on that. Good." While I was there, I might as well start searching for the amulet. I began shifting books to the side and looking for hiding places. "So why did you want to come in here again?"

"Because I saw this earlier." He pulled a thick leather-bound book off a shelf and set it on a long oak table in the center of the room.

I drew closer. There was a title on the cover in gold leaf, but it was in a language I didn't understand or recognize. "What is it?"

"A book on the subject of djinn." He opened it. The pages were old and yellow. The dusty scent of decaying paper wafted under my nose.

A book about djinn. Yes, that would be remarkably helpful right about now.

"What language is that?" I asked, scanning the pages that were filled with tiny writing.

"Andalusian."

I looked at him in surprise. "You read Andalusian?"

"I have a mild grasp of it. Hopefully it'll be enough to find the answers I seek. I need to know if djinn are immortal or if they're vulnerable when they take form in the mortal world."

I would think it would be better to find out how to stuff whatever magic had escaped back into the amulet when we found it, but then something occurred to me that made my heart beat faster.

"You think the djinn escaped from it, don't you?" I asked. "And you think it's going to cause problems if no one's controlling it."

Thierry glanced up from the page he'd started to read, his index finger swiftly skimming along the foreign words. "If I'm right, I think it's already causing problems. That . . . echo of the original coven of witches . . . They said the magic had to be returned to the amulet. The magic *is* the djinn. If the djinn has escaped, we must find a way to contain it again."

The thought that a genie might be prowling the halls of this mansion as we spoke made a shiver run down my spine. "If that's true, I'm guessing it won't want to go back to its prison just because we asked nicely. Not after it has a taste of freedom after, what, fourteen hundred years of being stuck in a tiny amulet?"

"Which is why I'm trying to find another solution."

"You want to know if it's immortal. Why? So you can slay it?"

"We don't know what we're up against tonight. Information is power and the more I can gain, the better off we'll be."

He sounded very certain, very confident in this, but that tension was still in his expression, the sheen of perspiration still on his brow. It worried me.

"Answer me honestly, Thierry. How are you feeling right now?"

His knuckles whitened on the edge of the table. "I've been better."

I watched him as he scanned the book, line by line. "Can I do anything to help?"

His jaw tightened, but he said nothing. His attention remained fixed on the page.

"Tell me the truth," I said after a moment, carefully. "Is it really bad?"

"I don't think you want a completely truthful answer, Sarah."

Frustration gripped me out of nowhere at his evasive answers. "Actually, that's all I've ever wanted. We're married now. We're together through thick or thin, sickness or health, richer or poorer, et cetera. Don't you think I can handle the truth in all its ugliness?"

His gray eyes flicked to mine. They were troubled, pained. "I don't think you can handle it nearly as well as you believe you can. I hold back certain truths because I want to protect you."

I shook my head. "You don't need to protect me."

Without warning, he slammed the book shut. "Don't I? It's all I've tried to do since you first came into my life."

"Thierry . . ." I took a step back from him, but he closed the distance between us, slid his hand around to my back, and pulled me closer. His gaze slid down the line of my throat.

When he spoke again, his voice was very low, very serious. "You push me for the truth, but there are some truths a twenty-eight-year-old can't possibly accept the same way as someone who has lived as long as I can. The things I've seen and experienced. The things I've done. Despite the many challenges you've faced, you have no true comparison for it."

"I understand, Thierry. I do."

His eyes met mine, pinning me in place. "You

don't understand. You *can't* understand. Because, if you did, Sarah, you never would have followed me into this room."

I was about to speak—to talk him down from the ledge, so to speak—but he pressed his index finger lightly against my lips to silence me.

"Sebastien's blood spell has triggered something very dark inside of me, something that grows with each moment that passes. My control is threatened like never before." He stroked my hair back from my throat, his touch light but firm. "My greatest fear is that this curse of mine will take me over completely. Sebastien knew that—he's exploiting that fear. And I'm afraid he may succeed."

"He won't," I said as calmly as I could. "I'll talk to him. I'll make him see reason. He's trying to get revenge against the wrong person. I want to help you."

Thierry squeezed his eyes shut, his face tense. When he opened his eyes again, they'd turned pitch-black. "If you really want to help me, then leave here, Sarah. Please."

He let go of me, and I stumbled back a few steps. "I'll talk to Sebastien."

He nodded and turned from me. "Go."

Even I wasn't crazy enough to stick around for a second longer. He was in a bad place—I hadn't even realized how bad until now. All I could do by lingering was make it even worse.

I turned and left the library as quickly as I could, my heart racing.

Okay, Sebastien, I thought grimly, but the bright glow of determination now fueled me. *When you mess with Thierry, you're messing with me. This game of hide-and-seek has officially begun.*

Chapter 9

As I left the library, I mentally recapped the evening so far.

Atticus had been accused of murdering two elders on his way to becoming boss of the Ring, with Thierry potentially next in his power-hungry crosshairs.

Sebastien, sired by Thierry who-knows-how-long ago, recently broke out of his three-centuries-long imprisonment/coma in a tomb who-knows-where, and wholeheartedly blamed Thierry for this.

As such, he'd taken the first step of his revenge by slipping Thierry some blood that had a "lose control and start biting people" spell on it.

A djinn might be loose in the mansion we were currently trapped in till dawn, and if we didn't stuff it back into its currently missing amulet, we were toast.

Oh, and I'd also had a conversation with a severed head who'd asked for my help to solve his murder.

Couldn't forget that. Not again, anyway.

I'd known it was a mistake to come here tonight. Chalk one up to the gut instinct of the brunette fledgling in the red dress.

I still felt like Sebastien was the element in the mix I had a chance to control. If I could find him and explain the situation, he might believe me enough to break Thierry's spell. Thierry worked much better under pressure when he wasn't fighting his thirst.

As far as what might happen at dawn if we couldn't fix this situation and find both the djinn and the amulet, I couldn't waste time thinking about that. Not yet, anyway.

As I searched for Sebastien, I also searched for the amulet. The first room I checked was the parlor. I turned over the edge of the rug, I checked the shelves. I even felt along the wallpaper in case there were any mysterious bumps. Nothing. And not even the slightest magical tingle to tell me I was close.

When I left the parlor, I decided to head up to the second floor. I'd seen Anna and Frederic, and Atticus, too, who'd started their search on the main floor. Only Veronique had gone upstairs, but that was to chase after Jacob.

In the foyer, I found Melanie sitting on the stairs, her head in her hands. Given that she'd been possessed less than half an hour ago, I approached her cautiously.

She looked up at me through glossy eyes. "I've been told I was a conduit for a message from the otherworld."

Put that way, it sounded so professional. "Has that ever happened to you before?"

"Never." She shuddered.

"Is that why you're upset?"

"No, that would be due to the news that we're hours away from certain death." She looked up at me beseechingly. "I know you don't believe me, but I didn't know about the blood. Honest. If I had, I wouldn't have put it in your husband's cranberry juice."

She did seem earnest enough. Part of me wanted to believe her. "A werewolf with morals."

"I am. Always have been. That's probably why I'm on my own at the moment."

I looked up at the second level. A little remorseful chitchat was delightful, but right now I had a million other things to do. Still, I didn't want to abandon anyone who seemed upset if I could do anything to help.

"A lone wolf," I said.

"That's me."

I nearly smiled at that. "I knew another werewolf once—the only other one I've known personally, actually. He was on his own, too. You two might make a good couple if I knew where he was."

"I'm more into vampires at the moment. Werewolves don't interest me. Way too alpha." She grimaced. "Then again, it's not like it matters. The guy I like's involved with somebody else."

I remembered how she'd looked up at the butler after he'd caught her in his arms. "Is it Thomas?"

Her brows shot up with surprise. "Good guess."

"He's very good-looking."

"He is." A smile now played at her lips, chasing her sadness away. "Too bad he's taken, even though he won't tell me much about her. Some old, rich woman."

"Sorry. Money talks, even to vampires. Sometimes at very high volume."

After reminding Melanie that we were all to meet in the foyer at three o'clock to regroup, I wished her luck on her search and headed up the stairs on my own.

I'd known the mansion was huge from the moment the taxi drove up the long, winding driveway, but seeing more than the main floor, which was gigantic all on its own, was incredible. This was the kind of house some reclusive billionaire might own, the kind of house that would make even *Architectural Digest* start to sweat. Really, with the number of rooms I saw lining the second-floor hallway—and there was another floor above this—it qualified more as a hotel than a private home.

To summarize, this place was freaking huge.

How were we going to search all of it by dawn?

Same way, as the saying goes, you eat an elephant. One bite at a time.

One room at a time.

I pushed open a door to my left to discover it was a sitting room that mirrored the parlor downstairs. Cream walls, a large Oriental rug, sofas that fit in some specific historical era rather than simply the La-Z-Boy one. I did a quick check, running my hands along shelves and peeking behind the crimson-colored curtains. I tried opening, then breaking the window, to find that it was every bit as impenetrable as the one in the foyer. Ditto to the phone on an end table being the same as the one downstairs. No dial tone, only silence.

After inspecting the sofa and upholstered chairs, I walked around with my eyes closed, my hands stretched out, trying to feel that magical tingle I'd felt before.

Nothing.

Not wanting to waste too much time in any one room, I slipped out, closed the door, and was about to go into the next room when I heard a familiar voice coming from down the hall and around a corner. It was Veronique.

"Please, darling. Just open the door and we'll talk. No one means you any harm here, I assure you."

I let go of the door handle and moved toward her instead. She stood in front of a closed door with her right hand pressed up against it. She gave me a tense smile as I approached.

"Jacob is very upset," she said. "He's locked the door and won't let me in."

"A locked room is good. Maybe he can steer clear of Anna's appetite in there." I leaned against the wall and crossed my arms over my chest. "Veronique, I need your help."

She glanced at me with surprise. "My help? Whatever for?"

"Sebastien."

She nodded. "He is acting foolishly."

"The spell . . . it's worse than I thought. Thierry is in a bad place right now, and I don't just mean this mansion from Hell. He's worried the spell will make him lose control."

Veronique pressed her lips together, her forehead furrowing. "Thierry is a realist. If he's worried, then there is most definitely cause for true alarm."

The confirmation made me feel queasy. "Can't we think a little more positively?"

"Not when it comes to Thierry's thirst." She tempered her words with a smile that felt slightly condescending. "You haven't seen what I have over the years, my dear. He is dangerous when in the grip of his hunger. This may not end as well as we'd like it to."

I bristled at the suggestion that a happy ending was not guaranteed. "He can handle a stupid spell."

"We will agree to disagree on that."

Agree to disagree? How about I was right and she was wrong? But I didn't think she meant any real offense. She simply didn't believe in Thierry nearly as much as I did, and she was a woman who didn't mince words.

"Fine," I said as calmly as I could, although I felt just the opposite. "The others can keep looking for the amulet. Jacob can stay safe and sound in his nest. But you have to help me find Sebastien and talk him into breaking the spell."

I expected an argument, but instead I got a firm nod of agreement.

She knocked lightly on the door. "Jacob, darling, will you be all right in there for a little while? I'm off on a quest with Sarah, but I'll be back as soon as I can."

There was no reply.

A grandfather clock farther down the hallway gave a loud ticking sound from its pendulum, and I counted off ten of them before I spoke again.

"Are you sure he's in there?"

She considered this. "I saw him enter this room. And a few minutes before you arrived, he did let out a rather high-pitched shriek as I requested entry. He kept calling me 'monster' over and over, which I tried very hard not to take personally."

I cringed. "'Monster,' huh?"

"I have grown increasingly frustrated with him since earlier at the cocktail party. Can you believe, I heard him talking to Tasha about publishing *her* memoir?"

Frankly, I could believe it. And I would totally read that memoir—no offense to Veronique.

Although this probably wasn't the right time to admit that out loud.

So why wasn't Jacob saying anything now that there were not one but *two* monsters standing outside his door? Had he been scared silent?

I knocked louder. "Jacob? Are you in there?"

Veronique pulled a compact from her purse and checked her makeup, running her finger along her right cheekbone. "Maybe he escaped through the window."

"That would be a neat trick considering that all the windows in this place are locked up tight like Fort Knox." I pounded on the door. I didn't really like Jacob, but I wanted to make sure he was okay. "Hey, Jacob, just say something so we know you're still breathing and we'll leave you alone. A casual grunt would be fabulous."

Veronique snapped her compact shut and regarded me with confusion. "Do you think he's unwell? Perhaps the shock of the evening has given him a heart attack. After all, he *is* of a certain mortal age."

Nine hungry vampires equaled one freaked-out human. It was simple math, really. "Stranger things have happened. I think we shouldn't go anywhere else until we know he's okay."

"Stand aside, my dear."

When I did as she asked, she took hold of the door handle. One modest shove and I heard the lock splinter.

It was a good reminder that this woman was about a million times stronger than she looked.

"You could have done that earlier," I told her.

Veronique brushed off her hands after checking

that her French manicure was unblemished. "I was being polite and giving him privacy, not that he likely appreciated it, given his cruel words."

"Probably a good idea," I agreed.

She pushed the door open to glance into the room. Her face fell. "Oh, dear."

"What?" I moved past her to enter the room completely. It was a bedroom, with a canopied bed, a large armoire against the wall, and floor-to-ceiling windows covered in luxurious brocade drapery. Much like in the previous room I'd checked, an Oriental rug adorned the floor.

Jacob lay on top of the rug, staring up at the ceiling.

"His throat," Veronique whispered.

I'd already seen the bite marks.

She moved toward him, crouching down next to him to check the other side of his throat for a pulse. She didn't have to tell me he was gone. Along with seeing ghosts, I could also sense death. I'd describe it like a weird cold spot, an absence of life. And I sensed big-time absence here.

Then again, the glossy eyes staring at the ceiling were also an excellent giveaway of this sort of thing without the need for any psychic ability at all.

"I'm sorry," I managed as she rose to her feet after closing Jacob's eyes. "I know you cared about him."

She gave me an incredulous look. "I think that would be stretching matters, my dear."

"You were dating him."

"Romance is for the young. I am much too mature and I've seen too many things to ever have my head filled with silly fantasies like that. Writing it is another matter altogether. Fiction is fiction, real life is real life."

That was as blunt as it could get. "Okay."

"Did Jacob deserve an end like this?" She glanced down at his body. "Many might argue that he did, but I would disagree. He was useful to me and now he is not. His death is an inconvenience, to say the least. Whoever did this is a very selfish, greedy vampire. They gave absolutely no consideration to how difficult it may be to find another publisher as eager for my writing."

I didn't believe she was taking this nearly as well as she seemed to be. Even Veronique wasn't this cold. If I had to guess, this was a survival tactic she'd built up over the years. Care too much about anyone and you'd only get hurt.

"That sounds . . . tough," I said.

She nodded. "It's not easy to be a mistress of words, you know."

"I can imagine." I scanned the room. "So who did this?"

"Clearly, the suspicion falls on Anna Dark. She threatened him publicly." Veronique's heels clicked as she moved off the carpet onto the hardwood floor and walked the length of the room, deep in thought. "He has been bitten, but a broken neck is what caused his death."

She was good at this. "So if he was in here and you were outside the only exit, where is the murderer?"

Veronique's gaze lowered to the bed where the bed skirt draped all the way to the floor.

I nodded and stepped slowly and cautiously toward the potential hiding spot, then grabbed hold of the bed skirt to reveal . . .

Nobody.

Relief washed over me. I hadn't been ready for a

confrontation right now with some murderous vampire.

I'd dismissed the possibility of the murderer being Veronique immediately. She was right—Jacob had been an asset to her and her burgeoning book career. If a vampire could be considered "normal," then Veronique fit that bill. She didn't need to drink. She didn't have that uncontrollable thirst to deal with that Thierry did.

There was no reason for her to kill him. But somebody had.

And, no, I'd given no thought whatsoever to that somebody being Thierry and his black-eyed hunger needing to be directed somewhere.

This was Anna Dark's doing.

But if she had been in here, how had she escaped? It wasn't out the window. It wasn't out the door.

I started exploring the room more carefully. Veronique watched me as I moved slowly around the area.

The armoire. I felt something coming off it. It wasn't precisely the same as the tingles from the amulet earlier, but it was close.

"That is a huge piece of furniture." I pointed at it. "Like a lion-and-witch-level wardrobe."

"You are quite right."

I grabbed the handle and yanked it open, half expecting Anna to burst out at me like a ninja through the musty-smelling clothing inside.

When she didn't, I inspected it closer. "I wonder why it's on wheels."

Veronique regarded me curiously. "Likely so it's easier to move."

"Good point." I pressed my hands against the cool,

polished wood and pushed it to the side to reveal an opening in the wall hidden behind the wardrobe.

A secret passageway! All the coolest mansions had them.

Veronique eyed it with interest. "Where does it lead?"

"My guess would be to the next room, but we should check it out. And then we're definitely finding Sebastien." I glanced over her shoulder at the floor and cringed. "Sorry, Jacob. You're a priority, too. Promise."

Veronique nodded. "Lead the way."

There was that tingling sensation again. What was it? "Maybe the amulet's in here. I feel something."

"The magic?"

"I don't know yet. Maybe."

Veronique took hold of my elbow as it got even darker—even for our vampire sight, it was still pitch-black for twenty feet. Then I saw a room through a small opening ahead. The opening was big enough to step through sideways.

I'd expected a similar room to the one we'd just left, but this one was . . . different. Very different.

"Where are we?" I asked, stunned by what I saw before me.

Veronique swept her gaze over the area. "It seems we have a bit of a problem."

I turned back to the passageway, only to find that it had disappeared, leaving a solid wall behind.

Let me emphasize that: *The passageway had disappeared*.

"I think I understand now what happened during the server's possession," Veronique said. "The moment when she mentioned containing the magic somehow and my book disappeared in a flash of light. Do you remember?"

I stared at her, my heart pounding hard. "I remember. What about it?"

Veronique swept another pained glance around the room, which looked a great deal like a well-populated European tavern from hundreds of years ago. "I believe this may be chapter ten."

Chapter 10

I believed in time travel. I believed in ghosts and possessions. I believed in vampires, werewolves, witches, and demons. But books magically coming to life?

"Are you sure this is a chapter from your book?" I asked, my throat tight.

She nodded. "Quite positive."

The tavern had stone walls. Wooden frames and pillars. Long wooden tables and chairs where a few dozen patrons, an even mix of male and female, were seated with tankards of ale before them. A bar stood at one end, with unlabeled glass bottles on shelves behind it. Flickering light from a multitude of candles on the tables and from an ancient-looking chandelier, a wooden disk set with many lit candles and hung on a heavy black chain from the ceiling. The scent of roasted chicken and boiled potatoes infused the musty air.

"We were warned that some of the amulet's magic would be contained. This must be how she decided to contain it," Veronique said quietly. "Perhaps she was deeply inspired by my prose. I will choose to take this as a supreme compliment." She hooked her arm through mine. "In any case, now we must hide."

I tore my gaze away from a group of large, hairy, drunken men. "I'm sorry? No, no hiding. We need to find a way back!"

"If this is indeed taken from my book, bad things are afoot."

"Afoot?"

She yanked me along with her as she began moving through the tavern.

"Veronique!" one of those large, hairy men called out. "Good to see you this evening!"

"Yes, you too," she replied with a tight smile.

We passed closer to his table and his bushy brows drew together as he eyed her tight black dress with its high slit. "Your clothing is rather unexpected. Then again, you were always one to try new things."

"My friend and I are only passing through. Pay no attention to us." She announced this to everyone and no one in particular.

"Are you *sure* this is from your book?" I asked, still wanting to fight the idea that this could be true. "Maybe we've literally gone back in time."

For some reason, that seemed much less crazy to me on a scale of one to crazy.

"I'm sure."

"How do you know?"

"Because this is the French tavern I wrote about, yet I hear no one speaking French."

"Oh." That actually made a weird kind of sense. The book was written in English. Therefore everyone here speaks English.

Mon dieu.

I almost went over on my ankle as she took a corner quickly. I'd decided to accept this as real and try to find a solution. If we'd found ourselves in a patch of contained magic, we needed to get back to the mansion as soon as possible.

"What's the rush?" I asked.

She gave me another tight smile. "This tavern is about to be attacked by a group of vampire hunters who are searching for me in particular."

My stomach lurched. "What?"

"I'm afraid so. That is, if I'm correct about this being a magical representation of chapter ten . . . and I'm so very rarely wrong it's not even worth mentioning." We'd reached the end of the narrow hallway, which hadn't led to an exit, if that was what she'd been looking for. To our right was a door, which she shoved open, pulling me into a small room the size of a closet. If it wasn't for the lit lantern on the wall, we'd be in pitch-black darkness. She closed the door and pressed her back against it. "I'm sure we'll be fine here."

"You're sure, are you? Veronique, we can't stay here!"

"Humor me, darling, for just a few minutes, would you?"

I tried to remain calm and think this through. "Do you think the others are here, too?"

Her face grew thoughtful in the shadows of the room. "Perhaps whomever used the passageway to escape what they'd done to Jacob has journeyed here as well."

A muffled scream pierced the air, making my blood run cold.

Veronique nodded, and a smile lit her face. "And, as expected, I was right. The hunters have arrived right on schedule."

And we were now sequestered in a tiny room with no escape. Even if this were fiction, it didn't fill me with confidence. "We have to do something."

She gave me a patient look. "And what would you suggest we do?"

"Something? Anything other than waiting in a place that doesn't even actually exist? I mean, it's not like we're really in danger, right? This place isn't real and any hunters here aren't real, either. Let's go out there and find a way back."

She pinched my arm. Hard.

"Ouch!" I yelped. "Why did you do that?"

"To prove to you that this might have originated in fiction, but it is every bit as real as if we were back in the mansion. I believe we can be hurt here and we can be killed. This was one of the more exciting and potentially bloody chapters of my book."

I stared at her. "Exciting and potentially bloody."

"Oh, yes."

"You sound proud of that."

"I am." Her pleased expression faded. "However, had I known I would relive this scene, I might have made some additional edits."

Okay. This was an unexpected development, and not one that made this already difficult evening even a tiny bit better. But Veronique had obviously lived through whatever dangers were around the corner, so I had to take comfort in that. We would both survive this chapter.

"We can handle this," I mumbled.

"Of course we can." She patted my arm. "This is excellent bonding time we're having. We're becoming even closer friends than we already were, don't you think?"

She never failed to find the bright side, did she? "Oh, yes. Best friends forever."

"You say that as if you don't truly mean it." Her brows drew together. "I've sensed some animosity from you since earlier when I gave you the book. I'm not blind, Sarah. I understand your misgivings."

"Veronique, let's not talk about this now, okay?"

"You should know I did not go into great detail about my relationship with Thierry. You have nothing to fear."

I gave her a squeamish look. "It's an erotic memoir. It says so right on the cover."

She waved her hand dismissively. "My book is much more of a romance, but certainly not one focused on your new husband."

Even with that assurance, I still didn't want to read it. "Forget it, Veronique. Let's focus on here and now. We have to get back to the mansion and find Sebastien."

"The hunters are here looking for me. They mean to use me to extort the location of a very powerful master vampire who is their true target this evening."

I eyed the door behind her. "Who? Thierry?"

"No, darling, not Thierry. He had no part to play in this particular chapter." She was quiet for so long I almost had to prompt her to keep talking. "It was the love of my life. My sire, Marcellus."

I'd heard the name before. Of course I had. Thierry might have been a long-term relationship, peppered with frequent decades apart, but for Veronique, Marcellus was The One. And he was a legend among vampires.

So the hunters were here looking for information leading to Marcellus. And we were hiding in a tiny room at the back of the tavern.

"So what do we—" I began.

There was a knock at the door and I clutched Veronique's arm.

"Veronique, I know you're in there. Please open this door!"

She sighed. "Alas, we've been discovered."

"Veronique!" I managed, but she'd already opened the door.

Three men stood in the hallway. The one in the middle was tall and handsome, with dark hair, blue eyes, and broad shoulders. The other two were equally good-looking. Like, Hollywood actor, airbrushed-perfection good-looking.

He flashed a smile. "Such a pleasure to see you again, Veronique."

She raised her chin. "I can't claim the same, Stefan."

"You are as beautiful as the last time I saw you. Stunning, really."

My heart pounded hard and fast, but I glanced at her skeptically.

She cringed, then looked at me. "Well . . . it *is* a fictional memoir, darling. I may have taken some liberties with characters and dialogue."

Well, that explained it. "Obviously."

"And your friend, whoever she is," Stefan said. "She is also quite beautiful, but not as beautiful as you. No one is your equal, Veronique. You are more angel than vampiress."

"Well, thank you, Stefan," she said, clearing her throat. Then to me, "Perhaps I did exaggerate his character just a little."

No comment.

"This does not mean that I will not slay you tonight if I must, and your friend, too." There was deep regret in Stefan's voice. "But to take such beauty from the world would be a desperate shame. Alas, one is not given many choices in a life like ours. Is one?"

His comrades shook their heads solemnly. "One is not," they replied in manly unison.

Oh boy.

On the bright side, the hunters I'd dealt with in the past were much less cordial than these ones. Maybe I could talk our way past them so we could find the nearest passageway back to the mansion from Hell.

"Listen, guys," I said. "I'm sure we can work something out here."

Stefan frowned deeply at me. "Your speech is unusual."

"Sarah is not from around here," Veronique explained.

To put it mildly.

"And your clothing . . ." He swept his gaze down the front of my tight red dress and high heels, then did the same with Veronique's black dress. "Are you out in public in your undergarments?"

Seriously, this was one of the friendliest and chattiest hunters I'd ever come across.

"No, they're not my . . . undergarments," I replied. "I . . . rather like them, whatever they are."

"Great." I forced a smile. "Can we move this along a little? I need to get back to finding a way to de-spell my husband and find and fix a leaky amulet before dawn."

Veronique straightened her shoulders and looked Stefan right in the eye. "What do you want from me?"

"You know very well what I want from you," the hunter said lustily.

She gave me a squeamish look. "Yes, well, that was chapter nine. Things happen."

I renewed my promise to myself never to read her book. Like, *never*. "I don't want to know. I really don't want to know."

"You're both coming with us," the hunter said. His friend grabbed my arm and I kneed him between his legs without a moment's hesitation. He staggered back from me, whimpering in pain.

"Why would you do that?" he gasped.

"Uh, because you were attacking me."

He stared at me incredulously. "I was politely guiding you out of your hiding space, that is all. Attacking? I am a gentleman!"

These romanticized hunters were the last thing I needed to deal with right now.

But this wasn't a dream. I wouldn't wake up from this, stretch my arms, and go make coffee. Thanks to at least some of the amulet's magic being contained in Veronique's book, this was potentially as real as real life.

If these fictional hunters did pull out their fictional wooden stakes and use them, I would not be fictionally dead. I'd be really dead.

That was a sobering thought that made me choose to play along and see this chapter through to its end. I took solace in the fact that Veronique had survived to write more chapters beyond this.

I allowed the gentleman hunter to take my arm and politely guide me out of the room, followed by Veronique and her . . . whatever he was to her.

Marcellus was her true love, Thierry was her husband, and Stefan the hunter was—a casual dalliance?

She didn't seem to discriminate very much when it came to boyfriends.

As they led us along the hallway back to the main

tavern, I tried to get the image of Veronique's most recent boyfriend out of my head. Jacob Nelson, trapped in a room with a vampire only a short time after he came to the unfortunate realization that vampires were real.

So who killed him?

I hadn't. Veronique hadn't, either.

Melanie was out, since she was a werewolf, not a vamp.

Anna and Frederic—either could have easily done it, in my opinion. Suspicion did point first to Anna, since she'd made no secret of wanting to bite him.

Thierry—well, we'll get back to him later, shall we?

Atticus? I wouldn't put it past him, although it seemed much too common a crime for the head elder of the vampire council. Bad press to randomly kill humans, especially high-profile ones like a billionaire publisher.

Sebastien had been stuck in a tomb for three centuries. That had to work up quite a thirst, so . . . maybe he was guilty.

Tasha—she was probably very well fed with the best blood that money could buy. Besides, she'd had her talk with Jacob about her own memoir. That was incentive for him to keep breathing, in my opinion.

And Thomas the butler—maybe. Those old mysteries always claimed that the butler did it. Maybe he did.

Too many suspects and not nearly enough time to figure this out.

Especially not at this exact moment.

In the tavern, the patrons cowered in the corners, leaving a large space clear in the middle of the wooden floor.

"I do hate to do this to you, my beautiful Veronique." Stefan swept her dark hair back off her shoulder affectionately.

"Really?" I couldn't help but say it out loud. "You're the first hunter I've ever met who has a problem pushing vampires around."

"Veronique is an exception," he said. "I am entirely enamored with her. Last night I begged her to run away with me, but she declined. It broke my heart to think she may never be mine."

"Maybe she's changed her mind," I said hopefully.

"Absolutely not." Veronique straightened her shoulders. "I could never give myself to one who takes pleasure in destroying those of my kind."

I glared at her. Couldn't she just play along? This fictional hunter guy—who in any other book would likely be the hot hero type—was putty in her hands if she'd be willing to go with it. She needed to take a page from Tasha's book—so to speak—and do a little acting to help get us out of here without more problems smacking us in the face.

Stefan drew a shaky breath. "If I can't have you, no one can."

There couldn't be anything worse than a vampire hunter with a broken heart, especially when his heart had been broken by a vampire.

This could get messy. And magical manifestation or not, I could get dead.

It was all the fault of that amulet and whoever tampered with it to release its magic and its djinn. I swore that if I managed to find it, I'd have no trouble stuffing that genie back inside the amulet, no matter what it took.

"Let's talk about this," I said to Stefan. "Like, really

discuss the details. I'm sure she might change her mind. You're very good-looking. From what I know about Veronique's past relationships, that's more than enough for a real love connection."

"I know there is only one man for her," Stefan said sadly. "The same man we wished to lure here with the threat of his true love's life in jeopardy. It is he whom we wish to slay tonight, but alas, Veronique—and you, whoever you are, strangely dressed woman— must also die."

More confirmation that there was more than enough reason for me to start panicking.

The frantic look she gave me confirmed that this turn of events was a surprise even to her.

The door to the tavern swung open and crashed against the wall. A man stood in the doorway. He was tall, blond, and even more handsome than the ridiculously handsome vampire hunters.

His gaze swept through the tavern and landed on the group of us. "Did someone call for me?"

Veronique gasped. The hunters gasped. The rest of the patrons, cowering in the shadows, gasped.

I just stared at him with disbelief.

Cue Marcellus's entrance for a dramatic cliffhanger.

Chapter 11

Once the gasping had ceased, Marcellus entered the tavern and assessed the scene before him.

"Well, well," he said slowly, "we meet again, Stefan."

"I was wondering when you'd arrive," the hunter replied.

"My good fellow, are you under the impression that you will apprehend me tonight?"

"I am indeed."

"That is wrong of you to think."

"I don't believe it is."

"You are not man enough to defeat me."

"I am indeed man enough to defeat you!"

I looked at Veronique to get her reaction, but her attention was wholly fixed on the two men. The dialogue between Marcellus and the hunter was amusingly bad. Was this a true representation of the conversation that had taken place—or a reflection of her writing ability?

Her face had gone very pale at the dramatic entrance of her infamous sire.

"Didn't you expect to see him?" I asked. "If he's in chapter ten . . ."

She shook her head. "We were in chapter ten. Now we're in chapter eleven."

"How many chapters are in this book?"

"Fifty-eight."

Crap. That was an offensively long book. Which made sense, since she'd lived an offensively long time. So we were only a sixth of the way through her memoir, which did nothing to ease my mind. Would we have to go through every single chapter to get to an exit?

"We have to get back to the mansion," I growled under my breath.

Her attention didn't leave Marcellus for a moment. "Yes, of course we do, darling. But presently, I can't quite think clearly, faced as I am with my long-lost love."

I swear, there were stars in her eyes. I'd never seen a more dreamy look on her face. "You do realize it's the fictional version of him, not the real one, right?"

She finally flicked a look at me, her lips thin. "Of course I do, my dear."

Debatable. Definitely debatable.

"What do you want?" Marcellus asked the hunter. "What will have you release the beautiful Veronique so she can be free to return to her regular life?"

"Only your death!"

Marcellus put his hands on his hips, threw back his head, and laughed heartily at this. "This is not to be, hunter. Do you know how long I've lived?"

Stefan's expression grew thoughtful, as if he was pondering the rhetorical question. "A long time?"

"A very long time. So long, I don't remember when I was born. But do you know the day I truly became alive?"

"When?"

"When I met Veronique."

A plump barmaid in a tight corset, crouched at my left, sighed dreamily at this. The remains of a chicken disappeared off a table as a group in the corner grabbed it to have something to nibble on while they watched the entertaining standoff.

"Oh, Marcellus," Veronique whispered, loud enough for only me to hear her. "I've missed you so much."

For someone who'd claimed she didn't have time for romance, this was a one-eighty. There was such sincerity in her voice that my heart began to ache for her, for what she'd lost. Marcellus was long gone, killed by hunters centuries ago. Since then, she'd had many affairs, with vampires, humans, and hunters alike.

But none had made her forget her true love.

I wondered what Thierry would have to say about all of this.

Very likely, something along the lines of "We must focus on what's important, Sarah."

Focus on what's important—breaking his spell and finding the amulet. I could totally do that. But first I had to get out of magical Vampireland and back to the mansion with everyone else—including Thierry.

I'm coming, Thierry, I thought. *Just hold on tight and try not to bite anybody.*

However, even though I was currently held in place by a surprisingly gentle hunter, I wasn't quite sure how far I could push this before somebody actually got hurt.

For the moment, I would stay silent and wait for the right opportunity.

Marcellus casually strolled toward the bar, then turned to face Stefan again. Several cowering patrons looked up at him with awe. His reputation preceded him, even in fictional memoir.

"I have a fortune in gold and jewels," he said. "I will buy Veronique's freedom from you."

"And Sarah's freedom," Veronique added.

He raised a blond eyebrow. "Sarah who?"

"Darling, this is Sarah Dearly. Sarah, please meet Marcellus Rousseau."

She said it as if we were making friendly introductions and weren't at the mercy of a vampire-hunter negotiation that could turn sour at any moment.

I waved my hand. "Hi there. Great to finally meet you."

He nodded at me. "Likewise. Veronique, yet another beautiful friend you've brought into the fold."

"She's with Thierry," she said.

"Thierry has excellent taste. Then again, he always did since he first chose you, Veronique my love."

"Not to split hairs, darling, but I chose him."

"Ah, yes. The plague. A pile of burning bodies. You liked his eyes, if I recall."

"That's right."

Thierry did have great eyes, but seriously. Ugh. They were chatting as if they were having a coffee date, not negotiating a hostage release.

It seemed I was the only one able to focus at the moment. I only wished I knew what to say to guarantee that this scene would have a favorable outcome for the main characters.

Namely me. And Veronique, of course.

"To answer your question?" Stefan interjected, holding up his finger. "How much fortune are we talking about here?"

Marcellus inspected his sleeve and casually brushed

off some invisible lint. "More than you could fathom in a hundred years, good sir."

"Can you put more of a number on it?"

"Perhaps I shall show you the treasure personally, and you can decide then."

Stefan looked skeptical. "Right. Because you're going to lure us out of here and into some alley, then tear out our throats."

"Why would I do something like that? If you treat me like a gentleman, I will do the same in return."

Stefan moved to a dirty window and peered out at the dark street beyond. "It's too late for that. We're looking for both you and for Thierry de Bennicoeur. Where is he?"

My breath caught. Would I be seeing the fictional version of Thierry soon?

"Not here. The last I heard, he'd journeyed to England. Perhaps he's planning on staying there indefinitely."

This was both a disappointment and a strange relief. I wasn't sure I wanted to experience the Veroniqueized version of him.

Stefan looked surprised by this news. "He would leave France, abandoning a wife as beautiful as Veronique and a mistress like this other one?"

It was a step up from "mere fledgling." But still.

I chose not to correct him on the wife/mistress thing because I knew it would be a waste of breath. Since their conversation was going on longer than I'd expected, I took a moment to try to get a feel for this place. To try to sense that tingling magic I'd felt by the passageway. I even squeezed my eyes shut for a few moments and really concentrated.

It was there, very faint now. I wondered how big

Vampireland was and how much of the amulet's magic it had successfully contained.

And what would happen to this place at dawn?

I thought I already knew the answer to that, and I definitely didn't want to be here when it happened.

"Thierry and I are currently estranged," Veronique said. "I don't anticipate he'll be back anytime soon. At least not until chapter twenty-three."

"I've never seen him, but he is another vampire on my list," Stefan said ominously. "A vampire I will personally kill."

"Oh yeah?" I said under my breath. "Guess you weren't all that successful, were you, Stefan?"

He approached, looming in my face with anger now blazing in his blue—no, wait. Were those *violet* eyes? "What say you, vampire who is attractive, but not as attractive as Veronique?"

Call me crazy, but I very nearly took that as a compliment. "What say me? I—I'm just saying that Thierry is nobody who's going to be easy for you to kill. I have a funny feeling he's going to live a very, very long time."

"With a thirst like his?" He raised an eyebrow at my look of shock. "Of course I know about it. Very few don't. It's what makes him unpredictable. It's what makes him dangerous. It's what makes him someone who must die."

There was a lot of hot air coming out of this guy. He needed to be taken down a notch. "Even fictional, your breath is pretty lousy. You might want to fix that with some historically accurate mouthwash."

He reared back from me, his hand at his mouth. "My breath is divine! Why do you say such outrageous things?"

His breath was fine, of course. Better than fine. He smelled like cinnamon and peaches, as all sexy hunters with violet eyes in a fictional romantic memoir should.

I stared past his shoulder at the exit, which would be my target if this was any other situation. The passageway had been in the tavern, so there was no reason to believe we'd find one anywhere else.

But we would find one. If there was a way in, there had to be a way out.

"Can we move this along?" I asked. "If Thierry isn't here, I'd really like to get back to the real one who actually needs my help right now."

"The last thing Thierry needs, my darling," Veronique said, "is your help right now."

"Excuse me?"

"Your very presence would be torture for him in his current bespelled state."

I shot her an unpleasant look. "Gee, thanks. Don't try to sugarcoat it or anything."

Despite being loosely held in place by one of Stefan's henchmen, she looked very calm as she tried to reason with me. "I'm sure it's not usually torture for him, of course. He's been taken with you from the beginning. I can't claim to entirely understand it, but I accept it as truth. This spell Sebastien has had cast upon him, unfortunately, may be an insurmountable obstacle."

The calmer she was about this, the more anxious I became. "It's definitely surmountable, Veronique, but thank you for your opinion—which I didn't actually ask for. This is all the more reason for us to—"

Something caught my eye. Like a zipper had appeared in the wall to my left and unzipped to reveal another dark passageway. Nobody else seemed to notice it, but I felt the familiar tingling sensation moving over my bare arms.

It was our exit back to the mansion.

Thank you, faulty, leaking, hidden amulet and malevolent missing djinn.

"Veronique . . ." I'd been worried that we might have had to endure the rest of Veronique's book before we could escape this strange place. "Time to vamoose."

Marcellus regarded me with bemusement. "What strange words this one uses. Wherever does she hail from?"

I tore my gaze away from the passageway. "Canada, originally. But I'm international now."

He frowned. "I don't know of this place. Ka-na-dah."

Veronique waved her hand dismissively. "It's a long way away, darling. She's a foreigner."

"Clearly."

Passageway? Veronique? Hello?

"Let the innocent people in this tavern be on their way," Marcellus said to Stefan, waving his hand at the audience now lining the walls and watching us curiously while munching on chicken bones and draining their tankards of ale. "No one needs to get hurt here."

Stefan shook his head. "You continue to delay. I want no treasure from you, Marcellus. Only your head separated from your body and details on where I can find de Bennicoeur. Preferably, the details first."

"My head in exchange for Veronique's life?" He spared a quick glance at me. "Oh, and the other woman, as well."

"Sounds fair to me, doesn't it?" Stefan puffed out his chest, as if he'd already won. "Unless you'd like to show us your cowardly side and run away."

Marcellus's expression darkened. "I don't run from my battles, good sir."

"He didn't," Veronique said to me under her breath. "He really didn't."

"Was he really that good-looking?" I asked her. I mean, we were talking Brad Pitt from *Legends of the Fall* hotness here.

She nodded gravely. "Even more so. My memory of him is as crystal clear today as it was back then. He was the perfect man in every way."

I chose not to remind her that he probably *wasn't* the perfect man, since I knew Marcellus had left her high and dry to go chase some medieval skirts, which was when she'd met Thierry.

Her memory wasn't nearly as good as she thought it was. Or perhaps it was merely selective.

"Then"—Stefan spread his hands—"we seem to be at a standstill."

"I am no coward, sir," Marcellus said. "But I cannot do as you ask and sacrifice my life for Veronique's."

"I'm not surprised." Stefan turned to Veronique and grasped her chin so she'd look right in his eyes. "You see, my beauty? This man you place upon a pedestal, forsaking the promises and declarations of love from others, does not deserve your devotion. He would not give his life for yours."

"And would you?" She didn't flinch from him. "You are a hunter, trained to kill anyone with fangs. Am I supposed to leave everything behind for someone like you?"

She was really getting into this. It was like dinner theater with sharper butter knives.

Despite myself, I found it utterly fascinating to watch.

Maybe Veronique was a better writer than I'd thought she was.

"Remember"—the henchman holding on to Veronique spoke up—"she is our enemy. Choose wisely, Stefan."

"Would I choose you, Veronique?" Stefan asked. "To leave behind my entire life, choosing to spend eternity by your side? If any other vampire asked me this very same question, the answer, of course, would be no. But you—you are different. You have always been different. I love you, Veronique."

"Really? You love her?" Even Marcellus seemed mystified by this outpouring of over-the-top devotion.

"Yes!" The hunter fell to his knees and grasped Veronique's perfectly manicured hands in his. "Even in this unusual frock you've chosen to wear this evening, I find that I am completely bewitched by you. I want no one else."

Veronique turned her face away, as if she couldn't bear to look at him. "But you are betrothed to the duke's daughter."

"I do not want her! I want you!"

Meanwhile, back in reality-ville, I continued to keep a close eye on that passageway in case it disappeared on us again. "Veronique, we need to go. Now."

She touched Stefan's cheek, drawing his gaze up to meet hers. "I only wish it had been this nice at the time."

"What do you mean?" he asked, confused.

"You were a horrible, smelly little man. I reimagined you to suit a more palatable image of what might capture the imagination of my readers. Fear not, I did plan to write a sequel where you will get the girl. But that girl is not to be me. It never was. My heart belongs to Marcellus and no one else but him."

Stefan rose to his feet, his fists clenched. "No!"

"I've endured quite enough of this," Marcellus said.

He moved so quickly I could barely see him. Stefan's henchmen released me and Veronique so they could fight him, but they were outmatched. Marcellus's fists arched through the air like . . . well, like really fast fists, smashing into jaws and stomachs.

Stefan pulled a razor-sharp silver stake from the sheath at his belt and slashed it toward Marcellus, catching him in the arm before Marcellus kicked the weapon away. With another punch to the jaw, Stefan flew backward, crashing into a table.

"There were more casualties during the actual event," Veronique told me with a sweeping glance at the enthralled patrons, many of whom were now applauding. "In fact, very few survived, even in the version I retold in my book. I much prefer this version where everyone potentially lives."

Living was good. I was definitely on the side that favored living. "Me too. So . . . let's go."

"Stay down if you know what's good for you, sir." Marcellus jabbed a finger at Stefan as he began to push up from the table, shoving away empty goblets and plates of half-eaten food.

With a scowl, Stefan stayed where he was.

Marcellus then turned to me and Veronique with a bright smile on his handsome face. "That was rather exciting, wasn't it?"

I nodded in wholehearted agreement. "You really kicked some butt. We appreciate it. That could have had an—" I paused. "Okay . . . you're not even paying any attention to me at all right now, are you?"

No, he certainly wasn't. His gaze was entirely fixed on Veronique and hers on him.

"It seems as if you've been rather busy in my absence entertaining the likes of Stefan," he said with disapproval.

"Oh, darling, you know he never meant anything to me."

"Like that husband of yours?"

"Are you still jealous of Thierry?" She smiled. "I will admit, I'm very pleased to hear that."

"Was that your plan in marrying him in the first place?" I asked. "To make Marcellus jealous?"

"Of course not." Her expression shadowed. "My heart was broken at the time, and my choices were questionable at best. If I were to go back and do it all over again, I'm not sure I would. He and his unnatural thirst have been troublesome over the years, to say the very least."

I glared at her. "Then I guess it's good he's not your problem anymore, isn't it?"

She nodded. "Yes, very true, my dear."

She had absolutely no idea how frustrating she was.

Marcellus stood to the side, his arms crossed tightly over his chest, his expression tortured. "Do you have nothing more to say to me, Veronique? After all this time?"

"It has been a long time." There was a catch in her voice as she said this. "Longer than you might think. It was good to have a reminder of how things were between us, Marcellus."

"And how is that?"

Everyone in the tavern, including Stefan, collectively leaned forward to hear her reply.

"That you could not have given your life in exchange for mine," she said.

Silence hung heavy in the air as we waited for his answer.

"How could I give my life?" His eyes locked with hers. "*You* are my life, my darling. I would never sacrifice that."

Several women and a few men made swoony noises at that answer.

I was about to argue the logic of such a sweepingly romantic statement, when Veronique pushed past me to stand directly in front of Marcellus. Her eyes flashed with anger.

"You dare to say such things to me."

"Yes, I dare. Every day of my life since I met you, I dare."

She threw her arms around him and kissed him passionately.

I waited patiently. Thirty seconds. A minute.

The patrons cheered as if this were the ending of a movie about two star-crossed lovers who'd finally found their way back to each other.

"Veronique?" I tapped her on her shoulder. "Hate to interrupt, really, but we can't wait any longer. Passageway? Mansion? Potential death at dawn when the amulet self-destructs? Remember?"

She stepped back from Marcellus, touching his face, stroking his hair. "Go back without me, Sarah."

I stared at her blankly. "Excuse me?"

"I'm not leaving."

"Again, I say, Excuse me? This is fiction—it's not real."

She raised her chin defiantly. "I don't care what it

is. I'm happy here and it's exactly where I need to be. Take me home, Marcellus, my love."

He clasped his hand in hers and they walked toward the door. He looked over his shoulder at me. "It was a pleasure to meet you, Sarah. Good night."

Could I get an edit here?

Veronique was not supposed to leave through that exit with her fictional ex-boyfriend. She was supposed to leave through the other one with me.

Nonfiction only!

I glanced over my shoulder at the passageway that I hoped would lead us back to the mansion and the drama still waiting for us there.

"If you disappear," I informed it, "I'm really going to be mad."

When the passageway didn't reply either negatively or positively, I turned toward the door and chased after the lovesick author.

Chapter 12

I couldn't just leave her there.

Veronique and I had had our share of differences, but letting her wander off to her fictional happily-ever-after with Marcellus would . . .

Well, I honestly didn't know what would happen for sure, but I had a sneaking suspicion that it was nothing good, especially since all of this was due to a djinn and its amulet needing some significant repairs in the next few hours.

I had to talk her out of this. Even if she was safe here—which I didn't think she was—I still needed her help to talk sense into Sebastien.

Veronique and Marcellus emerged on a moonlit cobblestone street. There was a cool breeze in the air. I followed at a respectable distance to give them a couple of minutes to say what they had to say, and then I planned to swoop in and do what I had to do to save her from making a deeply bad decision. They stopped every couple of moments to kiss.

"Helloooo? Are you still there?"

I froze in my tracks at the sound of the familiar voice. It was one I recognized now whether I wanted to or not.

Ghost head!

"Where are you?" I said under my breath.

"Oh, good! You can still hear me. Do you know you're the only one who can?"

I scanned the dark street. Some of the patrons from the tavern had begun to spill out of it, scattering in every direction, but not following us. "Lucky me. The resident ghost-whisperer."

"I'm not a ghost. At least, I—I don't think I'm a ghost." His voice now held trepidation. "Do you think I'm a ghost?"

"You said yourself you'd been murdered when you were in the freezer."

"It was a reasonable deduction, don't you think?"

I wasn't going to debate it. I had about fifteen other things on my current to-do list and, sorry to say, the head was low on that list of priorities.

"Definitely reasonable." I chewed my bottom lip nervously as I passed by a street lantern that lit a small area so I didn't have to pay quite as much attention to the jagged cobblestones threatening to trip me up. "What do you want?"

"Isn't it obvious? You're the only one who can hear me, so you're the only one who can help me."

I inwardly cringed at his pleading tone. "I don't even know who you are. Who are you?"

"I don't know. My memories are hazy right now."

"Why did I forget you?"

"Maybe whatever forgetting problems I have temporarily spread to you."

I considered that. "That sounds vaguely logical."

He sighed. "Maybe you're right about me being a ghost."

He sounded so depressed about that possibility that I wasn't sure what to say next.

No one else had followed in this direction, which made me the only one currently stalking Veronique and Marcellus. They turned the corner up ahead and I followed without hesitation. They didn't even notice me twenty feet behind them talking to myself like a lunatic.

Still, I couldn't ignore the head. He sounded so lost and alone.

"What's your name?" I asked.

"I don't remember. What's yours?"

I hesitated. "It's Sarah."

"Sarah! What a lovely name for someone willing to help a lowly ghost in need."

So now he'd accepted that he was a ghost. Progress. "How can I help you?"

"You need to find my body. I think. Yes, that's it. My body needs to be found!"

I repressed a shudder at the reminder that this poor guy had been decapitated at some point in history. "Why? Is that the reason you're stuck haunting that mansion? Because someone killed you years ago and hid your body behind the plaster and wallpaper?"

"You don't sound very sympathetic to my plight— if that *is* what happened to me."

"I am sympathetic." A thought occurred to me. "You haven't seen an amulet around the mansion, have you? Small green bottle on a thick chain? Somebody hid it."

"Sorry. I have no idea what you're talking about. And the last thing I saw was you staring at me with horror before slamming the door shut on my frigid prison."

I frowned. "How come I can hear you without seeing you?"

"I don't know. We must have established a connection, Sarah. Yes! One that transcends sight!"

I kept talking to the ghost head while staying on Veronique and Marcellus's tail. How far were they walking? "I promise I will try to find your body and make sure it gets a proper burial. Maybe that will free you to go to Heaven, or wherever you want to go next."

"That sounds very nice." He sounded relieved to know I wasn't trying to give him the brush-off. "I do feel like there's something else I'm forgetting. All I know for sure is I'm all alone, and it's so dark and cold, and"—his breath hitched—"and I'm scared."

I hated the thought of anyone being in pain, even if they were already dead. "I swear I will do whatever I can to help you. Okay?"

He sniffed. "Okay."

"First, though, I have to help steer a friend back onto the reality highway." I waited for a reply. "Hello? Are you still there?"

He didn't say another word, so I figured he was gone. I didn't know where ghosts went when they disappeared, but I had a very strong feeling that he'd be back. And when he was, I hoped to be in the mansion again so I could actually do something to help him.

First thing first.

Marcellus and Veronique arrived at a stone building and entered the front doors through a carved archway. Before it closed, I slipped in behind them.

"Oh, Sarah." Veronique glanced over her shoulder. "You secretly followed us."

She sounded so casual about it, I barely felt guilty. "I wasn't trying to be all that secret about it."

She leaned against Marcellus, her arm tight around his waist. "Don't think I don't appreciate your concern, because I do. But I am fine."

" 'Concern' isn't the word I'd use. 'Frustrated'? 'Flummoxed,' perhaps?" I tried to stay calm and reason with her. "Think about what you're doing, Veronique. You know this can't go on."

She looked away without answering me.

"I welcome you to my home, Sarah Dearly," Marcellus said with a sweeping gesture.

It was a stunning stone villa, the likes of which would have been owned by only the richest men at the time. I'd seen pictures of similar dwellings in history books back in college.

But I didn't care about architecture. I cared about getting Veronique back to safety. Or, well, back to the mansion from Hell. Close enough.

I couldn't feel the tingle of the amulet's magic at all here, which worried me. We had no idea how long this would last or when that second passageway might close up. Why didn't she seem to care?

A short man with a thick beard approached from down the long, shadowy hall.

"Marcellus," he said, "there was a problem while you were gone."

"What's the problem?"

"An old acquaintance of yours has unexpectedly returned. I discovered him on the street nearby, draining a man almost dry. Had I not stopped him, the human would be dead."

My breath caught. Was that acceptable in this era? Killing humans? Or had it always been frowned on by more refined vampires?

"I see." Marcellus exchanged a look with Veronique. "Whoever it is must know the rules as well as we do if he's an acquaintance."

"He's a danger to us all and he should be eliminated," the man said.

"If what you say is true, then I see no other answer," Marcellus said, then glanced at me. "Sarah, this is my manservant, Francois."

Francois was close enough that I noticed something strange.

I sniffed. "No offense, but do I smell . . . wet dog?"

Marcellus smiled broadly, showing off his perfect white fangs. "I'm not surprised you would notice that. With your enhanced senses, you would easily be able to tell that Francois is a werewolf. Humans can't sense this, but vampires can."

A werewolf manservant who smelled like a dog.

Man's best friend indeed.

"It is my great honor to serve Marcellus," Francois said, bowing deeply. "Now, if you'll follow me, I have the culprit restrained in the basement. I had to knock him out. He's incredibly strong."

"Lead the way," Veronique said.

I caught her arm. "Veronique . . ."

She slipped away from me. "We must see to the prisoner."

At what point should I give up on her and head back to the tavern? There didn't seem to be any reasoning with her now that she'd rediscovered her true love in the fictional flesh. Had he really been so great that she was willing to sacrifice everything to stay by his side?

Would I do the same thing if it was Thierry?

Damn it. I probably would.

Fine. Five more minutes.

The stairs creaked with every one I descended. They led to a small, sparse basement with a wooden chair in the direct center.

An unconscious man was tied to that chair. A very familiar unconscious man.

My heart sank right down to the dirt floor.

"Thierry," Veronique whispered. "But, I don't understand. He was not in this section of my book, so what is he doing here?"

I knew why. In fact, it was fairly obvious to me. "Unless they had black tailored Hugo Boss suits back in the old days . . ."

This was not fictional Thierry. This was real Thierry.

His chest hitched and his eyes popped open. But they weren't gray right now, they were pitch-black. His gaze took us in one at a time, ending on me. A frown creased his brow.

"Sarah. You're here."

"I am." What had Francois said? He'd attacked someone out there, draining them nearly dry?

Thierry glanced down at his bindings. "Why have I been tied up?"

I grimaced. "Somebody please untie him."

"Are you mad, woman?" Francois said, gesturing at Thierry. "I told you what he did. Look at his eyes."

Marcellus peered closer. "Are you out of control, old friend?"

"Marcellus." Thierry scanned the length of him. "This is a surprise, but perhaps not nearly as much as I would have thought."

Marcellus pursed his lips. "I was under the impression you were in England."

"You were under the wrong impression."

"Veronique tells me you are now involved with this young woman." He gestured to me.

Thierry's expression was maddeningly unreadable. "That is very true."

"Thierry, what are you doing?" I asked. "Was the werewolf right about you attacking someone?"

His expression didn't change as he turned those black eyes on me. "This isn't real. That was obvious from the moment I found myself here. This is your book come to life, Veronique."

"How do you know that for sure?" I asked, testing him.

He shrugged. "Because no one is speaking French."

Veronique cleared her throat. "That seems to be the case, yes."

"You knew your victim wasn't real," I said, trying to piece this together as best I could and avoid freaking out over Thierry giving in to his deadly thirst. "So you knew you weren't hurting anyone who could actually be hurt."

He didn't either confirm or deny this.

"He must be eliminated," Francois stated bluntly. "There is no other way. It's clear that he's lost his mind."

Marcellus had been carefully watching all of this, confusion etched into his handsome face. "What on earth are you all talking about? Fiction? French? I am speaking French—what other language would I be speaking?"

Perfect English, actually. With the slightest edge of a French accent.

"It doesn't matter, darling," Veronique said, patting his arm. "All is well."

"No, all is not well!" I literally shouted this. "And

you all need to get a serious grip or I'm going to go ballistic. Nobody is eliminating Thierry. And, you—" I pointed at the werewolf, who now had a wooden stake in his hand. "Put that down right now."

"This is what we do to those who cannot follow the rules," he explained.

"Put it down or I will have you spayed and neutered. I swear I will."

"She protects me at every turn," Thierry said with wry amusement. "Even after I've attacked an innocent."

"Fictional innocent," I said. "Not a real one. There's a difference and you knew it."

He shook his head. "The spell is rendering me unable to know the difference between right and wrong. All that will soon exist is the thirst, and then Sebastien will fully have his revenge. You are in grave danger anywhere near me, Sarah. You all are."

"Damn spell." I rubbed my forehead and paced back and forth. Thank God I hadn't taken the passageway back to the mansion and left Thierry to the fate of a werewolf with a wooden stake. "Why did Melanie have to put that blood in your drink? Do werewolves always follow orders to the letter?"

Marcellus nodded. "The well-paid ones do."

Francois was the second werewolf I'd met tonight, but there was one very big difference between him and Melanie that had just occurred to me.

I stopped pacing and turned to face Marcellus, his face lit from the flickering lanterns set into the stone walls. "Do all werewolves smell like wet dog to a vampire?"

"Yes," he said. "Some more than others, but there is always that barest scent to discern what they are."

I took a big whiff. Yes, wet dog—just a hint, but it

was definitely there. "Melanie didn't smell like Francois."

"Which means what, darling?" Veronique asked.

"Which means she was lying to me. She's not a werewolf."

"What difference does it make?" Thierry growled.

Maybe nothing. Maybe everything. I sorted through it before I answered him.

"I think it might make a big difference if she's actually a *witch*. I mean, she seemed to have some psychic ability. That could be witchy, right? Maybe she was the one who put the spell on the blood to begin with at Sebastien's command."

"This is all quite fascinating." Marcellus watched us discuss this as if he were watching a tennis match. "But I really don't understand a word of it. And it's not because we're not speaking French, because we absolutely are."

And he really seemed to believe it.

"Again, I must ask," Veronique said as she walked around Thierry's chair, her stiletto heels sinking into the dirt floor, "what difference does it make, other than exposing her as a liar? The spell is still on Thierry and it's making him exceedingly unpleasant."

She was right, I was guessing. Wild-leap guessing, actually. Besides, at this very moment, Melanie being a werewolf or a witch didn't make any difference at all.

"You can fight the spell," I told Thierry firmly, touching his shoulder. "I know you can."

He looked down at my hand on him. "When I chose my victim outside, it wasn't because I knew he was fictional. It was because I needed his blood. That he ended up not actually existing was incidental at that point. My first intention was to harm him."

I shook my head. "You're not thinking straight right now."

"His blood tasted like ashes. Not satisfying at all. It was then I knew he wasn't human."

"Didn't you already satisfy your thirst with Jacob?" Veronique said, her voice soft.

Thierry's black eyes flicked to her. "Pardon me?"

"Jacob is dead. Someone fed on him and then broke his neck, likely so he wouldn't be able to identify who did it."

"And you think I did."

"That room is what led us to the passageway here. And here you are as well." There was no hiding the accusation in her voice.

"No way," I said, feeling sicker to my stomach with every second that passed. "Thierry didn't kill Jacob."

"He's already shown his murderous intentions. If Francois hadn't stopped him—"

"He would have stopped on his own."

"You don't know that."

I hissed out a breath of frustration. "I do know that."

"I found another passageway to this place," Thierry said. "But it wasn't in a room that also contained Jacob."

More than one passageway here. That meant there might be more than one passageway back.

But I only knew of the one for sure. I really hoped it hadn't closed up yet.

"It would be rather lovely," Marcellus said, "if someone might spend just a moment explaining all of this to me."

Thierry was watching me very closely, so closely I felt the heat of his gaze on the side of my face. I turned to see his incredulous expression, as if my words constantly surprised him.

"You believe that I would have stopped," he said.

"I do," I replied firmly.

"But Veronique doesn't."

"No." She sighed. "I have seen too much, my darling. There is a spell on you—a powerful spell, it would seem. You are a danger now, even more so than you usually are. Everyone acknowledges this except Sarah, but she is a mere fledgling. She doesn't understand."

"Enough, both of you," I snapped. "All I care about right now is getting back to the mansion so we can find Sebastien and get him to break this spell. And if the witch who cast it in the first place is still lingering around pretending to be a werewolf, all the better!"

"He is a danger!" Francois insisted. "A danger to us all!"

"No, he isn't," I told him.

"Yes, actually I am." With a snap Thierry easily broke free from his restraints and stood up. "And I strongly suggest that each and every one of you—fictional or not—start running as fast as you can."

Chapter 13

Twice tonight Thierry had told me to run from him. I took him seriously both times.

Marcellus grabbed Veronique's arm and ushered her up the stone stairway ahead of him. Francois was right behind them. Now that Thierry was freed from his restraints, the werewolf had lost all of his stake-carrying bravado.

I found my feet weren't working.

"Thierry—"

"Ten seconds, Sarah." Thierry's jaw was tight, his hands fisted at his sides. "And then I fear I won't be able to protect you any longer. Ten, nine, eight . . ."

The countdown worked like a charm.

I was out of there.

I took the steps two at a time to get back to the main level. The werewolf was already racing out the front door.

"Save yourselves!" he hollered.

"Come with us, Sarah!" Veronique beckoned to me as Marcellus pulled her out the front door.

"I'll catch up with you," I promised.

"He's dangerous," she said. "Please don't underestimate him. I've seen him at his darkest and it was still nothing like what I saw in his eyes downstairs.

He is dangerous and what happens to us here is real. Please remember that!"

With her words echoing in my mind, I took a left out the front doors and emerged on the street. I ran back toward the tavern. If I could get to the passageway . . .

My heart wrenched at the thought. What would I do? Abandon both of them here in Vampireland?

Veronique hadn't been the only one to see something scary in Thierry's eyes. Something dangerous. Something deadly. I saw it, too, and it had made my blood turn to ice.

The spell had him tightly in its grip.

Was it unforgivably naive to believe he could still fight something like that?

Maybe he wasn't Thierry anymore. He was a vampire with no control who needed to feed.

It was my worst fear come to life.

I focused on putting one foot in front of the other as I headed back in the direction of the tavern. Marcellus's villa was the better part of a half mile away, so it wasn't a quick sprint. My feet ached and I had more than one blister by now.

Then someone stepped into my path on the cobblestone road a block from my target location.

"Sarah Dearly." Stefan the vampire hunter stood directly beneath a lantern, which lit up his handsome face. "You left far too soon."

"Oh, hi. Nice to see you again," I lied.

He scanned the area. "Where is Veronique?"

"Not with me anymore. Obviously." I glanced around. "Where are your friends?"

"Also not with me. It seems to be just the two of us now. Let us talk."

"About?"

"About what I can do to win Veronique back."

Was he for real?

Oh, wait. He wasn't. That explained a lot.

I tried to give him a patient smile. "Obviously she has you tied up in knots, but you could do so much better. I saw a barmaid in the tavern who was seriously giving you the eye."

"Greta?" He raised an eyebrow. "I have had her before. Every man in this town has."

"Okay, well, maybe she isn't your soul mate, but my point is that neither is Veronique. And listen, I'd love to chat a little longer, but I have to see a witchy werewolf about a blood spell."

I tried to sidestep him, but he blocked me.

"Not yet." He frowned deeply. "Are you trying to tell me I've been a fool?"

He was a good-looking guy with a tender heart, but I couldn't forget he was a card-carrying vampire hunter. I needed to tread softly on this dangerous ground.

"Oh, no. Not a fool. You're a romantic. A really fantastic, lovely romantic who probably writes poetry in his spare time."

"I do. I write poetry for Veronique." He raised his face toward the sliver of moon in the jet-black sky and lifted his hand. *"Her hair the black of a raven's wing / her lips so red they make me sing* . . . Shall I go on?"

I repressed a grimace. "Um, no. But thank you for sharing. That was really lovely."

He drew in a quivery breath. "She is my life."

"No, she's not."

"That she would turn her back on me to return to that man who casts her aside at his whim . . . It infuriates me."

How was I supposed to get away from him? This

dude was seriously obsessed. But I could only blame Veronique for that. It was how she wrote him.

"I have heard he's a little fickle. But when you've lived that long . . . well, maybe . . . Oh, I don't care. Listen, Stefan, all I'm saying is you could do better and I'm sure you will. I think you have about forty-five more chapters left to find happiness. And if she ends up writing that spin-off she was talking about, I know things are finally going to go your way."

What was I babbling about? I was giving romance advice to someone who didn't even exist.

Stefan pulled his stake from the sheath on his belt. Now *that* looked like it existed.

He held it up to the moonlight. "A gift from my father on his deathbed. He slayed over a hundred vampires with this. He didn't trust wood—only silver."

I took an automatic step back from him. "I'm more of a platinum fan myself."

His gaze moved from the sharp tip of his weapon to me. "Are you a fledgling, Sarah, or are you a full vampire?"

"I mean, I like to consider myself a full vampire, but technically speaking, I'm a fledgling."

"So you will leave a body behind when you are slain."

A chill slithered down my spine. "No reason to get nasty, Stefan. I thought we were having a nice talk."

"We are. And now you will help me leave a message for Veronique that I can't be cast aside so easily. She must know that I matter." A tear slipped down his cheek. "And my love won't be denied, not by her. Not by anyone. She has taken me for granted for the last time."

I stumbled back another step and raised my fists. "Don't come any closer. I might not look it, but I can fight."

"I would hope that you will. Everyone should fight when their life is in jeopardy."

Stefan came at me, grabbing the front of my dress and yanking me closer. I punched him in the face and his head snapped to the side. He laughed. "Definitely a fledgling. Veronique is much stronger than you are."

"Let me try that again." I punched but met only air this time as he shoved me to the ground. The air was knocked out of my lungs, and I gasped for breath. He loomed over me, but all I could see was that stake. I scrambled to get to my feet, but it was too late. He lunged—

—and then stopped in midair before being yanked backward. Thierry spun the hunter around, glanced at me and then at the stake.

"Who are you?" Stefan sputtered.

"No one you want to know." Thierry grabbed his head and twisted.

I winced when I heard his neck crack. His body crumpled to the ground in a heap. Before I could register what I'd just witnessed, Stefan's dead body vanished in a flash of light bright enough that I had to shield my eyes.

Fictional characters didn't leave corpses.

I stayed on the ground, staring up at Thierry. He didn't offer me a hand. He just turned that dark look on me.

I scrambled back from him, crab-style. "You just saved my life. That's a very good sign, don't you think?"

"I told you to run."

"I did and I was getting good distance even in these shoes. Unfortunately, I was interrupted."

"That is unfortunate."

I pushed myself up to my feet. "Feeling thirsty?"

His eyes narrowed. "You have no idea how thirsty I am right now."

"Oh, my God!" I cried, waving. "Veronique's on her way. Hey! Over here!"

When Thierry glanced over his shoulder, I took off at a sprint in the opposite direction.

Thirsty vampires were gullible. I'd use it to my advantage.

Thirsty vampires were also very fast. Especially ones not currently wearing four-inch heels.

Thierry caught up to me and pulled me to a halt, then he hoisted me over his shoulder and began walking away from the tavern. Panic tore through me.

I needed time to figure this out. This was not in my plan at all. "Where are you taking me?"

"Elsewhere. I don't want Veronique to interrupt us."

He walked until we reached the edge of this strange little town. Beyond the buildings, shops, and villas, darkness stretched out before us. Since I couldn't see anything beyond it, I guessed that was where the magic that had created this place ended.

Thierry set me down on my feet next to a stone building with a thatched roof. He easily held me in place with his hand flattened against my upper chest. His gaze slid down my throat.

My heart beat like the wings of a trapped hummingbird.

Every fear I'd had, every whisper of doubt about falling in love with a vampire who lost his mind when he drank blood . . . they were all rising up like smug ghosts to say that they told me so, that this would happen, that he would one day kill me, no matter how much I believed in him.

But that was just it . . . I did believe in him. Even now, when there was so much stacked against us.

I'd believe in him till my last breath.

"You're not going to let this spell beat you, Thierry," I told him.

"Too late."

"No, it's not too late. You're still talking. You're still listening to me. You haven't lost your mind."

"My mind is very much here. It's my empathy that has departed. To nearly kill that innocent earlier without blinking an eye—"

"But you didn't kill him."

"The intent was there. An intent you lack. I don't think you'd be able to kill someone face-to-face, even if it was an artificial situation."

I pressed Stefan's silver stake against Thierry's chest. I'd snatched it up earlier, but I guess Thierry hadn't noticed. The silver burned my hand to hold it, but I gritted my teeth against the pain.

I'd heal quickly. That was, if I lived through this.

He looked down at it.

"How about face-to-face when it's not an artificial situation?" I asked.

A cold smile curled his lips. "You wouldn't."

"Try me."

He shook his head, but didn't budge an inch. "So foolish, so naive. But you always have been. You thought you could tame me." He pressed closer to the tip of the stake. "This is who I really am, Sarah. Don't you see? For so many years I've fought it, until it weighs on me every day. I thought it was right to ignore it, but *this* is right. When one is thirsty, one must drink. It's natural."

I had to stay calm. He wasn't lost. He was talking way too much to be lost. "This isn't natural and you know it."

"It is."

"No, you just happen to be a total freak of nature, Thierry. You and Sebastien. Normal vampires can control their thirst. They don't let it control them."

"The spell has made everything so much simpler." His gaze lingered on my throat again. "If I hadn't bitten you earlier this evening, I might be able to stop this, but I can't."

"You *won't*, you mean."

His gaze snapped to mine. "Why must you continue to argue about everything I say?"

"Annoying, is it?"

"Deeply."

I chose to see that as a good sign. "Too bad. You know what I think? I think if you were completely psychopathic right now, thanks to that little spell, you'd already have finished me off. But instead we're talking at length about how bad you think you are."

He bent over so we were eye to eye. "I've always been bad."

I forced myself to hold his gaze without flinching. "Have you always lied to yourself, too?"

"Veronique saw my darkness. She ran from my darkness—she always did. Why don't you do the same?"

"I was running. You caught up to me and snapped the neck of that hunter before he killed me."

"I needed you alive."

Okay, enough of this. This had been an issue for us for our entire relationship—this unnatural thirst of his. I was so tired of dealing with it that, actually, I almost wanted to thank Sebastien for bringing it to the forefront so we could deal with it once and for all. I refused to be afraid of the man I loved. And I refused to let him continue to think the worst of himself just because everyone else did.

"I'm getting a little bored with this conversation, Thierry. Go ahead and bite me." I tucked my hair behind my ear and bared my throat.

His brows drew together. "Thank you for your permission."

"You're welcome. Go ahead. I'm waiting." I shivered, trying to remain completely convinced I wasn't making a horrible mistake.

He hesitated. "You're not fighting me or trying to get away."

"No, I'm not."

"Any reason why?"

"Because of what you just said about Veronique."

"I don't understand."

I poked him in his chest. "She ran from your darkness, but I don't. You know why that is? It's because you're not as dark as you think you are and I seem to be one of the few people who can see it. You are not your thirst, Thierry. You identify yourself so often by that one failing, but it doesn't define you. Your choices define you—and you have a choice right at this very moment."

Confusion slid through his black eyes. "I have no choice. The spell—"

"Isn't stronger than you are. It can't change who you are. That we're still discussing this proves it to me. Can't you see that? Just like this town, it might look real, but it's not real down deep where it counts. It's weak. You're the one who gives it strength. You haven't bitten me again. And you won't."

He shook his head. "You don't know what you're saying. You're making assumptions."

"Maybe I am. But maybe I'm right. And if I am right, and this is nothing but a weak spell by some fly-by-night witch poking at your inner monster, then you can cage him up nice and tight again without a problem."

Now there was pain on his face, although I wasn't sure if it was emotional or physical. "You think it's easy to fight this?"

I wasn't making light of what he was going through. Just the opposite. "What I'm saying is that I know you love me, Thierry. I *know* it. Getting a fresh copy of Veronique's memoir earlier tonight triggered a bit of my self-doubt—about how someone as incredible and long-lived as you could ever want to spend his life with somebody like me. But it was only for a moment. You love me, despite every reason why you shouldn't. And I feel the same for you. I think that's more than strong enough to break a stupid spell like this."

"Sarah . . ."

"You won't bite me again." I looked into his eyes. "I know you won't."

"You're betting your life on this."

"I know."

He let go of me and took a step back. His entire body began to shake. "Run."

This was a very good sign, but I was going to hold back my victory dance for now. "No way. I'm not running anymore."

He let out a harsh groan. "You are so incredibly frustrating!"

"I'm not running." I said it again, firmer. "Look at me, Thierry."

He was breathing hard, but he raised his gaze to

mine. It was still black, but now it didn't hold the coldness that I'd seen before. There was pain and struggle.

He was fighting the spell.

"This isn't easy," he gritted out.

"I didn't say it would be."

He fell to his knees and grasped his head in his hands. I took a step closer and he glared up at me. "Stay back."

I faltered, still clutching the stake. Then I threw it away from me. It clattered and clanged to the ground ten feet away.

Thierry let out another groan. "Why are you doing this? Are you completely out of your mind?"

"Possibly." But I'd never felt more sure about anything in my life. "You won't hurt me."

"I bit you earlier in the library."

"I'm not counting that one. The spell took you by surprise then."

He still glared. "You are a fool when it comes to me."

"Oh, absolutely. No question about it."

He went silent for a few tense minutes, crouched on the ground, his body shaking from head to foot. Then, finally, he slowly pushed himself up to his feet. When he looked at me, I was relieved to see that his eyes had begun to shift back to their normal pale gray shade.

However, the fierce glare was still there.

"I'm extremely angry with you," he informed me.

I couldn't hold back my smile. "I can deal with that."

"Damn it, Sarah. You shouldn't have risked your safety like that."

"You're feeling . . . ?"

"I believe you were right about the strength of the spell—it was not cast by a strong witch. But believe me, Sarah, you were most certainly in danger. There

was a dark hunger inside me that needed to be sated."
His glare intensified. "This is not a statement that
should be greeted with a smile that wide."

It was true, I was definitely smiling. "I can't help it."

He hissed out a breath. "Why do you put up
with me?"

"Obviously, I'm completely out of my mind." I closed
the distance between us, took his face between my
hands, and kissed him. He pulled me closer to him.

"I adore you," he whispered. "Do you know that?"

"I know. But thank you for the confirmation." Now
I couldn't stop grinning even if I tried. "Now let's go
find your ex-wife and get the hell out of here."

He had no argument with that. Inwardly celebrat-
ing our victory over Thierry's thirst monster, I took
his arm, and we headed back to the tavern. It wasn't
too far, only a couple minutes' walk, and I could see it
in the distance on the right of the cobblestone street.

But I saw something else, too, lying in the middle
of the street between us and the tavern.

A body.

My throat tightened. "Crap. Who is that?"

"I don't know."

As we got closer to the body, I realized with a sick,
sinking feeling that it was someone I recognized.

It seemed that Frederic Dark had found a passageway to Vampireland like the rest of us had. Unfortunately, he wouldn't be making the return trip.

The enchanted dagger he'd won in the auction was
sticking straight out of his chest.

Chapter 14

Thierry crouched down next to Frederic's body and felt his throat. "I can't find a pulse."

Fred was dead.

Which didn't make sense. Vampires older than a century disintegrated when they were killed, and I'd gotten the impression Frederic was at least that old. "Why's his body still intact?"

"It's rather unusual." Thierry continued to inspect the body. There was a bloody wound on his forearm. "This is likely where he attempted to block the dagger."

A shadow fell on us and the very next moment a man-sized object hurtled through the air, knocking Thierry to the ground.

The man-sized object was Marcellus.

"Stay down!" Marcellus snarled. "I will not let you harm these fair ladies, you beastly man!"

Veronique pulled me to my feet and shielded me with her body. "You will not hurt anyone else tonight. Sarah is hereby under my protection!"

"That's not necessary," I told her. "But thank you. I do appreciate it."

She frowned at me. "Whatever do you mean? He is driven by his dangerous thirst!"

Despite everything, I was actually touched by the fact that she seemed to care enough to intervene. "Actually, he managed to break that spell. He's fine."

Thierry nodded from beneath Marcellus's tight hold on him.

"I would not go as far as to say I'm fine, but I'm certainly better than I was." He glanced up at Marcellus. "You would be well advised to release me now."

Marcellus scowled down at him. "How do I know these are not lies?"

"They're not," I said. "Spell is broken. He's back to his regular level of bloodthirstiness, so probably like a three out of ten."

"Six at the moment," Thierry said.

"Six out of ten?" I grimaced. "That's not great."

"It's much better than a ten, believe me."

Marcellus finally, reluctantly, released Thierry and stood up, offering his hand to help Thierry stand.

Thierry stood on his own without help, brushed off his suit, and walked a slow circle around Marcellus. "It's uncanny, Veronique. He looks just as I remember him."

Marcellus regarded both of them with confusion. "Of course I do. How else would I look?"

"It doesn't matter, darling," Veronique said, but there was a thread of sadness in her voice. "Thierry is cured of his dreadful problem. Quite a miracle, I must say. Most problems such as this are not solved so easily."

"It wasn't exactly easy," I said.

"Actually, Sarah, it was, all things considered." Thierry appeared to contemplate this for a moment. "But let's hope that the problem has, in fact, resolved itself. Sebastien tried to ruin me and he very nearly succeeded. If he learns he's failed, we don't know what else he might have planned. It would be best if we kept this between us so he doesn't know I've fought against the spell and won."

Veronique nodded. "I agree. But at least we know all is well."

"I wouldn't say *all* is well." I glanced down at Frederic.

"Yes, this is a problem." Veronique looked down at the body. "Who did this?"

Good question. "Well, it wasn't us," I said.

Veronique eyed it with surprise. "That is the Amaranthian Dagger he acquired during the auction."

"Yeah. Sebastien said it could help a mortal lengthen his life if he drank blood using the dagger and it could help a vampire become totally immortal." I grimaced. "Wild guess, but I think that legend is wrong."

"Such a weapon kills as surely as any wooden stake," Marcellus said. "This man is dead."

Thanks for the confirmation, Marcellus.

Thierry studied Frederic's body, which was partially lit by a nearby flickering lamp. "His body should no longer be intact. Perhaps that is another side effect this particular dagger has when used to slay a vampire."

I looked down at Frederic. "He must have found a passageway like we did—maybe even the same one as Veronique and me. He could have been the one who killed Jacob, not Anna."

Veronique's expression grew thoughtful. "That could be."

"So you don't think it was me anymore?" Thierry said wryly.

"I am sorry, my darling. But what was I to think? You were not yourself."

"You could have given me the benefit of the doubt."

She smiled. "Next time I shall do just that. Thank you for the suggestion."

Marcellus gazed at her with adoration. "Veronique only acted as she could. She is a forgiving woman." He gestured toward me. "Especially when it comes to forgiving your indiscretions with this fledgling."

Thierry sighed with weary patience. "Sarah and I are married."

Marcellus looked shocked. "Sir, you are admitting to bigamy!"

"No. Veronique and I had our marriage dissolved and . . . why am I explaining this? You're not really Marcellus."

He stomped his foot. "I most certainly am Marcellus!"

I tried to tune their voices out so I could focus on Frederic for a moment—from the wound on his arm to the dagger sticking out of his chest.

Who had done this to him?

One suspect in particular seemed to keep coming up again and again.

"You know, earlier I heard him and Anna arguing," I said. "They might seem like a matched set, but I think they were having marital difficulties. They said some pretty nasty things to each other."

"All marriages have their stresses," Veronique said dismissively.

Very true. Some more stressful than others. "Yeah, but she used to be a vampire hunter. If she decided she'd made a mistake by marrying Frederic, by living a life as a vampire Purist under his thumb for all these years, maybe she wanted to end things between them by going back to her roots."

Veronique's heels clicked against the cobblestones as she drew closer. "You believe she murdered him?"

I'd say it was a good bet, actually. "We already suspected her of Jacob's murder, right? She mentioned how thirsty she was."

"This is true." Veronique crossed her arms and paced back and forth. "Very true. We don't have any idea what kind of a woman Anna Dark really is, do we? We have only a few tidbits about her that certainly do not paint the most attractive portrait."

Anna could have killed Jacob, then taken the passageway here with Frederic and offed him, figuring that she'd leave his body in a place that wouldn't really exist if it wasn't for the temporarily contained magic from the amulet. Sounded very neat and tidy—and, well, *contained*.

I considered this for a moment. "Maybe she was surprised that his body didn't turn to goo."

"I'm sure she was."

"Who is this Anna you speak of?" Marcellus asked. "She sounds like a true villainess who must be defeated."

"Don't worry about it, Marcellus. We have it under control." Which was a lie, but I didn't see how he could help. It wasn't as if he could return to the mansion with us. I turned toward Thierry. "We should take his body back with us. We can't leave him here."

"Agreed," he said.

"We should probably begin by putting this dagger somewhere safe so it doesn't end up in someone else."

Veronique leaned over and pulled the dagger from Frederic's chest.

In seconds, Frederic's body disintegrated right before our eyes on the cobblestone road.

"Oh dear." Veronique stepped back quickly before her expensive shoes could get soiled by his remains. "That is rather unfortunate."

To put it mildly. I would never get used to seeing that. One moment a solid body, the next moment a black puddle.

Still, it made me wonder why Anna hadn't done exactly what Veronique just did.

"Why would she leave the dagger behind?" I murmured aloud. "She could have sold it for big bucks and gotten rid of his body at the same time."

"It's possible she was in a hurry to get away," Thierry replied. "Perhaps she saw us approaching."

I suppose that made sense. But maybe Anna simply didn't care about the dagger for any reason other than using it to kill her husband.

"It's likely she's already gone." Veronique handed the dagger to Thierry with distaste.

Thierry drew a handkerchief from his inner jacket pocket, wrapped the blade in it, and tucked it into his jacket.

"Be careful with that," I told him.

"Trust me, I will be very careful."

"We must apprehend Anna Dark so she will answer for her crimes," Veronique announced.

"That is my Veronique," Marcellus said, nodding proudly. "A champion of vampire justice, of right, of glory. So beautiful and so brave. All women should aspire to be like her."

"Oh, my darling. You always knew me better than

anyone else." She embraced him and kissed him deeply.

I exchanged a look with Thierry, who looked perplexed by their public display of affection.

"This reminds me a great deal of how it was in the past whenever they were together," he said.

"It's kind of adorable."

"Not the word I would use."

No, there were plenty of other words for it, but "adorable" worked for me. Seeing Veronique so infatuated was a major revelation. "Let her enjoy him while he's still here."

Marcellus took a step back from Veronique, frowning at me. "What do you mean, while I'm still here? Where would I be going?"

Veronique slid her arm around his waist. "Pay no attention to Sarah, my darling. She's not much of a romantic."

"I will always be by your side," he told her. "Today and always. I swear this is true."

Her face shadowed with such raw pain that my heart ached for her.

Although, for the record, I *am* a romantic.

"I wish you were real," she whispered. "But this is not to be. You were lost to me a very long time ago, but know that no other man has ever claimed the place in my heart that you held—that you will continue to hold forever."

I was starting to choke up. She really loved him. I wished he was real, too, so Veronique could get her happy ending after all these years.

"Veronique, what is going on?" Marcellus said.

"It's too much to explain. You might not understand anyway."

"No, I mean . . . what is going on with the street?"

I glanced over my shoulder to follow his line of sight and saw that he was right to be concerned.

A fog had begun to roll in.

Not just any fog.

Whatever it touched blurred and then vanished from sight.

Veronique inhaled sharply. "*Mon dieu.* I knew this would happen."

A chill raced down my spine. "What's happening?"

Her expression was bleak and fearful. "The magic contained here must be draining away. I will assume it's not enough to sustain this place any longer, especially since we've gone so far off the original story-line."

I grabbed Thierry's arm. "I think that's our cue to leave. Like, now."

His gaze moved from the fog to lock with mine. "An excellent plan."

"Back to the tavern. I sure hope that passageway is still there."

As the fog drew closer, the four of us began running away from Frederic's remains and toward the tavern in the distance. It was good to see that Veronique was as adept at running in high heels as I was.

Practice made perfect.

One big problem when we got there, though: Stefan's two henchmen blocked the entrance.

"Veronique. You've returned," one said.

"Step aside," she hissed.

"We cannot do that. We must hold you until Stefan returns."

"Stefan's dead," I informed them. At their aghast

looks, I shrugged. "I guess he won't be getting that sequel after all."

Maybe it sounded heartless, but Stefan was fictional. *And* he tried to kill me.

Those were two big strikes against him.

"No!" the other hunter wailed, shaking his fist at the sky. "Not Stefan! He was the best of all of us."

Veronique winced and exchanged a glance with me. "The book's production schedule was rushed, but I do wish I'd had time to fix a few things in copyedits."

"Overly dramatic vampire hunters?"

"Perhaps I could have pulled back just a tad."

Marcellus grabbed one hunter and Thierry grabbed the other, shoving them out into the street. They stood there stunned, then began moving back to the tavern entrance just as the fog reached them and wrapped them up in its misty fingers. They disappeared from sight.

I frantically turned toward the busy tavern and scanned it. "Where's the passageway? Damn it. It was right there!"

Where the opening had been earlier was now only a solid wall.

The fog drew closer and closer.

I clutched Thierry's arm.

"There's another one over there," he said.

I looked where he indicated toward a crowd of people who magically faded from sight. One by one, all the tavern patrons disappeared so only the room now remained visible.

And I saw it. Another passageway, smaller than the previous ones.

"We must move," Thierry commanded. "Now."

We ran across the room, which began to feel less solid, the floor more mushy and slippery, like pudding. I nearly lost my footing, but Thierry kept hold of my arm to steady me.

"I feel it . . . " I managed.

"Magic?"

I nodded.

"I feel it, too," he said.

"I feel nothing, but I will trust you both." Veronique's voice held both panic and deep regret. "Farewell, Marcellus, my love! I will never forget you!"

Once we made it to the opening, I slipped through without another thought. Thierry was right behind me, and Veronique was on his heels.

The fog reached the passageway just as we did and tendrils of mist wrapped around my ankles, tugging, slowing my progress before they finally, thankfully, drew back.

It was dark in there, but I kept moving, slowing down just a little to put my hands out in front of me. We finally came to a wall, and I felt around until I found the shape of a door and a cold brass knob.

I held my breath and turned it, then pushed forward.

The door opened into a room, which I staggered into, heaving a great sigh of relief.

"We made it!" I threw myself into Thierry's arms as he came through the doorway. "We're okay!"

He squeezed me tight, then glanced at Veronique as she emerged from the passageway.

"We have successfully returned." She sounded sad and weary. "Alas, only the three of us."

My heart ached for her. I'd seen it in her eyes—what she felt for Marcellus, even the fictional version of him, had been as real as what I felt for Thierry. "I'm sorry, Veronique. I know part of you wanted to stay there with him."

"For a moment, I thought it might be possible." Her eyes shone with tears. "But of course, such things are not. Fantasy is not reality. My life is here and Marcellus must remain only a memory for me. There was never any other choice."

She went to close the door, but something was blocking it.

It pushed open again and Marcellus stepped into the room.

He regarded us all with a bright smile. "That was rather exciting, wasn't it? I certainly can't explain it, but—" He frowned. "Where are we now?"

My mouth fell open.

Thierry stared at the man with surprise. "There has to be an explanation for this."

Marcellus had followed us back here through the passageway.

That shouldn't have been possible. He was a fictional character created by Veronique for her book.

This was the real world. Yet he was standing right in front of us.

Veronique stared at him, her eyes wide, her mouth forming a perfect "O." "Marcellus . . ."

"Do you understand what has happened?" he asked.

"Yes, I think so," she whispered. "The magic from the amulet made this possible. It was contained within that place, making real what was only fiction—because you followed me here. Here you're real. It's a miracle!"

Marcellus regarded her with confusion, as if every

word that left her mouth was a puzzle he couldn't solve. "All I know for sure, my love, is we have a task at hand. We must find a murderess and bring her to justice."

Another item for the lengthy to-do list.

And another surprise guest now invited to the party from Hell.

Chapter 15

It was edging close to three o'clock in the morning. Only three hours remained before dawn broke.

Half our time had been squandered in Vampireland.

However, for a second there—between Thierry's spell and the fog—I wasn't sure if we'd make it back at all.

But we did.

I watched Thierry, trying to see if there were any signs of stress, any indication that the thirst still tortured him or that the spell hadn't been broken. He looked every bit as much in control as he ever had.

Point for me. Negative five million for Sebastien.

Not that I could rub it in his face. Who knew what else he might have planned as a backup?

"The others should be gathering in the foyer soon." Thierry moved toward the door leading out to the hallway. "Remember, tell no one about my spell. Sebastien must continue to believe it holds."

Marcellus had gone silent and looked around at everything we passed, his jaw tight. His eyes widened as Thierry pulled his cell phone from his pocket and checked to see if there was a signal yet. "You will explain all of this to me soon, Veronique. This strange place, that bright and magical object Thierry holds, your oddly revealing clothing, and what happened back there that we needed to escape from."

She gave him a tense smile. "Yes, my darling. Of course I will. For now, please try to play along."

"I will do my very best."

Thierry tucked his phone away and reached down to entwine his fingers with mine.

"Thank you again for believing in me," he murmured.

"Anytime." I squeezed his hand. "Although, if you want Sebastien to think you're still thirsty for my blood, it would probably look more legit if you keep your distance."

He nodded. "Yes, of course you're right."

Still, he didn't let go of my hand until we reached the bottom of the stairs in the foyer.

"Where is this Anna villainess?" Marcellus asked, turning around in a circle.

"Shh, darling." Veronique grabbed his arm. "Let Thierry explain when the others arrive."

And they did as the hour reached three o'clock, just as we'd planned. Sebastien arrived, his brow furrowed as he saw Thierry . . . and then Marcellus. I wondered if he had ever met the man before—the real one, anyway. He remained silent, but I could see the questions in his eyes.

Atticus was right behind Sebastien, and he looked extremely grumpy. By now, Thierry had put a dozen feet between us, as if keeping distance between himself and temptation. Atticus's sharp eyes caught everything. I still didn't know what to make of the man. Was he really as bad as the other elders suspected? Were they right to assign Thierry to figuring out if he was behind the murders?

Or was he someone, like Thierry, who'd been suspected of being evil when all he wanted to do was help?

"Who is this?" Atticus asked sharply, pointing at Marcellus as Tasha and Melanie appeared through an archway to join the group. "And how did he enter this building?"

Marcellus raised his chin. "My name is Marcellus Rousseau. My reputation should speak for itself among our kind. Who are you, sir, that you would speak so rudely to me?"

Atticus flicked a look at Thierry, "But Marcellus was infamously killed by hunters more than four hundred and fifty years ago," he said.

"I most certainly was not!" Marcellus blustered. "I think I would remember something like that!"

"Let's just say," Thierry said slowly, as if choosing his words with great care, "that Marcellus has joined us for the evening in a . . . magical manner."

"What's that supposed to mean?"

"It seems to be a side effect of the amulet's magic. I have no further explanation for it at this time. Nor do we have the time to waste discussing this."

"I would disagree. This seems significant."

"I am here to help," Marcellus said proudly. "You can take my help with open arms or you can resist. It makes no difference to me."

I'd kept a close eye on Melanie since she'd entered the foyer. She glanced from Thierry to me and gave me a sheepish look.

A *guilty* look.

I would expect so if she'd been lying to us about being a werewolf. About being the blood deliverer, but not the blood enchanter.

That drink server was a witch working for Sebastien, and even if she felt guilty about what he'd had her do, she was still a threat.

I would never, ever underestimate a witch—that was for sure.

"Where's Anna?" I asked, trying to sound conversational and not accusatory.

Be cool, Sarah.

"I haven't seen her," Atticus said, "or her odd little husband. I'm fine with that, since both of them despise me."

No need to blurt out the news of the murder. Better to wait and see if anyone looked guilty. "Why would they?"

"I am the leader of an organization they feel represses their ability to embrace all that it is to fully be vampire. No matter who might lead the Ring, Purists would not embrace that person as a friend. It doesn't matter. I have plenty of friends."

Is that so? It sounded as if he was killing off his friends at the Ring one by one.

Still, innocent until proven guilty. I had to remember that about Anna, too, even if all the evidence now pointed a big neon arrow directly at her.

"Thomas isn't here, either," Melanie said.

"We can't wait for him." Thierry had climbed a few stairs so he could address us all easily as well as keep a "safe" distance. "Time is slipping away. Has anyone had any success?"

Sebastien stood near the front door, his arms

crossed tightly over his chest. "I'm surprised you're still coherent. Aren't you feeling the pinch, Thierry?"

Thierry's cold gaze tracked to him. "I will deal with you later."

"I see you're keeping away from Sarah. Probably a good idea if you value her safety. Who would have thought the one she'd have to fear the most was her own husband?"

I forced myself to remain silent in case I might say something to give away the fact that Thierry's spell was already broken. I wanted to feel bad for Sebastien, that he had so much hate inside him directed at the wrong person that he wanted that person to suffer—that he was willing to put other people's lives at risk . . .

Okay, I didn't feel as bad as I should. I guess my empathy had an expiration date.

"I searched as many rooms as I could in the time I had," Tasha said, sounding frustrated. "This mansion is seemingly endless."

"I found some rooms on the third floor that are locked," Melanie added.

"There's nothing in those rooms," Sebastien said.

"So says the host of this party from Hell," I mumbled.

"Did you say something, Sarah?" he asked.

"Oh, no. Nothing. Nothing at all." I didn't try to smile at him. Just how much of this was Sebastien Lavelle, resident vampire with a grudge, responsible for? I was starting to think he had his fingers in many evil pies. "Where's the amulet, Sebastien?"

"I don't know."

I moved closer to him, peering at his face to see if

I could see anything helpful there. "I think you're lying."

He regarded me blandly. "Too bad I don't have a polygraph on hand. I'd prove you wrong about that."

"Why don't I be the polygraph and just say you're lying?"

"I'm not."

He was incredibly frustrating. "You are! Do you want us all to die at dawn if you don't grow up, you spoiled brat?"

"Control your wife, de Bennicoeur," Sebastien growled.

"Why?" Thierry replied. "Her assessment of both you and the situation at hand is perfectly reasonable to me."

Sebastien shot him a withering look. "I had nothing to do with the amulet going missing."

"And why, precisely, would any of us believe that, given some of your other nefarious decisions tonight?"

Sebastien's cheek twitched. "If I had hidden it, don't you think I would tell you? I took the warning we received earlier very seriously. We need to fix this mess before dawn or we'll all perish."

I still couldn't tell if he was playing a game with us or not. I now sensed he was telling the truth, but maybe I was a lousy lie detector tonight.

"No one found anything?" I asked. "Nothing at all?"

One by one, everyone, including Atticus, Melanie, and Tasha, said no.

No sign of the amulet. No sign of the djinn. And no one else mentioned that they'd randomly walked into a scene or two from Veronique's book.

Thierry hadn't breathed a word about Frederic's

death yet. Perhaps he was attempting to rule out every-one present as a suspect. It had to have been Anna. I was sure of it.

Thomas finally joined us, entering through the archway to the right.

"What about you?" Thierry said.

Thomas didn't reply. His face was pale and sweat coated his brow.

"Good Lord!" Tasha exclaimed. "What's wrong with him?"

He staggered close enough to me to clutch my arm, then dropped heavily to his knees on the marble floor.

"Thomas, are you okay?" I asked with alarm.

He just shook his head, licked his lips, and whis-pered, barely coherently, "Please, you must fix what went wrong. . . . Seven oh five. Attack. Seven oh—"

And then he slipped all the way to the floor.

I clamped my hand over my mouth as everyone else drew closer. Atticus helped me roll him over on his back.

"He's not dead," I told them. "Just unconscious."

Given the deadly night we'd had so far, this was very good news.

Melanie stroked the hair off his forehead. "We need to get him somewhere softer than the floor. Poor Thomas! What happened to him?"

"No idea," I managed.

"What did he say to you?" Atticus asked.

"I couldn't understand him." I'd heard him, although what he'd said hadn't made any sense to me.

Someone in this room may have done something to him. A vampire didn't just randomly faint. And the look in his eyes had been bleak and frightened.

If you asked me, he'd looked scared to death.

He'd seen something. Seen *someone*. And this was the result.

Maybe he'd come face-to-face with the missing djinn.

"Luckily, I was able to hear him," Marcellus said. "He said 'Heaven or life, a tick.' "

"Heaven or life, a tick?" Tasha's brows drew together. "What on earth is that supposed to mean?"

Pretty sure it was *seven oh five attack*, not *heaven or life a tick*. But I wasn't going to correct him. Not that I had any idea at all what it meant.

Marcellus rubbed his chin. "Perhaps he anticipated his own mortality and was choosing between embracing death and continuing to fight for his own survival and it was draining him, such as a tick might."

Veronique patted his arm. "That is an excellent assessment, darling."

Sebastien and Atticus hoisted Thomas and carried him into the parlor, placing him on a sofa. The rest of us followed.

Melanie stood by the doorway, wringing her hands. "Will he wake up?"

Tasha glanced at her. "Do I look like a doctor?"

"You were a great doctor in *Space Hospital*," I said weakly. "Which, you should know, is one of my all-time-favorite movies."

She looked at me with surprise. "Thank you so much. I had great fun on that one."

"I'd say so. That love scene with George Clooney was hot enough to—"

"Sarah," Thierry interjected, "perhaps we should leave the discussion of favorite films for later."

"Right. Right, yeah, that's probably a good idea."

Focus. I could do that. Even in the presence of someone who'd made out with George Clooney.

"We have just under three hours," Thierry said. "We will have to cover the rest of the house. Sarah and I may not be the only ones who can feel the magic from the amulet. Try to search not only with your eyes, but with your minds."

"And what if we don't find it?" Atticus said. "We're trapped in here like lambs to the slaughter."

Tasha hugged herself while giving him a worried look. "Don't say that. We're not. We'll find it. It's here—we know that much. And Thierry's right. We could be able to feel its magic if we allow ourselves the chance."

"I'll personally check the locked rooms on the third floor Melanie mentioned," Thierry said.

"And why should we trust you in the state you're in?" Atticus snarled.

"Touché, Atticus. I am willing to go with someone who'll ensure I properly behave myself."

"Who would volunteer for such a job? You are a danger to every one of us while you are dealing with your current difficulties." Atticus flicked a nasty look at Sebastien. "Break the spell."

Sebastien glared at him. "No."

"You're putting us all at risk by keeping him this way. You know his reputation just as the rest of us do."

"Even if I knew how to break it, I wouldn't," Sebastien said.

Atticus hissed out a breath. "There's our answer, then. This fool doesn't know how to break the spell. That's different from keeping the answer from us. We'll have to make do with what we've got. If Thierry slips up and bites anyone, I will personally kill him."

"You can try," Thierry said darkly.

Atticus ignored him. "And then I'll kill you for the inconvenience, Sebastien. We'll meet again in two and a half hours at five thirty and someone better have that damn amulet by then."

Atticus stormed out of the parlor without another word.

"Meeting adjourned," I said under my breath, sickened by the threat Atticus had just made, since I didn't underestimate him for a moment. "Fantastic. That went well."

Tasha glanced around. "Where is Jacob?"

"He's dead," Veronique said bluntly.

Tasha gasped. "What?"

Veronique had a way of conveying sensitive information in a far too jarring manner. I decided to take over. "We think Anna murdered him. And he's not the only one. You should all know that Frederic is also dead, and all signs point to her as the one who did it."

"We will find her," Marcellus said firmly, "and we will bring her to justice."

Melanie paled. "Frederic's dead, too?"

I nodded.

Tasha shook her head. "This is terrible. I've known them for years and I sensed that they were having problems recently, but why would she do something like this? It doesn't make any sense."

"Murder is an act of passion," Marcellus said. "Often, it doesn't make sense. All we can do is try to unravel the facts and ensure it will not happen to anyone else."

Tasha stared at him. "Are you for real?"

"As real as any Frenchman who lives and breathes

the fine air of France." He held his hand over his heart. "Our beloved homeland."

She frowned. "First of all, this isn't France. This is America."

Marcellus cocked his head. "America? What is America? What are these unfamiliar words you all continue to use to confound me?"

"I will explain everything later, my darling," Veronique assured him. "But first we must search for both the amulet and Anna Dark."

His tension seemed to ease as he met her eyes. "Very well, my love. Where you lead, I shall follow."

Veronique flicked a glance at me as she and Marcellus departed down the hallway, her eyes filled with equal parts happiness and dread.

I knew it very well as the look of true love.

Veronique had it bad for him. Which was appropriate, since I couldn't see much good in this situation. If we succeeded in finding the amulet and fixing it—which we had to do by dawn or else—what would become of Marcellus, who was here only *because* of that magic?

"I'll keep looking, too," Sebastien said sullenly, turning toward the parlor door after Melanie bade us good luck and followed after the ancient lovebirds.

I grabbed his arm before he could get away. "First I need to talk to you, Junior."

He gave me a sour look. "Can't it wait?"

"No. No, it really can't." Even though we'd broken Thierry's spell, I still needed Sebastien to see reason when it came to his sire. And if he wandered off, I might not get this chance again.

Tasha sighed. "I only wish the phones worked so I could call someone and tell them I'm going to be late for my arrival time on set—"

As if on cue, the phone on the end table near Thomas's unconscious body began to ring.

I stared at it with shock.

After a few rings, Sebastien tentatively picked it up and held it to his ear.

"Hello? Yes, just a moment." With a frown, he looked at me. "It's for you, Sarah."

Chapter 16

I gave Thierry a wary glance before I moved toward the phone, taking it gingerly away from Sebastien, and held it to my left ear.

"Hello?" I said as calmly as possible.

"There you are! Excellent. Have you found my body yet?"

It was the head.

"How are you calling me right now?" I asked.

"If I could answer complicated questions like that I'd be in a much better place. I don't know. I don't know what's going on. All I know is I need to be reunited with my body or I—I don't know! Do you think I want to be dealing with this?"

I covered the receiver and spoke to Thierry. "It's the ghost."

He regarded me with a lowered brow, then nodded once. "I've heard of ghosts using telephones to communicate. It's unusual, but not an unheard-of method to speak with the living."

"Sarah's talking to ghosts?" Sebastien said.

"There are ghosts in this house?" Tasha took a step back from me. "I don't like ghosts. I even refuse to do ghost movies."

"He's harmless—he's just a little confused." At least, that was the hypothesis I was going with. I hoped I was right.

I returned to the conversation. "I said I'd help you and I meant it. Can you tell me anything else that might be useful? Where can I find your body?"

"It's around."

"In the mansion or outside? Buried? Hidden? What?"

"If I knew, I'd tell you. If I knew, I'd try to find it myself."

I wasn't sure how he would conduct this search, being that he was only a head, but okay. "Where are you?"

"I don't know. Somewhere dark and cold."

Thierry drew closer to me. Sebastien didn't take the opportunity to slip out of the room; he remained by the entrance, where he'd been. Tasha sat down in an upholstered chair and began to wring her hands.

"Can you remember anything at all?" I asked.

"I feel like there was a blade, like a sword or . . . or a scimitar. I don't even know what a scimitar is, but that word pops into my mind. I think that's what killed me."

I grimaced. "Sorry."

"Don't be sorry. Just help me find my body."

"And then what?"

"Then—then I know I'll be able to put myself back together."

"You don't know anything else, but you suddenly know that you're Humpty Dumpty?"

He sighed again, a defeated sound. "All I know for sure is that someone—"

The line went dead.

"Are you still there? Hello?" I waited several moments, my heart pounding, before I hung up the phone. "He's gone."

Tasha grabbed for the phone and held it to her ear, already dialing a number before her shoulders hunched and she stared at the receiver with frustration. "It's still not working."

I think I was in a little shock at talking to the head again in such an unexpected way. "Only for ghosts, apparently."

She hung up. "This is so incredibly frustrating. Why can't it just be over already?"

"Let's not wish our time away." I blinked and turned to Thierry. "Wait. . . . *Wishing*. There's a genie loose and nobody's wishing us out of this mess?"

He shook his head. "The amulet's magic is not working as it should. Making large, arbitrary wishes could backfire."

He was right, of course.

"Why don't I test the theory by wishing for something specific and not threatening?" I suggested.

Thierry's jaw was tight, but finally he nodded. "It's worth a try. You officially won the auction. You are the current owner of the amulet, even though it's missing, so you would have the best chance of getting a response. If your wish is granted it's possible we can try to manipulate this magic to help us."

"Wish for something small," Tasha said eagerly.

"Okay." I cleared my throat and tried to center myself. What should I wish for? Something minor, but something I legitimately wanted. "I wish I had a refreshing glass of water right now."

I held out my hand and waited.

No glass of water magically appeared to quench my thirst.

"Try again," Tasha urged.

Okay. How about: "I wish my dress was green instead of red."

I looked down. Still red.

No magic tingles. No nothing.

"It's not working." Which was disappointing, since I'd really thought I might have figured out how to help us. But apparently it wouldn't be that easy.

"And now we're wasting time." Tasha shook her head, twisting a long piece of red hair around her index finger as if considering her next move. "I'll head upstairs and keep checking rooms. I hope one of them contains something useful."

"You and me both. Good luck," I said.

She nodded, then turned and started up the staircase, leaving me, Thierry, and Sebastien alone.

I turned my attention back to Sebastien. "I haven't forgotten you, Junior."

His lips were thin as he regarded me. "There's nothing to discuss, Sarah."

"I disagree."

Thierry didn't budge from where he stood near me, and Sebastien noticed.

"He still protects you, even when you have no one to fear but him."

"Arguable. There are plenty of shady people here tonight I don't feel comfortable spending much time alone with. You're on that list."

"Got something to say?" he asked Thierry.

"For now I'll let Sarah do the talking. She's excellent at summing up difficult subjects in a highly concise manner."

Such compliments made me feel all tingly, and magic didn't have anything to do with it.

"This isn't my fault," Sebastien griped.

"Wrong." I poked him in his chest. "This is one hundred percent your fault. You're the one who threw the party, held the auction, had Melanie put the blood in Thierry's drink. You were trying to hurt him because you think he hurt you."

"I don't regret what I've done."

Big surprise. But I knew it was important for him to see reason. If he was the one hiding the amulet, that might make him come clean. "You should, because you're wrong. Everything you did was to get back at Thierry for what he did to you. The only problem with that plan is Thierry didn't do anything to you. He's innocent."

Sebastien rolled his eyes and sat down heavily in a chair next to the sofa the unconscious Thomas currently occupied. "I think we've covered this already, Sarah. You defend him because you're in love with him. I understand love, I understand what one is willing to do—what lengths one will go to—for love. But you're wrong. He destroyed my life."

It was like a dog chasing its own tail. All we were doing was talking in circles. "He didn't do it. Read my lips—*he did not do that*. Do you remember Thierry personally shoving you into that tomb?"

"He hired men to do it for him."

"But you didn't see him with your own eyes, did you?" I countered.

"What I saw doesn't matter."

"Oh, but it does matter. He's innocent. Someone else put you in that tomb. And I'm sorry. I really am. That seriously sucks beyond anything I can possibly

understand. But you're blaming the wrong person—
and that single-minded hatred is going to get everyone in this mansion killed when dawn breaks."

I'd basically accused him point-blank of hiding the
amulet. So be it. I believed it was true. Who else could
have done it?

He just stared at me.

"As I said," Thierry said, "Sarah has an excellent
way with words."

Sebastien gave him a tense look. "You couldn't say
the same thing to me?"

"You wouldn't believe me. I know you, Sebastien. It's
been a long time since I last saw you, but I know you.
You hated me then as you hate me now, only now you
feel you have reason for this hatred. I don't know who
conspired against you, but it wasn't me. I swear it."

For the first time that night, the slightest edge of
doubt crept into Sebastien's eyes.

"You hated me, too," he whispered.

Thierry shook his head. "I never hated you."

"I had your thirst, and it reminded you of what
you had to deal with every day."

"Yes. Perhaps I was disappointed in that, but only
because I knew it would cause you difficulties I
wasn't sure you could handle."

"I didn't handle them well."

"You handled them as well as anyone could in the
same situation."

Sebastien went silent. "Who else would have done
that to me? It had to have been you. She told me it was
you."

A breath caught in my chest. "Who told you that?"

"It doesn't matter."

"Oh, yes, it certainly does matter. Whoever told

you specifically that Thierry was the one to lock you away has some secrets of their own—or a vendetta against Thierry, too." I let out a frustrated sigh. "Seriously, Thierry. Does anyone have a really solid and friendly history with you without any violent and backstabbing hiccups?"

"Many," he replied. "Unfortunately, none are present with us this evening."

"Forget it. You can try to fool me," Sebastien growled, "but I don't accept it. I won't accept it. Now leave me alone, both of you. And I swear I'll never break the spell."

"Who's your witch, Sebastien?" I asked. "Is she here tonight with us?"

Namely, a drink server named Melanie currently posing as an innocent werewolf?

He shot me a look of surprise. "Why would she be here?"

"That felt like a yes to me."

"Leave it alone, Sarah. And stay away from Thierry if you value your life. I don't care how restrained he might appear. He can't be far from losing control completely by now."

If only he knew the truth. "I'll take my chances."

"Then you're a fool for love." His expression grew wistful. "I lost my love when I was trapped like that. Three centuries without her by my side. Do you remember her, Thierry?"

Thierry shook his head. "Not particularly."

His expression soured again. "No, you wouldn't. You were far too focused on your own life to worry about mine. This conversation is over."

When he left the parlor I shut the door behind him, then turned to face Thierry.

"Honestly, I was willing to give that guy the benefit of the doubt, but he's seriously a self-obsessed, evil idiot, isn't he?"

"Sebastien is not evil or an idiot. He's hurt, emotionally, physically . . . and mentally, I'm sure, from all that time locked away. It takes years to recover from such an ordeal and he's been out mere months."

"Now you're defending him?"

"If I believed heart and soul that someone I trusted had betrayed me so completely, my vengeance would also be single-minded."

"He messes with you, he's messing with me. And I don't like to be messed with." When I leaned my head against his chest, he wrapped his arms around me and pulled me close. I looked up at him with surprise. "This is okay? The spell is really gone?"

"I believe so."

"Still a six?"

"A five point five."

"Marginally better." At least one thing had gone right tonight. I glanced over toward Thomas. "He said something to me before he collapsed. 'Seven oh five attack.' I didn't want to tell the others just in case it's dangerous information."

"What does it mean?"

"Your guess is as good as mine." Not a single thing had occurred to me that made any sense of it at all. "So what now? Should I join the others in the search for the amulet or look for the ghost head's body? I wonder if he pesters whoever normally lives here about this?"

"The problems of a ghost can wait, no matter how intensely they wish to find help. The amulet and the djinn are our priority."

Thierry led me out of the parlor and down the hallway to the library we'd been in before. Once there, he retrieved the book he'd been reading off the shelf.

"Did you find anything in there?" I asked. "How to slay a djinn, perhaps?"

He flipped through the pages, his index finger skimming over the strange words. "I found some information that could be useful if we had the right weaponry. A djinn is not like a normal supernatural being, such as a vampire or a werewolf. They can take both corporeal and incorporeal form. They are flesh or they are smoke. It makes them difficult to kill. But I feel we may need to do just that before dawn." He looked up from the book and said, "I believe the djinn is free from the amulet and has taken on a familiar face, one we are likely to trust."

Of course. I wasn't sure why this hadn't occurred to me. There had to be a reason our paths hadn't crossed with the djinn's yet. "Who?"

He drew me closer and lowered his voice as if someone might be eavesdropping. "Marcellus."

My eyes widened. "What?"

"A man Veronique knew who's been dead for centuries suddenly lives again because she wrote him back into existence? It's too much of a miracle for me to believe."

Marcellus was the djinn. Could it be possible?

"Wow." I raked my hands through my hair and paced back and forth to the bookcase. "So, if it's true, what do we do?"

He flipped forward a few pages in the book. "I don't think we can slay him, not while being trapped here. The translation from the original Andalusian is difficult, but from what I understand here, there is a sword that holds an ancient magic that must be acquired. When the djinn is summoned from the amulet . . ." He scanned the page. ". . . for a short time, his magic is apart from him. As he takes form from smoke to flesh, he is momentarily vulnerable. There is a window of opportunity during which he can be slain. When a djinn is slain, his magic will transfer to the slayer."

I cringed at the thought. "Slain? Like, stabbed through the heart?"

Thierry flipped back a page before he replied. "No, it specifically says that the djinn must be decapitated. The magic is then freed from him and this wild djinn magic will be fully claimed . . ." He frowned deeply. ". . . the following morning as the sun breaches the horizon."

I couldn't find words. "Decapitated."

"Yes."

"Uh, Thierry . . . I have a question."

"Yes, Sarah?"

"When you said 'sword,' could that word be translated to . . . *scimitar* instead?"

He closed the book. "Yes, I suppose it could be."

"Oh boy."

"What is it? What are you thinking?"

What was I thinking? Could it be?

"Marcellus isn't the djinn. I think I've already met the djinn." I took hold of Thierry's arm and looked up into his eyes. "It's the head!"

Chapter 17

Thierry took me by my shoulders. "Sarah, you're jumping to conclusions . . . I thought you believed the head was a ghost."

"That was only a guess. But what you're saying about the book—"

"A book written in an ancient language a very long time ago."

It couldn't be the only book about djinn. I was sure there would be a whole shelf of books on the subject at the library. Or an ocean of info on the Internet. "Somebody knew about the amulet, they acquired the magical sword, they summoned the djinn, and they whacked off his head!"

"Who would do this?"

He might believe in his fledgling's innocence, but I wasn't convinced. "Sebastien had the amulet in the first place."

"If Sebastien's plan was to steal a djinn's magic, why would he have bothered with an auction tonight with witnesses? He already possessed the amulet and has for centuries."

"You keep coming up with very good arguments that are not helping my theory at all." And my confidence in it was swiftly fading. "So you still think Marcellus is the djinn."

He rubbed his forehead. "I think, given the solid evidence presented, that is more likely to be the case."

"And the head is just some dude who got killed once upon a time and his body is hidden somewhere in this house."

"Yes. That is what I believe."

I tried to piece it all together and found my clues were less convincing than Thierry's. "But it's still a ginormous coincidence, don't you think?"

"I don't know that I'd use the word 'ginormous,' but yes. It certainly is a coincidence."

"Okay, fine. I'll go with your theory." Still, I couldn't give up that easily. "But you *might* be wrong. Can you at least admit that much?"

After a moment he nodded. "Yes. I might be wrong. All I know for certain is that we must find the amulet and keep a close eye on Marcellus during the next three hours."

"Sebastien is responsible for all of this, including hiding the amulet. You agree with that, too, right?"

"He's in pain. There's a distinct possibility he's responsible, but I can't bring myself to completely blame him for this." His jaw tightened. "I regret that I was not a better sire."

"The past is over. We need to focus on the present—and so does he. He'll come around."

"I hope you're right."

"What happens at dawn if we can't find the amulet?"

He took my hand in his and pulled me closer, brushing his lips against mine. "We'll worry about that at dawn."

I didn't want to leave Thierry's side, but after a few minutes of debate on how best to handle everything, we came up with a plan. Unfortunately, that plan meant we had to separate.

We could both feel the magic from the amulet and we had no guarantees that anyone else could, so searching separately meant we could cover twice as much ground.

Thierry set off to find Marcellus and Veronique so he could assess whether or not the fictional Marcellus was actually the djinn.

I went in the opposite direction and headed up to the second floor, where I'd left off earlier before my unexpected detour with Veronique to Vampireland.

Down the hall, I found a huge music room, one with pianos and harps and a whole orchestra's worth of instruments. An open archway led to what looked like a ballet studio, with bars set along the mirrored walls. There was a fine layer of dust on most surfaces. This wasn't a place used very often, so I was surprised the doors weren't locked like the unused rooms on the third floor.

I didn't touch anything and get dusty—I just tried to sense the magic.

"Where is it?" I whispered.

Thierry believed Marcellus was the djinn, but my gut told me he was wrong. Maybe he hadn't totally seen how Veronique looked at her lost love, but I had. Veronique, despite her superficial mannerisms, went a lot deeper than most people believed. She loved hard, even though she would deny it to anyone who asked. Her book might not be the greatest piece of literature ever written, but I'd bet my last dollar that it had tons of heart in its five billion pages.

She said it was a romance—a romance between her and Marcellus, one that spanned the ages. He was the true love of her life.

A djinn could certainly prey on that kind of weakness, but I honestly didn't think she was that gullible.

Marcellus was the real deal—or as real as any fictional version could ever be.

Combine that with a pinch of magic, and you had a recipe for . . . well, a whole lot of trouble.

I left the music and ballet studio and moved slowly down the hall, trying to sense something. Anything. I stopped and studied the portraits hanging on the walls. The oil landscapes. The carpeting, the vases, and anything else.

No magic.

And I did try my very best to avoid any dark passageways that might take me away from the mansion again.

Luckily, I didn't see a single one.

"Sarah." Atticus greeted me as I turned the corner. He was exiting a room. "You're not with Thierry."

At the sight of him, my self-defense instincts popped up like a cluster of Whac-A-Moles. "Not at the moment."

"Tell me the truth—how is he really holding up against that unfortunate spell?"

Are you asking out of concern or morbid curiosity? "He's . . . managing as best as he can."

Atticus pursed his lips and nodded. "I know his troubles. I wouldn't wish this on anyone. It was particularly cruel for Sebastien to prey upon this weakness."

"It hasn't been an easy evening for him for many

reasons. Any luck?" I asked, trying to change the subject. Atticus was the last person I'd confide in. I wasn't about to tell him that Thierry had broken his spell.

He glared at the walls going down the long hallway as if they'd personally offended him. "I'm afraid not. Whoever hid it did a fine job. I'd be very nearly impressed if I weren't deeply annoyed by this inconvenience."

I was still trying to figure out what Thomas could have meant by *seven oh five attack.* Was it an important clue or something a nearly unconscious person might randomly ramble?

And why was he unconscious, anyway? Was he trying to tell me who'd attacked him?

Seven oh five.

It was another piece of information I hesitated to share with Atticus. However, since he'd cornered me, I couldn't just scurry off. Not yet, anyway.

"I was just thinking about the otherworldly message we got earlier via Melanie," I said. "How do we even know to take it seriously? It could be as dangerous as a car alarm."

He shook his head. "I'm not sure we want to take the chance of ignoring it."

"No, of course not." I didn't trust Atticus, but there had to be something he was good for. He was old, therefore a natural wealth of information. "What do you know about djinn and their amulets?"

"Enough."

Something in that single word made me eye him with additional suspicion. He'd wanted that amulet really badly—but why?

When Atticus had first approached me in the hallway, I'd wanted to try to lose him immediately. But why would I want that? I bet he'd know about all things djinn, given his acute interest in the amulet. And I couldn't forget for a moment that he was suspected of offing a couple of high-level master vamps on his journey to the top. And if he was responsible for those murders, Thierry could be next on his list.

But if I could somehow get him to admit to those crimes . . .

"I know what you're thinking, Sarah," Atticus said.

My stomach lurched. "Oh, yeah?"

He drew closer, peering at me through the shadows of the hallway. "You're angry with me."

That would be one of the lesser emotions I felt toward Thierry's shady boss. "Why would I be angry with you?"

He glanced up and down the hallway, as if checking whether we might be disturbed. Then he took my arm. "Let's go sit somewhere more private and talk."

More private than an empty hallway? My high heels dug into the carpet. "We can't waste time talking."

"The others are searching. This mansion is large, but a group of motivated people scouring it from attic to basement will turn up something. I have faith."

"Do you? I wish I could say the same."

"Sarah, please, I mean you no harm. Trust me."

Spoken by someone I didn't trust. One I believed could definitely mean me harm.

I'd admit that my insistence on trusting people based solely on my gut instinct had gotten me in trouble before. But it had been a help many more times than not. Trust was a gamble, and sometimes it paid off.

Like with Thierry, for example. Most assumed him to be cold and emotionless and dangerous. Well, he certainly could be all three, depending on the situation.

But I'd seen something more in him and gone against the advice of others to prove it.

My gut had been totally right about him.

So what was it trying to tell me about Atticus Kincade?

It seemed seriously conflicted when it came to the big boss of the Ring.

Why not get it out on the table so we could stop wasting time?

"Do you want to kill me?" I asked bluntly.

His brows shot up. "Kill you? What in the world are you talking about? You're very paranoid tonight."

I remembered that he'd stormed out of the parlor before he'd had a chance to hear about the murders. "I think I have a right to be. Jacob and Frederic are both dead, Atticus."

He paled. "My God. Do we know who's responsible?"

Okay, he was either being completely genuine right now, or he was one a hell of an amazing actor.

"We think it was Anna. And she's nowhere to be found."

His eyes narrowed with disapproval. "And you're wandering the halls alone without protection?"

"I can look after myself."

Anger flashed across his face. "De Bennicoeur is an idiot if he's left you alone to face potential danger. Sarah, you must trust me. I have devoted my existence to protecting vampires from the world at large, from each other, and sometimes even from themselves. I want to help you and I swear on all that is holy that I mean you no harm."

Yeah, my gut was all kinds of conflicted when it came to this guy.

Fine, he wanted to talk in private? We'd talk in private. I might even get some important information out of him.

With renewed determination, I followed him to a nearby room with a large couch in it. There were also floor-to-ceiling shelves of books, but not nearly as many as the library downstairs held.

Atticus shut the door to give us some privacy, but he didn't get too close. He sat down in the chair opposite the sofa where I'd taken a seat.

"I know you must hate me," he said.

My brows shot up. "Excuse me?"

"Thierry works for the Ring because of decisions I made. Because of . . . threats I made."

Okay. So we were going to talk about this, were we? Now?

I glanced at a clock on the wall, which told me it was three thirty.

We didn't have time for this.

I crossed my arms. "He hasn't shared much about that, but I have a general idea of what happened."

"I believed he had feelings for you based on what I'd heard through the grapevine. Deep feelings that surprised the entire council of elders. You see, we had all known Thierry in the past, before he took his lengthy sabbatical from the Ring and from us. He was an admirable man, but he had his faults, as do we all."

Let's get to the point, shall we? "Go on."

"I was in charge and I had some difficulties with previous consultants. I kept thinking about Thierry and how capable he'd been as lead elder in the beginning, how focused he was on creating the council. When Thierry does something, he does it wholeheartedly. I needed him back. He refused several offers. He refused until I grew angry and impatient." He shrugged. "I am used to getting what I want and when I don't, I get very . . ."

Murderous? "Cranky?"

Atticus nodded. "I had also received information that he might have had contact with the Jacquerra Amulet, which had become a bit of an obsession of mine in the last few years. To make a long story short, Sarah, I refused to take no for an answer from him."

"So you threatened to have me killed." Saying it out loud left a nasty taste in my mouth.

He didn't speak for a moment. "I preyed on what I believed was Thierry's new weakness . . . you. I pressed buttons I never would have guessed he'd even possess. And it appeared to work like a charm. He agreed to sign on as a consultant for us."

That was as close to an admission as I was likely to ever get. "And here we are."

"Here we are." His forehead furrowed. "I now recognize my methods may have been more extreme than necessary."

"Thierry took you seriously."

"He did." He shook his head. "But I don't understand. Seeing you here together tonight, I'm questioning what others have told me about the strength of your relationship. I did wonder how it was possible that a fledgling could capture the full attention and devotion of a master vampire, not to mention the heart of one always assumed to be heartless. It seems . . . impossible. No offense intended."

Thierry wanted him to believe we had our problems, so I didn't argue this. I bit my tongue for a moment so I could stay silent long enough to gather my thoughts.

"Thierry's an enigma," I said.

"Yes, he is that."

"Was it just a threat?" I had to ask. "Or would you have followed through if he'd continued to say no to the job?"

Atticus pursed his lips, his expression strained. He didn't reply.

"I see." I stood up. "I think we're done here."

"You have nothing to fear from me, Sarah."

"Says someone who planned to have me killed. Or would you have done it yourself?" I swept my gaze over the length of him, my stomach souring. "No, you don't seem the type to want to dirty your own hands. You must have plenty of minions you can order around."

"I've never been much of a minion enthusiast." He sighed. "Am I a coldhearted, ruthless bastard, Sarah? One who would do whatever it takes to get what he wants and maintain his level of power? I am. No question about it."

"And I'll take that as a 'yes, I would have killed you.' Thank you for the clarification."

"I have no interest in death of any kind tonight. All I need is the amulet."

"Then we should be looking for it, not wasting time talking." I moved toward the door, but he stepped in front of me.

Any guilt left his expression as he gave me a focused and intimidating look. "Where did Thierry get the money that enabled him to bid so high tonight?"

The last thing I wanted to do was let on that the Ring suspected Atticus of nastiness, enough to bankroll Thierry's investigation of him. "Thierry's got lots of money squirreled away all over the place. He's pushing seven hundred years old. That and compound interest will do wonders for your savings account."

I tried to get past him, but he shuffled to the side.

"He's dangerous. More so than I even thought he was."

"He's under a blood spell, thanks to Sebastien."

"Apart from that. I have reason to believe that Thierry means me great harm."

This man was a serious question mark. Was he a villain or a victim? "Now who's paranoid, Atticus? Are you going to let me leave?"

"I have a few more questions."

Fine. He wanted to play this game? "So do I. What did you want the amulet for?"

"For my collection."

"Right. You're already the boss of the council. What more do you want to wish for?"

"My position with the Ring has nothing to do with this."

I found that very difficult to believe. "That amulet should be destroyed. It's trouble. And it's cursed, did you know that? Sebastien tells me that anyone who owns it gets saddled with a little curse. Maybe that's why he ended up in a tomb for so long."

"I thought Thierry put him in that tomb."

"He didn't."

"Why do you defend him when he is not here to protect you? When he publicly claims to consider you a temporary plaything, not a true companion?"

I still wasn't sure what he thought this conversation would accomplish. All I knew was that I was more than ready to get out of it. "Do I need protection right now?"

He spread his hands. "I'm happy to protect you."

"Look, Atticus, I don't mean to be rude, even though you're now literally blocking me from leaving this room, but I don't need your protection or anyone else's."

Frustration and a sliver of growing anger flashed through his eyes. "The more I think about it, the more I'm certain that the murders tonight—both Jacob's and Frederic's—are Thierry's doing."

Of course he'd think something like that. His saying it so bluntly made a knot form in my stomach, since I knew it would be impossible to convince him otherwise. "You're wrong."

He waved a hand as if dismissing my commentary. "Two very important elder vampires have been murdered in the last couple of months, Sarah. Vampires who were a part of the original council. Only myself and Thierry have survived. My theory is that Thierry was so angry about being forced back into the Ring that he took out this anger by murdering those he held responsible. I can only assume that I will be next. Of course I wanted the amulet, so I could have some means of protecting myself now and in the future."

Yes, I was seriously having this conversation right now.

Atticus was openly talking about the very crime he'd been accused of. But he believed Thierry had done it.

What the hell was going on here?

"I couldn't let him acquire the amulet, Sarah," Atticus continued. "He's wanted it for so long that I fear what he'd do with that power in his hands, especially with the threat of vengeance toward me."

This guy was delusional, paranoid, or crazy. Likely, all three.

And none of the above made me comfortable about spending another minute in his company with no one else around.

"I hate to admit it, but you might be right," I said slowly. Humoring him seemed like the best way to get out of here.

Relief entered his gaze. "I'm glad you're open to this unfortunate possibility."

"I'm not as naive as some people think I am. And I'm definitely not blind when it comes to knowing a dangerous man when I see one."

Or when I was stuck in a room with him.

Atticus rubbed his chin. "This blood spell may be a blessing in disguise. One day, perhaps I can thank Sebastien for giving me this loophole to take care of an ongoing problem." He watched me carefully. "Is this too much information for you to handle?"

"Oh no," I managed. *You talking about offing Thierry just because he's a little on the thirsty side?* "I can handle it just fine."

"I will stay by your side and ensure that no harm comes to you."

"That's really super-nice of you." I followed as he moved across the room and pushed open the door. "But not necessary. We can cover more ground if we—"

He cut me off. "Why do women always argue with me about every little thing? It's very annoying."

I glared at him. "Is it? I suppose I should learn my place."

"Yes. Try to learn it swiftly if you want my help now and in the future. Understood?"

I slipped past him to enter the hallway. "Don't worry. I'm a quick learner."

I slammed the door shut in his face and began running down the hallway.

Chapter 18

A couple of moments later, Atticus easily caught up to me, grabbed my arm, and pulled me to a halt.

He spun me around so I could see his flushed face. "What are you doing, you foolish woman?"

I tried to pull away from his bruising grip, but found I couldn't. "Let go of me."

"You need to behave yourself!"

I was about to start clawing at him with my free hand when I heard a *whack* and he stumbled forward a step. After a crash, he fell face-first onto the carpet.

Tasha Evans stood behind him holding a broken vase that she let drop to the floor. "Are you okay?"

There were red marks on my arm where Atticus had gripped me. "I—I think so."

"What did he think he was doing, manhandling you like that?"

"I don't think he was thinking."

She let out an angry grunt. "I thought he'd changed, but he's just as much of a jerk as when we dated. He thinks women are nothing more than arm candy and that we need to be coddled and protected and cared for like children, but he also thinks we're stupid and irresponsible and need harsh discipline to keep us in line." She poked him in the forehead with her open-toed shoe. "Jerk."

I looked down at the council elder who'd wanted me to "learn my place." Was he really evil or was it a case of not so simple misogyny? He was a manipulator who used people's weaknesses against them.

He was using the events of tonight to find a reason to have Thierry killed. And he'd actually thought I would help him.

Atticus Kincade was a bad guy—our enemy—and he'd gotten what he deserved.

"He won't be unconscious for long," Tasha said. She looked back over her shoulder. "I saw something that might contain him so he doesn't try anything else tonight."

A shiver went down my spine. "What do you mean, 'contain him'?"

"Trust me. Unless you want to wait around for him to wake up."

"No, not a good idea."

"Didn't think so. Help me carry him."

Together, without further argument, we got his unconscious body down the hallway and around the corner. Tasha pushed open a door to a cluttered room that looked as if it was used to store old furniture.

"Here," she said as we dragged his body over to a chest. "It's made of wood, but it's banded with silver. Don't touch the lid."

She didn't have to tell me twice. My hand was still stinging from clutching the stake back in Vampire-land.

Vampires couldn't break through silver because it burned our skin, which made it perfect for restraints. Legend said that a silver cross would repel and burn a vampire, but the cross itself actually had nothing to do with it. It was all about the silver, which was most definitely not my favorite precious metal.

Tasha carefully opened the lid of the carved chest.

I grimaced. "That looks eerily like a coffin."

"Yes, it does, doesn't it?"

"Who did Sebastien rent this mansion from, anyway? Morticia Addams?"

"Who cares? Come on, hoist him up."

I did as she instructed and Atticus dropped inside the large chest with a *thunk*. He was now snoring.

Tasha closed the lid. A bronze key was already in the lock. She twisted the key and pulled it out, placing it on a nearby shelf. "He'll be in there until someone lets him out."

I eyed the chest uneasily, suddenly thinking of Sebastien being locked in a tomb for three centuries. "Can he breathe in there okay?"

She inspected the lid more closely. "There are some holes, see? He'll be fine. Besides, it's much better for everyone if he's out of our way for now."

I let out a long, shaky sigh. "Thanks for intervening."

"No problem."

"It was sort of like that scene in *Kill or Be Killed*."

She nodded, smiling. "I played a wisecracking spy."

"Wisecracking spy by night, supermodel by day. Brilliant and hilarious. I own the DVD." My inner fangirl was threatening to rise up and spill over again. Since I didn't have time for her right now, I changed the subject. "When did you date Atticus, anyway?"

"It's got to be fifty years ago by now." She sighed. "Time flies."

She turned and moved toward the windows that

were blocked by furniture and I could see some of her tattoos on her back and shoulders. The woman seemed to ooze cool from every pore.

Despite this, and maybe only because I was paranoid, everybody in this mansion was currently a suspect for me. I couldn't give Tasha a free pass just because she was completely awesome.

I leaned against a stack of wooden boxes and attempted to look remotely at ease. "You said you knew Frederic and Anna."

She rattled the windows, but they were every bit as sealed shut as any others in this place. "I recognize them enough to speak to, but I wouldn't really call us friends. Anna was a sweet kid in the beginning, despite the crazy hunter family she escaped from, but now . . ." She turned toward me so I could see that her expression had shadowed. "Frederic's really gone?"

"Afraid so."

She wrapped her arms around herself and squeezed. "Maybe it sounds strange, but I feel so sorry for her. I knew they had troubles, but maybe if I'd been friendlier earlier and spoken to her, made her feel like she could talk to someone, she might have found another answer tonight."

"Don't beat yourself up about it. It's not your fault." I studied Tasha's face, trying to see any glimpse of deception.

Then a loud bang made me jump.

"Let me the hell out of here!" Atticus's voice boomed.

"Uh-oh." I eyed the chest uneasily. "He's awake."

"I swear on all that is holy, if you don't let me out of here I'm going to kill you!"

"Death threats," Tasha said. "I think that's our cue to leave."

"Sit tight, Atticus," I told him. "Behave yourself and we'll let you out as soon as—"

"Did you hear me? I'll kill you! Are you forgetting who I am? I tried to help you and you do this to me, you ungrateful little bitch! And you, Tasha, you'll never get another favor from me. Ever. You hear me?"

My empathy for his current predicament was fading away in record time. I knocked on the non-silver part of the lid. "Don't try to sweet-talk us like that, Atticus, because it won't work. Just try to relax and reflect on your more unpleasant life choices. Oh, and by the way? Bite me."

I left the room as he was hollering something about me being an idiot. Men. Always wanting to have the last word.

Tasha shut the door behind her and gave me a squeamish look. "Bite me?"

I shrugged. "I can't help it—some people bring out the worst in me."

"That's Atticus." She grinned, flashing a hint of fang. "Believe it or not, I actually had the idea I might go and work for the Ring once I'm done with acting. But that would mean working for him—thus his comment about favors."

"Not fun."

"No, it certainly wouldn't be."

I scanned the hallway, checking a drawer in a table and behind an oil painting. Why waste valuable search time? "How much longer will you act?"

"I don't know. It's been twenty years and I haven't aged a day. For now, everyone thinks I'm gifted with fantastic collagen. If they only knew the truth. I'm thinking angry mobs, pitchforks, and burning torches." She shrugged. "Then again, I've dealt with the paparazzi. What could be worse?"

"Good point."

"Seriously, though, I have two more movies in me, I think." She gave me another mischievous smile. "Maybe I'll give it another try in a century or so. I'll get myself a makeover."

"Those tattoos, though." I looked at the distinctive one of a black rose, which she'd famously bared for the cover of *Vanity Fair* a few years ago. "They're a bit of a giveaway of your true identity."

"Tattoos can be removed if necessary." She glanced at them. "But these ones are special. They're a part of me, way more than just skin-deep. I'd hate to have to lose them. But first, before any decisions can be made, we need to make it past dawn, don't we?"

"Good point." It was shadowy in the room, but I'd seen something that surprised me. "And you might also want to get back to your dentist. I'm seeing a bit of fang."

She grimaced and touched her lips. "I know. I keep them filed down, but it's a pain to maintain."

One of the many reasons why I'd never bothered. Getting regular manicures was trouble enough.

"I need to keep searching," she said.

Right. Enough with the chitchat. It was time to get back on track. "I swear," I said, "the answer is Sebastien. He's the one who had the amulet from the beginning."

"You think he hid it?"

I nodded. "Him, or maybe Thomas. They're the last ones who had direct access to it after the auction."

"Maybe he's waiting for something, some last moment where he can extort something out of us in order for us to leave safely."

"Or maybe he's in way over his head."

Head.

I couldn't forget the head.

That pesky gut of mine was telling me I needed to find his body as per his request. If only I had any idea of where to start looking.

I also had no idea if I was right about him being the djinn or if Thierry was right that he was just a ghost.

"Do you know anything about djinn?" I asked Tasha as we moved down the long hallway checking rooms as we went.

She gave me a sidelong look. "I was in a movie about djinn."

"Right, *Wishcaster*! That was . . . It was . . ." I grimaced. "Actually, it wasn't one of my favorites."

She stopped walking and peered in the next room to our left, its door creaking as she pushed it open. I tried to sense any magic in the area, but came up empty.

"I think you're being kind, since it was absolutely dreadful. But it was my first starring role."

I stopped breathing. "Wait a minute, I remember something. You killed the djinn at the end of that movie by chopping off its head."

She grimaced. "That was really disgusting. The purple blood they used smelled as terrible as it tasted. But, so what?"

"The screenwriter must have done his research, because that is actually how you kill a djinn."

"What? It is?"

My shoulders slumped after a moment's consideration. "Yeah, but it's also the way you can kill just about anything, so I'm not sure that makes whoever wrote it an expert on the subject. It doesn't really matter right now. All that matters is finding that amulet."

I didn't share anything about the head with Tasha. I loved her movies, but at this point in the evening's festivities I trusted only one person other than myself: Thierry. And he was currently somewhere else, hopefully acting as Veronique's guardian angel.

Tasha was silent for a minute after she closed the door to the room we'd just finished searching. She turned to face me. "So what do we do now?"

I wished I had all the answers, if only to impress my favorite actress.

I paced back and forth along the hallway. I could still hear Atticus's muted hollering from down the hall, and my stomach inexplicably twisted with guilt that we'd trapped him like that. Even if he *was* guilty, it seemed a terrible thing to do to anyone.

But a couple hours were not nearly the same as a few hundred years.

"Find Sebastien and keep an eye on him," I told her. "Watch him for any shady behavior and if you see any, make with the broken-vase action again."

Tasha gave me an alarmed look. "Aren't you going to come with me?"

"No, but I'll catch up to you as soon as I can."

She looked like she was going to argue this, but then she closed her mouth and nodded. "Sounds as good as any plan we already have."

"Which means it doesn't sound great, right?"

"Let's hope all the answers lie with Sebastien."

"And if you see Anna, be very careful."

"I can handle her."

She said this confidently, but I wasn't sure how

much of that was false bravado. If Anna was a murderer, that meant she was dangerous. No exceptions.

"Don't be so sure," I said.

"Fine." She nodded. "I'll see you soon."

"Good luck."

We moved away in opposite directions. I wished I had a specific plan of attack, but I felt at loose ends. Something wasn't fitting into the puzzle and I wished I knew what it was. If we found the amulet . . . what then?

If the head was the djinn, that meant I should focus on finding his body, just as he'd requested. And finding his head again, too, rather than his disembodied voice.

Wild-goose chase or a good use of my time?

All I knew was I had a lot to do in not a lot of time. But first I needed to quickly visit Atticus's room again.

When I got there, I whispered, "Are you still in there?"

"Let. Me. Out. Of. Here." He growled each word like an ugly troll living under a bridge. *"Now."*

"You didn't say pretty please." I scurried over to the shelf and grabbed the key, eyed it for a moment, then shoved it down the front of my red dress and into my bra.

"What are you doing?" A furious eyeball pressed up against one of the holes in the chest between two bands of silver. "Come over here with that!"

"Just sit tight for a while longer."

"When I get out of here, you will be very sorry!"

"Understood. See you later." I slipped out of the room, ignoring his hollering, and closed the door behind me.

It had made me uncomfortable to know the key

was sitting out in the open and anyone could grab it. Now it was in my possession, and Atticus wouldn't get out until I decided it was time.

He was definitely going to kill me.

It was a problem to deal with later—if there was a later.

I headed downstairs and scanned the deserted foyer. If I hadn't known there were other people currently exploring this mansion, I'd have sworn I was totally alone in the universe at this exact moment.

"Hope you're having better luck than me, Thierry," I mumbled. He wouldn't approve of my decision to search for the head's body instead of the amulet, but I had to. If I was right about him, he was the key to everything.

Seven oh five attack.

Had Thomas woken up yet? If so, I could ask him face-to-face what he'd meant by that. Maybe it meant nothing at all, was simply the ravings of someone in the process of blacking out.

I quickened my steps as I moved toward the parlor where I'd last seen Thomas. Just before I got there, I heard a piercing shriek.

I started running.

Melanie was already in the parlor. She had her hand over her mouth and her eyes were wide with shock and horror.

My gaze moved to the sofa where Thomas had been earlier.

Instead of a vampire, it now had a very unpleasant black stain on it.

Chapter 19

Thomas was dead. And if I'd just inadvertently walked in on his murderer, I was next.

I tore my gaze away from the stain and looked at Melanie with alarm.

She was shaking her head. "I didn't do it if that's what you're thinking."

A witch, a murderer, and a mind reader. Triple threat.

I raised my hands and backed away from her. "I'm sure you had your reasons."

She cut me off as I headed toward the exit. "I didn't do it! I wanted to date him, not kill him."

"Of course you didn't do it." I cleared my throat nervously. I had to get past her. I had to find Thierry and let him know that Anna wasn't the only murderer under this roof.

"I know you want to think the worst of me because of what happened with your husband, but I'm not bad. Really. I'm sorry I had anything to do with that and if I could fix it I would. How can I get you to believe me?"

"You can start by admitting the truth."

She frowned. "What do you mean?"

"That you're a witch, not a werewolf."

Confusion clouded her expression. "But I *am* a werewolf."

It would be so much easier if she'd just admit it. Still, I couldn't get a good read on her. She did seem sincerely stunned by Thomas's death.

But for all I knew, she was an accomplished actress just like Tasha. I mean, this *was* Hollywood. A cute blonde who didn't have acting aspirations around here would be a miracle in itself.

However, if I tried to think rationally—which was *difficult* at the moment—why would she bother trying to fool me?

If she was a powerful witch with murderous intentions and I was in her way, she could do the exact same thing to me without even breaking a sweat.

"What do you want?" I asked her warily.

"For starters? I want to get out of this crazy mansion. I'm not being paid nearly enough tonight to deal with all of this insanity."

That made two of us.

I watched her for any sign of deception. "You didn't kill Thomas."

"No! But somebody did. I don't think he woke up and decided to stake himself. Do you?"

"No need for sarcasm." I let out a shaky breath. "If you'd just admit that you're a witch, we might be able to move on."

She stared at me. "You're going to make me do it, aren't you?"

"Do what?"

She groaned with frustration. "Fine. Here you go."

I watched with shock as she shifted form right in front of me and her clothes landed in a pile on the floor. One moment she was a blond drink server I suspected of being a devious witch, the next she was a medium-sized shaggy doglike creature with fur a few shades darker than her hair.

She glared up at me.

I glared back at her. "Fine. You're a werewolf."

"*Ahh-roooo.*"

It sounded a lot like "I know."

She shifted back to human form and quickly got dressed again. "Satisfied?"

I shrugged. "Witches can also shape-shift. I mean, they can in *Harry Potter.*" I cringed at her sharp look. "Okay, okay. You're a werewolf and you didn't kill Thomas. Understood. So who did it?"

"No idea." She glanced toward the sofa, her expression turning sad. "I liked him. He didn't deserve that. Whatever I can do to find out who killed him, I'll do it."

I still had questions for Madame Werewolf. "How come you don't smell like a werewolf? I smelled another one tonight—he was mostly fictional, but he smelled like wet dog."

"Fictional?"

"Don't ask."

Melanie sighed. "It's a perfume that masks the scent of a werewolf from vampires. Like I said, I wanted to date Thomas if he ever broke up with his current girlfriend, and I know vampires aren't fond of the smell of wolf. Wolves have better noses than vampires, but this is one area where vamps excel: werewolf detection."

I had to admit, that explained it neatly enough. A perfume to improve werewolf/vampire romantic relations.

I'd heard of crazier things.

Then something occurred to me. "You have heightened werewolf senses."

"I do." She put her hands on her hips. "Not that they're much of a help, like, ever."

"They could be a help right now."

"How?"

"I need you to find a corpse for me."

She blinked. "Huh?"

I quickly explained about the ghost head, leaving out a lot of the gorier details. I didn't tell her I suspected him of being the djinn, only that he'd asked for my help to find his body.

Melanie looked confused by the time I'd finished my spiel. "I thought we were looking for the amulet."

"This is a secondary search. One I know is going to help us—and it could also lead to Thomas's murderer."

It wasn't a lie. I mean, you never knew what a search for a headless body might uncover.

Maybe Thomas hadn't been killed at all. He'd looked extremely ill when he'd staggered into the foyer earlier, before he passed out. Maybe he'd just . . . stopped living.

Although, with the track record we'd had so far this evening, it was much more likely that someone had strolled in here and put a stake through his heart.

But who?

"I'll help you," Melanie finally said with a determined nod. "And I think I know where we should start."

It was nice to know she was both furry and industrious when needed. "Where?"

"Earlier, I sensed something by the stairs down to the basement. But the door was locked."

"You sensed it?"

She shrugged. "Slightly psychic, remember?"

I hadn't even thought about a basement. That sounded like somewhere a murderer might stash a headless body.

I nodded. "Okay. Let's check it out."

"But the locked door—"

I sent a last look at the stained sofa as we exited the parlor. "Believe me, Melanie, a locked door is the least of our problems."

The door to the basement was indeed locked, but a firm kick from yours truly managed to break it open. I wasn't as strong as a master vampire, but I could hold my own when it came to doors.

Melanie nodded with approval. "Nice."

Then she shifted into wolf form, nudged her discarded clothes to the side of the doorway for safekeeping, and we descended the spiral staircase.

I wasn't sure what to expect. Maybe another floor of rooms like the rest of the mansion. Maybe a storage area. Maybe a dungeon.

You never knew what someone might have in their basement.

My first clue to what was down there was a strong scent that even I could pick up on.

Chlorine.

The basement of the mansion from Hell was the location of a large indoor swimming pool. It was lit by a few lights set into the ceiling, but the area was mostly in shadow.

Still, color me impressed. On the ceiling was a beautiful and colorful mosaic of a sky with clouds and a sun with twisting beams that stretched and waved out in all directions. Grecian pillars stood like sentries around the Olympic-sized pool's circumference. My high heels and Melanie's claws clicked against the ceramic-tile floor as we drew closer to the edge of the water.

I watched as she padded around the pool, sniffing at the tiles and the water. She looked up and cocked her currently furry head to the side.

"Smell anything other than chlorine?" I asked.

She raised her muzzle and let out a long howl.

The sound was alarming. "What is it?"

Then a weird sensation went through me, shivering up my arms. It wasn't the tingle of magic I'd felt before. It was something . . . creepier.

It felt like someone was watching me.

My breath caught and I stood very still and very silent as I peered into the shadows surrounding the pool.

"Somebody there?" I called out, my voice hoarse.

"Ruu-oouaoo?" Melanie replied.

"No, not you. Somebody else."

I waited, hardly breathing, but nothing happened. Nobody emerged from the shadows with a silver stake ready to kill me. Nobody appeared suddenly in a Speedo ready to dive into the pool.

We were alone.

I was just being paranoid. Considering the night I'd had so far, this wasn't a surprise.

Despite the attention to detail given to the basement pool by the millionaire owner of this mansion, I didn't like it down here.

"Anything?" I asked Melanie.

She'd come to stand next to me and she pawed at the ground. *"Roooh!"*

"Sorry, I don't speak werewolf."

She turned and quickly moved around the edge of the pool toward the deep end. *"Rooo-ruh-roooh!"*

I followed her to where she now sat next to the diving board.

She pawed at the water.

I edged closer to the water and looked down with growing dismay. There was a body lying at the bottom of the pool. It was a body I recognized, even from up here.

"Damn," I whispered.

It was Anna Dark.

A wooden stake stuck out of her chest.

I could barely believe my own eyes. "Another murder. And this time it's our main suspect for the other murders. What is going on here?"

Jacob—bitten and neck broken.

Frederic—enchanted dagger through the heart.

Thomas—unknown cause of death.

Anna—good old-fashioned wooden stake.

But what did this mean? Did she murder the others as we thought she had and karma had finally caught up to her? Or was something else going on here?

All I knew for sure was that the list of suspects was getting smaller and smaller as we drew closer to dawn.

Melanie jumped into the pool and dog-paddled out a few feet. She dove down to the bottom and surfaced with Anna, pushing the body to the edge of the pool so I could haul it out.

I grimaced as I looked down at her. For a terrible moment I half expected her to lurch back to life like something out of a horror movie.

"I don't know what's going on," I told her bleakly. "But I swear to you I will figure out who did this."

Anna had obviously left a corpse behind, which meant she was much younger than her husband. She was a fledgling with an older master vampire as a husband.

I guessed we had something in common after all.

That weird sensation came over me again, as if someone or something was watching me from the shadows.

We couldn't stay here any longer.

"Let's go," I told Melanie grimly, getting up and turning toward the staircase.

Melanie didn't budge. *"Ruuu-raaoo."*

I looked back at her over my shoulder. "Still not fluent in werewolf. What?"

She nudged Anna's hand, which I now noticed was clenched in a fist. I drew closer again, crouching down next to the body so I could take a better look.

There were strands of hair clutched in Anna's fist. I pulled them free and held them up to the meager light.

My heart started beating faster as I got to my feet. "Okay, I've seen enough. Let's get out of here. Now."

The werewolf didn't protest this time. I'd seen what she'd wanted me to see.

One might come to the conclusion that the hair in Anna's grasp belonged to her killer, ripped out during a fight for her life.

The hair in question was long and red—a shade I recognized immediately.

It belonged to Tasha Evans.

Chapter 20

I needed a moment to make sense of this.

Maybe Anna had tried to kill Tasha and Tasha had turned the wooden stake on Anna in self-defense. However, I'd just spent some time with Tasha upstairs, and she hadn't mentioned a single thing about that.

But why else would Anna be clutching Tasha's hair?

"This is crazy," I said under my breath as we went up the stairs. Melanie stayed in wolf form, sniffing each of the stairs as we ascended.

I kept thinking about Tasha and Anna. It *had* to have been self-defense. Maybe it had just happened, like, moments ago, and that was why Tasha hadn't said anything to me.

"We need to go and check on something," I said.

Melanie didn't protest, so I led her up to the second floor, passing no one on the way, to the room Jacob's body was in. We passed a grandfather clock on the way, and I grimaced at how quickly time was passing.

I moved toward Jacob's body. Melanie pawed at the floor and growled.

"Yeah, I know. Dead body number two." I crouched

down at Jacob's side and looked at him uneasily, specifically at the bite marks on his throat.

"Lip gloss," I said, with a sinking feeling in my stomach. My hunch was right. "There's a little lip gloss near the bite marks. See?"

Melanie's werewolf eyes grew bigger. "*Ruh-roh.*"

"Exactly. If it wasn't you and it wasn't me, and if there isn't a man here who favors this shade, it was Anna or Tasha. Veronique wears bright red, not this subtle pink."

But a bite wasn't a broken neck, and there was no way of knowing for sure that the biter had been the neck breaker.

"Sorry to interrupt."

I jumped to my feet at the sound of Sebastien's voice at the doorway. Melanie stood by my side growling.

"Sneaking up on us, Sebastien?" I said. "Why am I not surprised?"

Sebastien sighed and rolled his eyes. "Yes, sneaking up. That's why I announced my presence before I entered the room. Paranoid, Sarah?"

"I'd say that's a safe bet. We have an hour. Let me underline that for you. *An hour* before dawn."

"And then what? You think if we don't find the amulet we'll all implode because she"—he nodded at Melanie—"said so?"

"First of all, I think it's very possible that implosion is the very least that will happen to us. Second of all, you know Melanie's a werewolf?"

He shrugged. "Of course."

"How?"

"The wet-dog smell."

Melanie's wolf shoulders sagged and she whined.

"Sorry," Sebastien said. "It's subtle with that perfume you have over it, but it's still there."

His surprise entrance forgotten, I approached him and grabbed his arm so he'd look at me.

"Tell us where it is," I said. "I know you're mad. I know you're hurting. But you can't put everybody's lives at risk due to your personal vendetta."

Sebastien studied my face, frowning. "You really think it was me, don't you?"

"Maybe you don't feel like you have anything to live for, but you can't mess with stuff like this and expect everything's going to be okay. You have to stop dwelling on the past. Thierry didn't trap you like that. I'm sorry you think that, but it's not true."

"You believe that because you love him." Before I could protest, he shook his head. "I understand it. I had someone I loved like that in my life once. Do you know what I would have done for her, Sarah? Anything. I would have moved mountains. I would have waited a thousand years. I would have killed for her."

"Funny you'd say that since we're currently at four murders tonight."

His brows drew together as he glanced down at Jacob, then back at me. "What do you mean, four?"

I counted them off on my fingers. "Jacob, Frederic, Thomas, and Anna. All dead."

Sebastien paled. "What? Thomas and Anna?"

"Yes. And I really don't want the list to get any longer if we can help it."

"I don't understand what's happening."

The anger that had been building for a while now threatened to spill over. "Are you serious? I'll tell you what's happening. Your misguided need for vengeance against Thierry is what's happening—somebody who did nothing to you except, possibly, ignore you a little too much back in the day. Because of that you trapped a group of people in this place tonight and we're dropping like well-dressed flies. Some better dressed than others. You're responsible for those deaths."

"I didn't kill anyone."

"It doesn't even matter if you did. You're the one who sent out the invites. You're the one who planned this auction. If it wasn't for you, none of us would even be here."

"Thierry needed to pay for what he did."

"Read my lips, Sebastien. Somebody might have shoved you into that tomb, but it wasn't him." I took a step closer to him, all fired up now. "Who found you, anyway? Who knew where you were? And why did it take them so long? To me, that sounds kind of fishy."

He shook his head. "What you're suggesting is impossible."

"Nothing's impossible."

His eyes flashed with anger. "Really. So why do you constantly and incessantly protect Thierry when it's possible he could be guilty?"

Talking to Sebastien was like talking to a toddler having a very passive-aggressive temper tantrum. "I don't have the time or energy right now to drill down into that thick skull of yours. Are you so blind that you can't even see something when it's staring right at you?"

"*Roo-raooo?*" Melanie commented.

Sebastien blinked. "Question. Why is Melanie in wolf form right now?"

"She's helping me search the mansion for dead bodies. Unfortunately, I don't think she can smell a ghost. But . . . he's *not* a ghost. I know he's not . . ." I looked up at him. "Whoa. What did I just say about something staring right at you and you can't see it?"

"I forget. Something about my thick skull."

I grabbed his shoulders and shook him. "Skull. Staring at me. Earlier tonight and then poof, he disappeared."

"And—?"

"But what if he didn't really disappear?"

"Huh?"

I didn't wait for him to figure out what I was saying. My feet started moving, out of the room, down the hall, down the stairs. Melanie and Sebastien were both following me, but I didn't pay them any attention.

If I was right about this . . .

But how could I possibly be right? How could the head have been in the freezer all this time and nobody had seen it?

Only one reason that made sense and, well, it made zero sense.

Or maybe it made all the sense that it needed to!

"Where are you going?" Sebastien called after me.

"You don't have to come with me," I told him. "You can go back to alternately feeling sorry for yourself and rubbing your hands together with glee about your little blood spell. Just who cast that blood spell, anyway? Was she a reliable witch? Did she charge you a lot of money?"

His jaw tensed as he followed Melanie down the stairs. "No money at all. And yes—I trust her. I trust her exactly like you trust Thierry."

"Vampires trusting witches," I mumbled. "Yeah, that usually works out well."

I went directly toward the kitchen. It seemed like a small eternity since I'd been here. Twice tonight I'd entered this stainless-steel oasis. It was dark and empty and cavernous with the lights off and no one here. I moved toward the freezer, standing before it for a couple of moments and attempting to center myself.

"If this works, this will prove one very important thing," I said under my breath.

"What will it prove?" Sebastien asked.

I glanced over my shoulder to see that Sebastien and Melanie were still with me. He currently looked deeply mystified by everything I did.

"If you're the bad guy," I told him.

His expression tensed. "Sarah, you don't understand . . ."

"Oh, I understand perfectly. You've done some shady things tonight because you're in pain. But you're not evil—not really."

"*Rur-aooo*," Melanie added.

"See? Melanie doesn't think so, either." I inhaled slowly and tried to summon whatever courage I had left tonight. "Now, let's confirm it one way or the other, shall we?"

I pulled open the freezer and peered inside.

Sebastien gasped.

Melanie let out a throaty *woof.*

It was very nice to be right about something tonight. Even if it was . . . this.

"I'm so cold," the head said, shivering. "So very, very cold."

"Hey . . . *you*," I managed. "You've been in there the whole time, haven't you?"

"It was dark, so I had no idea where I was. I thought I was in Hell."

"No, but pretty close, I think."

I grimaced as I reached in and . . . oh, *gross.*

He was officially *not* an incorporeal ghost. No, he

was definitely a solid head. A very cold, solid head covered in ice crystals.

I pulled the head out of the freezer, holding it gingerly between my hands.

On the plus side, this gave me a whole lot more confidence that I'd been correct about him.

He looked up at me and smiled, despite his chattering teeth. "Thank you! You are a goddess!"

Despite everything, I couldn't help but smile back at him. "And you are the missing djinn. Hi, there. Nice to finally meet you."

"The missing what?" he asked, frowning, which broke some ice particles off his forehead.

Right. He had some faulty memories. Or no memory, as the case might be.

"Djinn," I repeated.

"That," Sebastien said, his voice strained, "is definitely a severed head that talks."

"It is," I agreed. "And this is my proof that you didn't kill him."

He gave me a very confused look. "How is this proof?"

I'd been working on the hows and whats and whys for a while now, ever since the head disappeared—and yet whenever I heard his voice, he always mentioned how cold and dark it was. "Whoever killed him didn't do a good job, since he's still, well, existing and thinking and talking. If the murderer knew that, they'd want to finish him off. How crazy is it to think he has some sort of survival instinct that kicks in like a chameleon hiding from its enemies. Does that make sense?"

"Magical self-preservation."

"Exactly."

"And you're saying *he's* the djinn from the amulet." He gave the befuddled-looking head a squeamish once-over. "So where's the rest of him?"

"Yes," the head said. "Where's the rest of me?"

"Good question." I scanned the kitchen.

Melanie had found Anna's body, but she hadn't happened on the djinn's yet. There had to be a logical reason for that. And I think I'd finally figured out what it was.

I slowly moved toward a large chest freezer in the far corner. Melanie kept pace with me, her claws scrabbling over the smooth tile. I nodded at Sebastien. "My hands are full. Do you mind?"

Wincing, he slowly opened the freezer door, lifting it up like the lid of a coffin.

I peered in. Sebastien peered in. Melanie jumped up and put her front paws on the edge and peered in.

Out of the dark, misty interior a frosty hand reached up and grabbed hold of the front of my dress.

Chapter 21

I swear, I nearly dropped the head in my frantic rush to pull away from the hand.

"A little help?" I managed.

Sebastien reached in and batted at the hand until I got loose.

Melanie ran around in circles, then stopped and shifted back to human form in five seconds flat.

Sebastien's eyes bugged at the unexpectedly naked woman. He pulled off his suit jacket off and tossed it in her direction.

I had mostly recovered from getting grabbed, and I peered down into the deep freezer again.

"You found me!" the head exclaimed happily. "Hooray!"

"I guess I couldn't smell a frozen body," Melanie said, cringing. "Sorry about that."

"You never checked this freezer?" I asked.

"No. All the food and drinks for the party were kept over there." She nodded toward the opposite side of the huge kitchen. "And Thomas told me not to touch anything else."

I looked down at the body that reached up helplessly toward me. "Did Thomas do this to you?"

"Are you asking me?" the head asked. "Because, in

case you forgot, I'm having some memory issues at the moment. I wish I knew."

That made two of us.

Sebastien drew closer again, his attention going between the head and the body, his expression stunned. "A djinn who wishes for things. Ironic?"

The head frowned. "Why do you keep calling me a djinn?"

I eyed the kitchen suspiciously. We couldn't stay there. Someone might be watching us. "Sebastien, can you and Melanie get the body out of there?"

"You should really put some clothes on," he suggested sternly to her.

"I will in a minute." Melanie looked down at her borrowed jacket that covered everything it had to. "Is it that difficult to look at me?"

Sebastien cleared his throat. "Trust me, difficult is not the problem I'm having."

Despite any references to past loves, it was obvious to me that he was attracted to the pretty blond werewolf. If this was another time and place, I might try to act as matchmaker. "Headless body now, naked body later. Okay?"

With no further protests, Melanie and Sebastien heaved the body out of the freezer and placed it on the floor.

It gestured frantically at its empty neck . . . well, as frantically as a mostly frozen body could.

I had a flashback to the performance of *Sleepy Hollow* that my drama group put on back in high school. "I think it's trying to tell us something. Any thoughts, head?"

"This is a guess," the head replied, "but maybe put me into place?"

Why was I asking somebody who didn't have any memories? "And you think you'll snap back on like a Lego?"

"Stranger things have happened," Melanie said with a shrug. "Tonight, anyway."

"Good point." Carefully holding the head between my hands, I placed it atop the neck.

"Wait," Sebastien said. "How do we know this isn't a bad idea? Can we trust a severed head?"

"A bad idea is better than no idea," Melanie said pointedly.

He eyed her. "Are you sure about that?"

The body's hands came up and held the head in place, swiveling it until I heard . . .

Yes, that was definitely a click.

So, pretty much *exactly* like a Lego.

A red line still circled his throat, clearly showing where the injury had been. I took a shaky step backward, waiting for him to show some sign that Sebastien was right about it being the wrong move to help him.

"That kind of stings." He winced, then his eyes widened. "Somebody cut off my head!"

"I'd say that's a safe assessment." I watched him warily, but saw nothing suspicious yet. "Can you stand up?"

"I . . . I'm not sure. I'll try."

Sebastien gave him a hand and he slowly and shakily got to his feet.

Finally, I took a good look at him—all of him. He was tall and he wore loose, emerald green pants. He was shirtless, but his arms and chest were covered in tattoos, black winding symbols and patterns. Some were faded to gray, some were dark black.

"Somebody cut off my head!" he said again,

gingerly holding that head between his hands. "Who would do that to me?"

Good question. I scanned the kitchen again nervously, but less worried he was an immediate threat to the three of us. "Can you walk around without that thing falling off?"

"I think so." Slowly, he removed his hands and tested his head, craning it to the right, then the left. He turned grateful eyes to me. "Thank you, Sarah. You did exactly as I asked of you."

A warm feeling took hold of me, chasing my misgivings away. "Sorry it took me so long."

"At least it's before dawn. Which means . . ." He frowned. "I'm not sure what it means, but it feels important."

I patted his arm, worried that he might be in one piece, but his mind was still messed up. "You're still a little broken, aren't you, Jack?"

"Is my name Jack?"

"If I'm right and you're the missing djinn, that means you're from the Jacquerra Amulet." I shrugged. "I figure it's as good a name as any."

"Jack." He nodded. "I like it. Maybe it is my name. But I have absolutely no idea who I am or how I got here."

"We're running out of time," Melanie said, her voice tense. "We have the djinn, but now we need to find the amulet."

I took Jack's hand in mine. "Maybe you can help us now."

"I can try."

Was it fair to get an amnesiac djinn to help us find his personal prison we had to put him back into?

Trapped. For centuries.

Seemed to be the theme of the evening.

"If you didn't hide it"—I looked at Sebastien—"it must have been Thomas."

He nodded. "It's possible."

So what Thomas said *had* to have been a clue.

"Seven oh five. Attack." I said these words over and over as we left the kitchen, my brain aching. Was it the ramblings of someone already half-dead? Or was it a clue that would help us from someone who knew more than he'd let on? "Attack. A tick . . ."

"Attic," Sebastien said.

I stopped walking and turned to stare at him. "What did you say?"

"Attic? Is that what you're saying?"

Seven oh five . . . attic.

Could it be? Or was it another false lead?

Only one way to know for sure.

I gave Sebastien a big smile. "That's where we're going. The attic."

First we quickly stopped at the basement entrance and retrieved Melanie's clothes so she could get dressed in more than a man's suit jacket. Once she changed, we went up to the third floor and found a trapdoor on the ceiling that Sebastien yanked down to reveal a rickety set of stairs.

"Where's everybody else?" Melanie asked.

"Not sure," I said. "This is a big mansion. They could be anywhere."

Or they could have mistakenly strolled into another magically created world and be fighting flowery-speaking vampire slayers this very moment.

Or they could be dead at the bottom of the pool just like Anna Dark.

A cold chill sped down my spine.

No way. If Thierry had found Veronique and Marcellus, I had total faith that the three of them would help one another stay alive.

The murderer was somewhere in the mansion. And she was trapped, just like we were.

If I was right about who to blame, she was very dangerous. Very deceptive. And currently feeling more desperate by the minute as we edged closer to dawn.

We took the stairs as quickly as we could and found ourselves in a large attic with a low ceiling. Sebastien found a few bare lightbulbs hanging from that ceiling and he clicked them on one by one to light the area, casting spooky shadows all around.

"So what now?" Sebastien asked.

Good question. I'd hoped a spotlight would immediately shine on exactly what we were looking for, but I knew nothing was that simple. Never had been, never would be.

I looked at Jack. "Any ideas?"

He gave me a blank stare. "About what?"

I sighed. He wasn't going to be very much help. "About where to find your amulet."

"I have an amulet?"

Like I said, nothing was simple.

"What do you remember?" Melanie asked.

Jack absently stroked the red line around his throat. "I remember being really cold. I remember being in the dark. I was trapped."

"In the freezer or in the amulet?" Sebastien asked. "You are a genie."

"I thought you said I was a djinn."

"Same thing."

Jack didn't remember anything helpful right now;

that much was crystal clear. Continuing to prod him would only result in more confusion. "What I don't understand is why Thomas was trying to help if he was the one to hide it. And why did he die? Did somebody really stake him?"

"He looked very ill," Melanie said. "Maybe somebody poisoned him."

"Maybe. And maybe he was working with somebody. And if it wasn't you, Sebastien . . ."

"It wasn't," he said, his expression tense. "He came with the mansion. He's the butler here normally and he seemed like a big help to me tonight, but I don't know what his game was."

Sebastien might be scummy when it came to putting the revenge spell on Thierry, but I'd decided that he wasn't a bad guy when it came to the amulet.

I scanned the cluttered area where it looked like old furniture from decades ago had gone to die.

"Seven oh five attic," I said again. "We have the attic part down. But what's with the numbers?"

"Could it be a labeling system?" Melanie suggested. "Maybe the seven hundred and fifth box of junk?"

I hoped not, since we didn't have the time to look through that many boxes. Still, it was worth a few minutes of looking. My magic intuition hadn't kicked in. I hadn't felt even a modest tingle yet.

I grabbed a nearby box. "Let's start searching. And Jack, if you remember anything, anything at all, please speak up."

"I remember that I'm eternally grateful for your assistance this evening, Sarah." His voice hitched. "I was lost and now I'm found."

Earlier, I'd assumed the djinn would be some sort

of fire-and-brimstone demonlike creature, furious about being imprisoned in the amulet and ready to destroy anyone who wanted to put him back in it.

But he wasn't a horrible demon. He seemed more like a lost puppy dog who didn't possess any magic at all.

Which was seriously too bad. A little magic would help right about now.

"During the auction, you said the three wishes legend is true, right?" I asked Sebastien.

"Yes. You allegedly get three specific spoken wishes before the djinn can begin to resist the compulsion to take your orders."

Three wishes. I'd already made two specific wishes, not that they'd come true. I wondered how many djinn masters had wasted their precious few wishes, not realizing that was all they were guaranteed.

I drew closer to Jack, who was standing there, his arms at his sides, his shoulders hunched. "Are you all right?"

"I can't go back," he whispered, shaking his head. "Please don't make me."

"Go back where?"

His gaze flicked to mine. "The cold, dark place."

I knew he didn't mean the freezer.

I wanted to promise that he didn't have to go back into the amulet, but since fixing it would likely require him going back into it, I couldn't say the words.

All magic that has escaped must be returned to the safety of the amulet by dawn.

Melanie and Sebastien were busily going through boxes trying to find the amulet.

"Any luck?" I asked after a few minutes.

"No, none." Melanie gave me a bleak look. "Maybe

coming up to the attic was a mistake. There are those locked rooms on the third floor. Maybe it's in there."

"Thierry said he'd check those. Keep looking. I don't feel anything yet, but something tells me there's something here that can help us."

That something might just be blind hope, but so be it.

Still, I hoped very hard that Thierry was having a great deal more luck than we currently were.

Boxes of junk. Old framed movie posters. Oil paintings. Furniture. A few broken grandfather clocks in the far corner. Piles of books.

I sneezed.

And dust. Lots of dust.

I shuffled through a stack of the old movie posters that were from the 1920s. They featured silent films all starring the same actress—Betty Levins, a cute but rather plain-looking girl-next-door type of brunette who grinned like she had a secret behind those big expressive eyes. I'd never heard of her before.

I moved a large oil painting of a sunset aside to reveal a portrait beneath.

"Well, hello again, Betty." It was a beautifully done portrait of Betty, but she wasn't smiling in this one; she looked quite serene. And she didn't look anything like a cute flapper. Maybe she was dressed as one of her many movie roles, since by the costume she wore, it looked a hundred years earlier.

Jack had taken a seat on the floor, drawing his legs up to hug them against his chest. His face had grown paler. He didn't look well at all.

I was getting really worried about him. How quickly could someone, even a supernatural, snap back from a decapitation?

"Who's that?" Melanie came up beside me and nodded at the poster.

"Betty Levins. A silent-film actress from the twenties I've never heard of before."

"She looks a little bit like Tasha, don't you think?" Melanie said, pointing at the portrait. "Around the eyes. Maybe they're related."

Then Melanie wandered off, not realizing that she'd just said something rather profound. And disturbing. And potentially puzzle clicking.

I stared at the portrait, then compared it to the movie posters. I was sure it was supposed to be the same woman.

"Sebastien," I said, indicating with a crook of my finger that I wanted him to come over.

"Yes, Sarah?" He glanced at the poster I had my hand against and his jaw tightened.

I studied him with narrowed eyes. "Tasha told me she hadn't acted before twenty years ago, not seriously, anyway. But she had. Tasha Evans is Betty Levins."

He didn't reply.

"You already knew, didn't you?" I asked. "You already knew because this is her house. And these images are her before, I don't know, some plastic surgery to make her look different. More beautiful."

"She's always been beautiful." He traced his index finger over the frame of the oil painting, staring down at Betty's face. "But I was the only one who seemed to see it."

I really hadn't wanted to be right.

It felt like someone had just punched me in the stomach.

Sebastien ran a hand over his mouth, his eyes

filling with worry. "She didn't want anyone to know this is her mansion."

I tried to stay calm, but it was a losing battle. "She killed Jacob and she killed Anna."

"How can you say something like that? Do you have any proof?"

I had to admit, a few strands of hair and some lip gloss didn't guarantee a guilty verdict. "Call it a gut instinct."

"Tasha wouldn't hurt anybody. She's wonderful and . . ." He touched the portrait again. "And . . . I love her."

He loved Tasha Evans, Oscar-winning movie star.

And I didn't think he meant only as a fan.

A few more pieces clicked into place with a sharp *snap*. "She's the one, isn't she? From your past? The plain girl Veronique said you were dating hundreds of years ago. Bettina. And now she's Tasha, a famous actress."

He gripped the edge of the painting, and stared down at it reverently. "She's more than that. She's the one who found me."

Melanie had drawn closer and we exchanged a worried look.

"Found you?" Melanie said. "In the tomb?"

Sebastien nodded. "She never believed I was dead. She said she worked closely with a witch to locate me and she rescued me just in time."

"What do you mean, just in time?" I asked, my throat tight.

"Vampires can't survive forever in hibernation like that—soon I would have wasted away to nothing. She nursed me back to health. She was there for me when no one else was. I'd do anything for her. *Anything.*" Anger flashed in his eyes as he turned to face me, his fists clenched. "That you'd accuse her of something so horrible when she's the only one who was there for me—"

"Forget I said that." I cut him off and pushed a smile onto my face. While I'd decided Sebastien wasn't a horrible villain, he was still recovering from his ordeal. He wasn't thinking straight. "Loose cannon" would be putting it mildly. "I'm being totally paranoid. Sorry about that. Tasha Evans is my favorite actress, like, ever. Of course she didn't do anything wrong, especially if you say she's the one who helped free you. She's obviously one of the good guys."

He seemed to relax a fraction. "I'm glad you're seeing reason."

And I was glad he was so easy to fool.

Then again, he believed Tasha had been a loyal and loving girlfriend throughout the centuries. Color me skeptical of anything to do with that woman at this point.

Still, I did have to admit, I had no solid proof she'd been anything tonight worse than a liar. Just because she owned this mansion but hadn't told anyone about it didn't mean diddly-squat. Maybe she owned a bunch of mansions and rented them out for parties.

I kept the sheepish smile on my face for accusing his immortal beloved of anything unsavory. "Let's keep looking for the amulet, all right?"

He nodded. "All right."

Jack had stood up from his spot on the floor and moved close enough to look at the portrait. His brows drew together. "This woman looks very familiar."

"Does she?" Sebastien's face lost its friendliness again. "How so?"

"I'm not really sure." He shook his head. "I can't remember anything."

I had a really sick and twisting feeling in my stomach that I might know exactly why Tasha looked familiar to Jack, but I didn't want to say it out loud. Not yet, anyway.

I might be able to prod Jack's memories, see if we were on the same wavelength. But I wanted to do this alone, considering how close to the edge of his emotions Sebastien currently was.

"Jack . . ." I touched his arm.

"Wait a minute. I do remember." Jack gasped. "The woman in the portrait is the one who cut off my head!"

Um. Yeah, that was pretty much what I was thinking, too.

Chapter 22

Sebastien may have been emotionally close to the edge all night, but this made him lose it completely.

He grabbed Jack by his newly mended throat, his eyes blazing with fury. "How dare you accuse her of something like that! She saved me!"

Jack sputtered, clutching Sebastien's arm. I ran over and tried to wrench Sebastien away from Jack, but it was no use. Sebastien now had both his hands on Jack's fragile neck. With a vampire's strength—especially a vampire who wasn't thinking logically—he might be able to pop Jack's head off again like a field daisy.

"She'd never hurt anyone!" Sebastien was shaking now, and sweat appeared on his brow.

"Jack, do something!" I cried.

"Do . . . something? Like?"

"You're a djinn! You must have some magic in you!"

Jack's face was turning red, but he focused on Sebastien before him and clutched Sebastien's wrists.

"Sleep," Jack managed.

The tingle of magic slid over my skin.

Sebastien's eyes rolled back in his head and he crumpled to the ground.

I grimaced. "See, Jack? I was right."

Jack stared down at the unconscious Sebastien with shock. "Maybe I am a djinn."

Melanie stood by with her arms crossed tightly over her chest, her eyes wide. "Where did that anger come from?"

I couldn't bring myself to blame Sebastien for any of this. To me, he was a pawn in someone else's game. Too bad he didn't realize it yet. "It's not his fault. He's having trouble controlling his emotions since he woke up on the wrong side of that tomb."

"I hope he'll feel better when he wakes up."

"Me too. Although I hope that's not anytime soon." I'd felt Jack's small burst of magic, but I hadn't felt anything else up here that might pinpoint where the amulet was. "Have you found something yet?"

She shook her head. "Nothing."

Jack gave me a bleak look. "I'm sorry I can't be more of a help to you."

Thierry, I thought, *wherever you are right now, I sure hope you're having more luck than we are.*

Maybe having Jack in one piece by dawn would be enough to stop anything bad from happening. He'd just proven that he did still have some magic inside him.

Melanie stood by the portrait of Betty aka Bettina aka Tasha, studying the actress's face with a frown. "You know, I never thought Tasha Evans was a very good actress. I have no idea how she managed to win those Oscars."

But movie stars didn't have to be great actresses. They needed the look, they needed the "it factor," and—as I'd discovered during my short time trying to be an actress—luck played a huge part in one's potential success.

Once she'd established herself, Tasha's roles trended

toward big-budget blockbusters. Sure, she made tons of money—enough to own a mansion this huge, for starters—but as far as acting skill . . . now that I thought about it, both of her Oscar wins had been controversial.

Melanie twisted a finger through her blond hair, her expression thoughtful. "Sebastien said a witch helped her find him. Maybe she had a witch cast a spell to make her more successful."

Of course, that had to be it. "And more beautiful."

"What?"

"A spell. Magic. If Tasha had a witch help her locate his tomb, then that witch could have helped her with other things on her to-do list."

Melanie's eyes bugged. "You might be right."

No "might be right" about it. This explained almost everything.

Unfortunately, if Tasha had magic like that at her fingertips and if she was also responsible for the murders and trying to steal Jack's magic, we were in more trouble than I'd thought.

I needed to find Thierry. He would know what to do to give us a chance to stop Tasha.

Jack had moved off to the side, near where Sebastien lay on the floor. I studied the black and gray tattoos on his back.

Maybe it was my imagination, but they seemed even more faded than they had earlier.

One darker tattoo stood out on his upper arm now, words in a language that looked a lot like the one in the book Thierry had read earlier.

I approached him tentatively. "Jack, what are these marks on you?"

He held out his arms and looked at his skin. "They hold my magic. And they also bind me to the amulet."

I stared at him. "You remember that?"

He turned to me and Melanie, his face a mask of confusion. "Maybe . . . maybe I do remember. Or I'm starting to."

That was a good sign.

Or it was a very bad sign. Maybe Jack was a nice djinn only when he didn't remember who he was. When his memories came back, would he turn into a demonic monster?

I had to remind myself that most people believed vampires to be monsters. Didn't mean we actually were. Well, not all of us.

"Do you remember anything else?" Melanie asked gently.

He shook his head, then touched his throat along the red line. "No, nothing else. Sorry."

"Come on." I offered him my hand. "Let's get out of here."

He eyed my hand warily. "You're going to force me back into the amulet, aren't you?"

He remembered enough to know what was to come.

I decided to be honest with him. He deserved that much. "That was the original plan, but there has to be another solution. Nobody should be forced to do anything they don't want to do because of a decision made more than a millennium ago."

"I don't want to go back."

"Then you won't." I gave him a smile. "And since we can't find the amulet anywhere, that makes everything much simpler. But please try to remember as much as you can by dawn so we won't implode. Okay?"

"Okay." He finally took hold of my hand and I began leading him out of the attic like he was a little boy lost at the zoo.

And, quite frankly, that was what he was starting to feel like. For all of my theories about him, and what I was certain he was—the djinn of the Jacquerra Amulet—he seemed harmless to me. Innocent. Lost.

Trapped.

"What's the plan?" Melanie asked.

"I want to find Thierry, but first I have to go get Atticus."

"Atticus? Where is he?"

"He's somewhere . . . safe."

My gut had been confused when it came to the boss of the vampire council, but now I'd almost decided that he was more of an asset out of the chest than he was in it.

Tasha had locked him up, but I doubted it was to protect me.

She needed him out of her way.

Which meant, I needed him *in* her way.

As we moved toward the stairs, I brushed against several broken grandfather clocks. "Tasha likes things that tell time, doesn't she?"

"Maybe it reminds her of how old she really is," Melanie said.

Broken clocks stuffed in the attic. They had to be worth money, but were currently useless until she had them fixed. Each one of them frozen at the exact time it had been when their inner workings died.

One froze at ten after eleven. Another at quarter past six. Another at five minutes past seven.

I stopped moving and I stared at that clock.

Behind us, Sebastien groaned. He was starting to wake up.

"Sarah?" Melanie whispered. "Are we going or what?"

Five minutes past seven.

My heart began to pound harder. "Seven oh five. This clock reads seven oh five. And it's in the attic."

"So?" Jack asked, letting go of my hand.

I closed my eyes and tried to feel something. *Sense* something.

And there it was. A tingle—a magical tingle.

My eyes shot open. "This is it."

I began touching the clock all over, searching for a compartment, a hole, anything.

Near the bottom, there was a wooden button. I pressed it and a hidden drawer slid open.

"Thomas," I whispered, grabbing hold of the amulet's chain, "if you'd been a little more specific, you could have saved us all a lot of time."

Another low, groggy groan came from Sebastien's direction and I tensed.

"Let's get out of here." I reached out to take Jack's hand again.

He staggered back from me. "Don't come any closer with that thing."

His eyes had turned bright emerald green, just like the amulet.

"I'm not going to hurt you," I assured him.

He nearly fell in his hurry to get away from me— away from the amulet.

"I'm claustrophobic. Do you know what it's like to be trapped in something that small when you're claustrophobic?" He reached the stairs first, and he practically fell down them because he was moving so fast. "It's not fun!"

What was with his eyes? It must show the connection between him and the amulet—that he was still bound to it whether he liked that or not.

"Jack, don't run away. It's okay, really."

"It's not okay! I could hear things, sense things, feel things, but I wasn't a part of them. It is Hell, Sarah. And my previous masters—the wishes they wanted. Not pleasant, let me tell you! They were all so greedy, hedonistic, horrible. And I had to do what they asked. Please—I beg you—don't force me back inside that thing."

The farther he moved away from me the more the green faded from his eyes. The magic that had begun coursing up and down my arms also dissipated.

Maybe that had been my window of opportunity to fix this, to return the magic—namely Jack himself—back to the amulet.

Even as I watched him, his tattoos faded even more until a few of them disappeared completely.

Jack looked down at his arms. "The magic is leaving me. Good. I don't want it anymore."

He disappeared down the ladder.

I exchanged a worried look with Melanie. "We can't let him get away," I said.

"I know."

We left the attic as quickly as we could and raced down the hallway after Jack, turning corners that twisted through the mazelike third floor.

But Jack was nowhere to be seen.

"What now?" I asked, clutching the amulet tightly in my hand.

Melanie didn't answer me. I turned to see if she'd caught up to me, but she wasn't there.

"Melanie?" I called, running back along the route I'd taken.

I'd lost Jack and I'd lost Melanie.

Damn. I had no time for another impromptu game

of hide-and-seek with a memory-challenged djinn and a werewolf that smelled like vanilla.

I stared down at the amulet in my palm. "At least I found you."

The amulet, thankfully, didn't reply.

Without wasting any more time, I headed down to the second floor to the room Atticus was in. This might go badly, but I had to try.

He might be a jerk and a womanizer, but . . . added up, it didn't necessarily equal villain.

At this point, I needed all the help I could get.

As I navigated the twists and turns of the second floor trying to retrace my steps, a shadow loomed up ahead. I flattened myself against the wall and glanced around the corner to see that the shadow belonged to Tasha.

She entered Atticus's room.

There was a sharp wooden stake in her hand.

There was no time to second-guess myself. I blew out a breath and approached the door.

"Hey, Tasha," I said as calmly as I could.

She spun around, now holding the stake behind her back and out of view. I'd slipped the amulet into my pocket, thanking the designer's brilliance of adding pockets to this dress.

"Sarah." She smiled at me. "I'm glad you're here."

"Have you found anything?"

"Not yet. You?"

"This place is like a labyrinth. I have no idea where to search next and it's nearly dawn."

She shrugged. "I honestly don't think anything bad's going to happen at dawn."

"No? I'm glad you said that. I've been thinking the same thing. I mean, ominous collective voice of a dead coven emanating from a werewolf cocktail waitress. Not too scary, you know?"

"Agreed."

We both went silent as I grappled for something else to say.

"By the way," Atticus growled from inside the chest, "this is a gentle reminder that as soon as I get out of here I'm going to destroy you."

Even though he sounded furious, I was happy to hear his voice. "He's still conscious. I thought he might slip into a coma."

"That takes a while," Tasha said.

Yes, I was quite sure she knew firsthand how long something like that might take.

"I'm not slipping into a coma, you bitches! Now let me out of here."

"That's not going to happen, Atticus," Tasha said. "And there's no reason to be rude to us. But you could never help that, could you? You've always been rude, from the very beginning. It's impossible to teach an old dog like you new tricks."

Atticus slammed his fist against the lid of the chest. "You've always had it in for me, haven't you, Tasha? I told you that you could work for me. I thought that would finally appease you. What more do you want from me?"

"I want a great deal more than a glorified office assistant position. I want to rule over the council."

"Rule over it?" I echoed. This was unexpected. "You're saying you want Atticus's job."

"Of course I do. Why aim low when you can aim high—the highest. Ever heard of the law of attraction, Sarah? If you believe you can, you will."

I fought to keep any accusatory expression off

my face. "I believed I'd win the lottery. It never happened."

"Bottom line—Atticus is in my way," she said bluntly, finally revealing her wooden stake.

My heart jumped into my throat. "I agree he's a problem, but I don't think this is the best way to deal with him."

She ran her thumb over the sharp tip of the stake. "Nobody has to know about this, Sarah. He won't leave a body behind. A mop and a bucket will get rid of any evidence."

"Is this how you normally handle problems?"

Her gaze flicked to mine. "Sure. Nice and easy. He's a brute, he's abusive, and he has way too much power, which he refuses to share."

"It was you, wasn't it?" Atticus growled. "The other elders . . . the path to my position with the Ring, anyone who would take it next if something happened to me. You're the one who killed them."

Tasha raised an eyebrow. "Do you really think I'm capable of something so bold, Atticus?"

I forced a smile, although it felt twitchy after that revelation. "Men. They can't understand how motivated a woman can be if she wants something badly enough."

"They really can't. But that makes it so much easier to manipulate them." She tapped the chest with the tip of the stake and stared down at Atticus through the small openings in the lid. "You're wrong about one thing, Atticus. I'm not ready to take over—not yet. I have someone else perfect in mind to temporarily head the council. Someone I can control. Someone who will take orders without giving me any problems. But first I need to get rid of you."

She glanced over toward the shelf where she'd left the key. "Where is it?"

I carefully kept my face blank. "What?"

"The key."

"It was over there. Why? Is it gone?"

Tasha gave me a smile that didn't reach her cold eyes. "I thought we might be friends, you and I."

"Tasha, that would have been really amazing. I wasn't lying when I said I thought you were a fantastic actress. Fantastic, yes. But Oscar-winning?" I gave her a mock grimace. "Debatable."

Her smile soured at the edges. "Where's the key, Sarah?"

"I can't let you stake Atticus."

"The world would be a better place without him in it. Don't you understand that?"

"Let me think about that." I paused. "No, I don't understand. But I do understand that you think you have the right to decide who gets to live or die, based on your own agenda. And I wholeheartedly disagree."

Her lips were now a thin line. "That's too bad."

"Did you kill Jacob?" I already knew she did, but I wanted confirmation. "Your shade of lip gloss was on his throat. And I know your fangs were fully filed down earlier this evening but now they're back."

A vampire could file her fangs down all she wanted, but as soon as she gave in to the need to bite someone, to drink blood from the original source, they immediately re-formed in all their pointy glory.

Those fangs were proof that she'd fed tonight.

She slid her tongue over the tips of her small but sharp fangs. "I thought if Jacob was willing to publish a piece of trash like Veronique's memoir, he'd be willing to publish something well written. *My* memoir. But he refused. That made me very angry."

My brows went up. "Where do you find the time, Tasha? An actress, a murderer, an aspiring council leader . . . and a writer, too."

She narrowed her eyes. "I can do it all."

"You're a famous actress—why wouldn't other publishers be scrambling to sign you on?"

"They're not willing to pay me nearly as much as I deserve for it. I asked Jacob to consider it, since I know he has the money. But he refused because it would compete with Veronique's book."

"So you killed him."

She shrugged her bare shoulder adorned with the black rose tattoo. "I was going to just have a quick sip, but then he made me mad. Humans. More trouble than they're worth."

My stomach churned. I noticed how silent Atticus had gone, but I knew he was listening very carefully to this increasingly disturbing conversation. "What about Frederic? Anna didn't kill him, did she? It was you."

Her smile returned, more amused this time. "You found him, did you? All tucked away in a little piece of contained magic. I'm almost sorry to spoil your naive, starry-eyed view of me. You must think I'm horrible."

Yes, I'd say I was officially off the Tasha Evans fangirl list. "Not sure that's the word I'd pick. But the thesaurus is another must-read bestseller, isn't it?"

"One day you'll understand, little fledgling. We're immortal. We don't have to treat this world as humans do with their you-only-live-once attitudes. We can have many lives, many loves, many adventures. And we make our own rules. You said you wanted to be an actress. Well, guess what? You can be. You can be anything if you're willing to do what it takes to achieve it. And if others get in our way, may the strong survive. And I'm very strong."

"So that's a yes to Frederic?"

She shrugged. "Old lover. He annoyed me tonight, that's all."

That was way too simple an explanation. I didn't buy it. "That's it? He annoyed you and you killed him?"

"His wife wasn't too happy about it. She tracked me down, confronted me, wanted me to pay. But she was also a fledgling, sired only twenty years ago. No chance against someone like me."

"Consider me warned."

She stepped closer to me and I fought to stand my ground. "Now you're going to give me the key and help me get rid of Atticus."

After all this, she actually thought I might help her? "Sorry, can't do that. Who's the naive one now?"

Without waiting another moment, I turned and bolted from the room so I could regroup elsewhere and figure out how to deal with this actress from Hell.

I slammed face-first into Thierry's chest.

I looked up at him with deep relief. "Thank God you're here. It's Tasha—she's the murderer. Atticus is locked in the prison, but he's innocent. She's responsible for killing the council elders. And I'm sure she's also the one who cut off the djinn's head trying to steal his magic. You can help me stop her!"

I sent a wary glance over my shoulder at Tasha, who now leaned against Atticus's chest without a flicker of worry in her eyes.

"That might be a problem," Thierry said.

I had a bad feeling in the pit of my stomach. "Why is that a problem?"

"The blood spell from earlier."

"What about it?"

"Tasha cast it herself."

"Wait. What?" I stared at him with confusion. "But she's a vampire. Vampires can't do magic, can they?"

"I'm special," Tasha said proudly. "And you don't want to know what I've had to do to get that way. Bad things, Sarah. Very bad things."

"Thierry"—I stared up at his face—"you broke that spell earlier. You have control over your thirst."

His face was tense and he wouldn't meet my eyes.

"Oh, little fledgling." Tasha strolled closer to us, her hair a shiny red curtain over her shoulder. "Did you really think it was that easy? The insatiable thirst was only a small part of the spell I cast on that blood. It was a test to prove it had properly taken hold of him. The rest was a spell of obedience. Thierry's mine now. He'll do whatever I tell him to." The smile on her face stretched from ear to ear. "Grab her, Thierry."

Heart racing, I tried to slip past him, but he got hold of me and hoisted me over his shoulder.

We'd been so cocky to believe it had been that easy to break the spell.

Nothing important was *ever* that easy.

Chapter 23

I felt the tingle of the amulet's magic in my pocket as Thierry began moving down the hall. Did he feel it, too? And if he did, would he say something to Tasha?

I held my breath as I waited for him to speak, but he stayed silent. Maybe under this spell he couldn't sense its magic.

"Damn it, Thierry! You have to fight this."

He squeezed me tighter against his shoulder. "I would advise you to be quiet now. You don't want this to get any worse."

"Worse than this?"

"Things can always be worse."

Something horrible occurred to me. "What did she make you do to Veronique and Marcellus?"

"They won't be a problem."

Tasha trailed after us and I lifted my head enough to glare at her.

"Sorry, Sarah." There was already smug victory in her eyes, contradicting the apology. "I was willing to cut you a little slack since you're a fan, but you're a do-gooder with a bleeding heart. Atticus doesn't deserve your mercy. I'll get to him later when this is over. There can't be any loose ends after tonight."

"At dawn, if we don't find that amulet and return

the djinn to it . . ." I hesitated, expecting Thierry to say something about the amulet currently pressed against his chest. "This mansion is going to be destroyed and we're all going to die. Remember?"

Her self-satisfied smile held. "I don't think so, little fledgling. I have other plans when dawn breaks. Big ones."

After Thierry descended the stairs and entered the parlor, he threw me unceremoniously down on the sofa—luckily the one opposite the one with the remains of Thomas on it. I sprang to my feet immediately.

"You would be wise to stay down," Thierry growled.

His expression was unreadable, impassive, but his eyes were very serious. He didn't want me to argue with him.

But that had never stopped me before.

"Just that easy, huh?" I tried in vain to come up with a fantastic plan to solve this mounting problem, but any such plans were currently hiding from me. "Vampire-witch here whispers a few magic words over a shot glass of blood and, boom, you're suddenly her loyal minion?"

"Seems that way."

"That's pretty pathetic."

"Your opinion is duly noted."

I scanned the room and spotted a few familiar faces. Veronique, Marcellus, and Melanie were all in here. Conscious, but bound and gagged.

And, thankfully, not dead.

"You did this to them," I said to Thierry with accusation.

He glanced with disinterest at the three of them. "It's what Tasha wanted."

I took a very small measure of optimism from the

fact he hadn't whipped out the silver-infused ropes and handkerchief to do the same to me yet. "What about Marcellus and your theory about him?"

Thierry stood coolly before me, his arms at his sides. He didn't bother to meet my eyes as he answered. "My theory was incorrect. Tasha told me what really happened to the djinn."

Tasha adjusted Veronique's gag so it fit more snugly over her mouth. She seemed to be taking great pleasure in this as she patted Veronique's head. "Don't you have anything to say, Veronique? That's a first."

If looks could kill, Veronique would already have the actress six feet under.

"What did you do to the djinn?" I asked Tasha.

She gave me an amused glance. "Why would I tell you?"

"Because I think you want to. Did you trap him somewhere?"

Of course I already knew what she'd done and that Jack wasn't trapped, but I wanted her to tell me. I wanted her to keep talking because I was very afraid of what would happen after she stopped wanting to explain her master plan.

And what would happen at dawn.

So very close now.

Wherever Jack was now hiding, I sincerely hoped he'd stay there.

"The djinn is gone." Tasha traced the tip of her wooden stake over Veronique's bare arm. "That's all you need to know about that."

"The amulet's gone, too."

"The amulet is far less important than you think it is. Frankly, I don't care if it's ever found."

Again, I waited for Thierry to reveal what was

safely nestled in my pocket. But he remained silent, standing between me and Tasha, his arms now crossed over his chest, looking like an obedient soldier in an expensive black suit.

He'd fought the thirst. Could he fight this obedience spell as well, or was that too much to hope for?

Tasha needed help. She couldn't do any of this on her own. And I didn't think Thierry was her first minion.

"Thomas was the one helping you before, wasn't he?" I asked.

She sighed. "He was very helpful . . . at least, until the end when I know he tried to tell you something. The spell holding him was wearing off. It was my mistake for not renewing it earlier this evening. Live and learn."

Of course. No wonder Thomas had tried to reveal to me—albeit cryptically—where he'd hidden the amulet. He was following Tasha's orders under duress. "The blood spell, the same one you put on Thierry . . . that's what made Thomas your willing servant."

She pulled her stake away from Veronique and rose to her feet. "I prefer the term 'slave boy,' but all right. 'Servant' is good, too."

The realization that someone I'd looked up to and admired since I was a kid could be so horribly evil and self-serving made me sick with disappointment. I'd tried to come up with so many excuses all evening as to why she couldn't be the one responsible for any of the crimes. Turned out she was responsible for *all* of them.

"I don't understand why you're doing any of this." I shook my head. "You have the perfect life. You have the perfect career. You have everything anyone could ever wish for."

A sneer curled her upper lip in a very unattractive manner. "Perfect life, perfect career. This can be such an illusion to someone not living that life, working that career. I achieved all I could as an actress. I crave more, but it will have to be out of the public eye for a while. God forbid that humans find out our little secret—the world might end. Or would it? Maybe it's time for us to let them know vampires really exist. Maybe that's exactly what I'll do when I become the head elder of the Ring."

That vampires would go public with our existence was the worst idea I'd ever heard. "It would be chaos."

"Or maybe not. Maybe they'd bow to us—that is, if they knew what was good for them. Maybe we need to accept that humans are a plentiful food source for vampires, but not anyone who has power over us."

Was she crazy or just completely delusional? "You definitely have big plans."

"The biggest. But first I want to finish a couple more movies. I'm not quite ready to leave the lime-light." She put a hand on Thierry's arm. "That's why Thierry will take Atticus's seat on the council and keep it warm for me. Yes, I think your husband will be a great help to me in the years to come, in so, so many ways."

Something very dark and unpleasant bubbled in my chest at the greedy way she was eyeing Thierry. I wanted to scratch those eyeballs out. "Is this how you get your boyfriends, Tasha? You have to put a spell on them so they can't say no? Kind of pathetic if you ask me."

She didn't flinch. "I guess it's a good thing nobody asked you."

"I think Sebastien might have a little trouble with your plan to use Thierry as your walking, talking slave boy. He's in love with you."

Tasha scanned me from head to toe as if assessing the competition and finding it unworthy. "He's been very helpful to me."

"If that's so, why did you forget about him for three hundred years after you trapped him in that tomb?"

Her brows went up. "You think I did that?"

"I think I need an itemized list to keep up with everything you're responsible for, Tasha. I'm actually impressed by your thoroughness. When you do something, you do it right."

"I'll take that as a compliment."

"You killed Jacob since he wouldn't give you big bucks for your book. You killed Anna and Frederic because they were in your way. Thomas . . . I still don't understand how he died."

"A side effect of that spell, I'm afraid. He'd been under it for so long he went into harsh detox in minutes."

Panic clutched my heart to learn that the same spell Thierry was under had a deadly side effect.

I shot him a look. "How do you feel?"

A frown creased his brow. "I feel fine."

"What about your thirst?"

"Currently muted."

I wanted him to snap out of this, to take control of the situation so everything would turn out all right, but he wasn't making any sudden moves. "I guess there are worse fates than being the minion to a gorgeous actress. And, hey, looks like you're going to get a promotion at work. Congrats."

"I have to respect your ability to make light of even the darkest situation. You're not going to beg me to try to fight against this spell, as you did earlier?"

"I'm hoping it's implied. I'd hate to sound like a broken record."

His jaw tightened. "It won't make a difference, anyway. Besides, you never believed in my ability to resist my thirst. You always thought the worst of me."

The accusation was delivered in a monotone, but it managed to ignite my anger like nothing else had this evening. I wanted to yell at him, to remind him that I was the one who'd believed in him when he didn't believe in himself.

But the words froze on my tongue before any escaped.

And I just stared at him.

"How sad." Tasha shook her head as she walked in a slow circle around the two of us. "Married only a short time, but already that marriage has reached its end. It's impossible for a fledgling to understand the needs of a master vampire, one with so much history, so much baggage. Believe me, Thierry, you'll be much better off with me."

Over all the months we'd known each other, I'd never lost my faith in him. Moments of doubt, sure. Moments of fear, okay. But overall? I knew he was a good man who didn't want to give in to his darkness. And I knew in my heart that he would never hurt me on purpose.

I'm not sure I could have made my faith in him any clearer in the time we'd shared.

Thierry's expression didn't change. His gaze remained cold and stoic.

But he'd just lied right in front of Tasha.

He *knew* I believed in him.

Maybe it was possible to teach an old vampire new tricks after all.

I cleared my throat and tried to compose myself. "You're right. I didn't believe in you, Thierry. Maybe I should have, but what was I supposed to think? Your thirst always gets the better of you and tonight's no exception. My neck feels like you used it as a chew toy earlier. And one pathetic little spell can make you snap to attention like a tin soldier. I almost feel sorry for you."

His shoulders stiffened, but he still wouldn't meet my gaze directly. "Your opinion is always appreciated, Sarah."

I turned back to Tasha. "So what exactly are you waiting for?"

She raised an eyebrow. "You think I'm waiting for something?"

"Actually, yes. You killed half the people who were stuck here tonight. You tied up three others. You've got Thierry at your beck and call." I exchanged a glance with Veronique, who looked very worried. For someone who was rarely concerned about anything, that wasn't a good sign. Marcellus just stared at Tasha with silent fury. "What about Sebastien? Is he still around or did you get rid of him, too?"

Tasha shook her head. "I didn't kill Sebastien. In fact, I have him to thank for all of this."

My stomach lurched to think I'd been duped by someone I very nearly trusted. "He's been in on this with you from the very beginning, hasn't he?"

She laughed. "Hardly. With all the time he was unconscious in his little tomb, Sebastien is barely more than a fledgling himself, ignorant to the ways of the real world. We were the same age in the beginning, supporting each other, helping each other. But then he misbehaved and had to be punished. All these years later, he's still that little fledgling who needed punishment, and I'm a master vampire who knows what to do and how to get what she wants."

I was trying very hard to understand their relationship. Sebastien loved her, but it didn't seem as if that love was returned. "What do you mean, he misbehaved?"

Tasha's hand went to her long hair as she absently smoothed it down over her shoulder. "I wasn't exactly the most beautiful girl in my village, but Sebastien and I connected. At the time, I thought he was my soul mate." Her eyes narrowed. "Then *she* came along."

"She?"

Tasha marched over to Veronique and roughly pulled her gag loose. "This woman seduced him."

"You," Veronique snarled, and I'd never heard her sound more dangerous. Those had to be silver-infused ropes or she would have broken free long before now. "I *knew* you looked familiar, but I hadn't thought of that mousy little creature in hundreds of years. *Bettina*."

Tasha flinched at the name. "That was my name once, but I've upgraded. However, my hate for you, Veronique, has never faded. You ruined my life."

"I ruined your life?" Despite her bound state, Veronique managed to look down her nose at Tasha. "You barely registered for me. I couldn't have cared less about you if I tried."

A muscle in Tasha's cheek twitched. "You seduced Sebastien knowing it would ruin his love for me. I couldn't compete with your beauty. Not then, anyway."

Veronique looked disgusted at the accusation. "Are you mad? Sebastien was like a son to me. I didn't seduce him."

"You're a liar. You've always been a liar, but I know the truth." Tasha shoved the gag back into Veronique's mouth to stop her from saying anything else.

I think I was starting to understand what had happened back then—fueled by love and jealousy, two very explosive elements. "You hated Veronique, but you had no chance against her as a fledgling. So instead you punished Sebastien by trapping him in the tomb and leaving him there to rot."

She gave me a withering glare. "I couldn't bear to look at him, knowing that he'd betrayed me."

"Why blame it on Thierry?" I asked, sickened by the thought of doing this to anyone.

"I didn't. Sebastien assumed it was him and I chose to let him believe the worst of his sire."

So why had she released him now, after all these years?

I think I knew.

"You freed him because you found out he had an amulet stashed somewhere. Right? If he hadn't had the amulet, you would have let him stay in that tomb forever."

Thierry hadn't budged an inch. His gaze was fixed on the wall behind my shoulder, and I couldn't even tell if he was paying attention. Melanie, Veronique, and Marcellus moved as little as possible, but they could hear every word spoken between us.

Her secrets were being revealed to a captive audience. Emphasis on the *captive* part.

Tasha's condescending smile returned. "Some time ago, I came across letters that he'd left for me detailing that he possessed the amulet—the same amulet Thierry had wanted. When I'd first read those letters I had no idea what it meant, nor did I care. But in recent years, my interest in the subject has greatly increased."

I remembered a conversation we'd had earlier tonight. "That movie you made—the first one. The lousy one. The screenwriter knew all about djinn."

She laughed and shook her head. "Oh, Sarah, perhaps you're more clever than I thought you were. That writer was a great asset to me, especially since he was obsessed with finding one of the legendary amulets. Yes, there are more than one. When we acquired one, together we killed the djinn with a special blade I purchased at an auction much like the one held earlier tonight, burned his body, and stole his magic. Or rather, I did. By then the writer was no longer a problem for me."

"Gee, let me guess. You killed him, too."

She shrugged. "Humans are greedy creatures, but very fragile. Jacob, for example, didn't take very much effort at all. Just a little twist after I quenched my thirst."

At this admission, Veronique attempted to stand, but didn't get far. Smoke rose from her wrists as she fought against her bindings.

"You burned the djinn's body," I said.

"Of course. Cutting off the head wouldn't be nearly enough to completely destroy a djinn."

Aha! So now I knew why Jack was still alive and kicking. They'd missed a step.

"Thomas helped you," I said. "You cut off the djinn's head tonight before everyone arrived and you let him take care of burning the body."

A blood spell had made him her yes-man. But tonight he'd started to say no.

Her gaze turned predatory. I knew there was no way she'd ever let me leave this room knowing what I did now about her and her nasty deeds. "Does it make you feel better to know all of this? Accomplished somehow?"

"Mostly it makes me sad that my favorite actress is a power-hungry, wannabe witch."

"Most famous actresses are."

I hadn't felt bad for Thomas earlier when I thought he was helping Tasha of his own free will. Turned out, he had very little free will to spare. And what he did have, he'd used to try to thwart her.

I scanned the room again, trying to look as much at ease as possible given the situation. "I have a question. Why are we trapped here? If you managed to successfully steal the djinn's magic, why are you still here with the rest of us?"

Tasha regarded me in silence for an uncomfortable moment, and I wasn't sure if she was going to answer. Then again, I already knew Tasha Evans loved the sound of her own voice. "There have been a few complications, but I'm patient enough to wait until dawn. We're so close now. Can you feel the sun about to rise as I can?"

She closed her eyes and held her arms out to either side. As I watched her warily, her famous tattoos . . . multiplied.

Literally. The ones she already had expanded, tracing along her flesh as if someone had taken a Sharpie marker to her. It was writing in a foreign language, symbols twisting and flowing over her skin all the way down to her wrists and over her throat.

Now that I was paying attention, I realized that her tattoos looked exactly like Jack's.

"The tattoos are the magic," I whispered.

This earned me an unpleasant look. "Don't be too clever, now, little fledgling. It's not healthy."

But I couldn't stop just when more pieces were clicking into place for me. "You got the first ones when you killed the original djinn and stole his magic. It's djinn magic you have, not witch magic. But it's fading because you're not a djinn. Now after all these years you need to recharge."

"Yes, every twenty years like clockwork." She flicked a glance toward Thierry. "I need you to do something very important for me, Thierry. Will you do whatever I ask of you?"

"Of course," he said without hesitation, his familiar voice so cold it gave me chills.

She held out her wooden stake, the one she'd been about to use on Atticus. "Kill your wife."

My gaze shot to Thierry as he turned to take the stake.

"As you wish, Tasha," he said.

Chapter 24

I spun to face Thierry as he stepped toward me, stake in hand.

"What are you doing, Thierry?" I asked, my voice shaking. "You're not going to resist at all?"

His jaw was so tight it looked painful.

I tried to get Thierry to look in my eyes, but he refused. Instead, he studied the sharp wooden stake in his hand.

"Kill her, Thierry," Tasha commanded. "*Now.*"

Thierry's eyes finally snapped to mine.

I didn't beg. I didn't try to convince him that he could fight this. He'd already given me a clue that he *was* fighting—that he believed there might be a chance, even if this was a much stronger spell than we'd originally assumed.

Life had been so much easier when we thought the werewolf cocktail waitress might be the witch in residence.

Although the rest of him looked completely cold-blooded, a trickle of perspiration ran down Thierry's left temple.

"Do what you have to do, Thierry," I told him, standing my ground. "You know how I feel. That hasn't changed. It will never change."

"I didn't believe in myself," he said through clenched teeth. "It sounds ridiculous, given who I am. How long I've lived. But you changed everything for me."

Thierry lunged at me and I staggered back. He grabbed my hand and placed the stake in it. "Defend yourself against me however you must."

Maybe he meant for me to stake him, but, please. That wasn't going to happen. Clutching the stake, I moved toward Tasha instead. Having a weapon made me feel a whole lot better about my odds against the murderous actress.

But then, out of nowhere, Sebastien was suddenly there and he stepped in front of me, yanking the stake out of my grip. He shoved me backward so forcefully that I stumbled and fell hard to the floor.

"Sebastien," Tasha purred, "you didn't have to worry. She wasn't close enough to hurt me."

"I know," he said. "But I am."

He turned and thrust the stake into her heart.

She shrieked and stumbled back, a mirror image of what I'd just done. She grasped the stake and pulled it out of her chest, letting it clatter to the floor.

Her wide-eyed gaze snapped to his. "Why would you do that?"

Sebastien's hands were clenched at his sides. "I heard what you said. It was you all this time, all because of your stupid jealousies. I'd told you that Veronique meant nothing to me, but you refused to believe me. And you'd want to hurt me like that when I trusted you more than anyone else?"

I flicked a look at Thierry. His brow was shiny with perspiration. He was a master vampire, much stronger than Thomas had been. He could fight this spell. I knew he could.

He already had, mostly. There was only a little left, trapping him in its magical grasp.

Tasha braced herself against the wall and glared at Sebastien, but the outrage and surprise swiftly faded from her eyes . . . just as the stake wound healed on her chest.

"What the hell?" Sebastien managed. "You should be dead!"

She grabbed his shirt and launched him backward. He hit the wall so hard he left a deep dent in it before he fell to the floor. "You think it'll be that easy to kill me? I'm immortal, darling. For real. Forever."

"Frederic's dagger," I whispered. "That's why you killed him. The cut on his arm. You used it to drink his blood. The dagger can give extended life to humans—"

"—and true immortality to vampires," she finished. "I wasn't sure if it really worked, but I guess I've proven it now, haven't I? I'm indestructible. I will live forever."

I stared at her in shock. This beautiful actress I'd admired for longer than I could remember was the scariest thing I'd ever seen in my life.

"There are now only minutes until dawn," she said, glancing at the grandfather clock in the corner of the parlor near Veronique, Marcellus, and Melanie. "And then this will finally be over."

"You'll have all the magic of the Jacquerra Amulet inside you," Thierry said.

"The sun is a powerful entity. Its arrival, its absence, makes all the difference when it comes to magic like this." She looked down at her arms and the slightest edge of worry crossed her gaze. "This is a bit different than last time, though. The markings should all be solid by now."

"That's strange," I said. "You didn't miss a step anywhere along the line, did you?"

She looked at me, her eyes narrowing. "Of course I didn't."

"Don't be so sure. You know what they say—if you want something done right, you have to do it yourself."

As if on cue, Jack walked into the room.

I looked at him with alarm. "What are you doing here?"

Tasha began to laugh. "Oh, this is quite a twist, but it doesn't matter. Look at him. He's barely holding himself together. Burning his body won't be necessary. I already feel myself powering up."

Sebastien had risen to his feet and began to approach her. With a flick of her wrist, she sent him sailing backward again.

"Stay down," she told him. "Or you'll be begging to go back into your tomb."

"You're the one." Any humor or confusion had left Jack's face. "You tried to kill me."

"Thought I did a pretty good job, actually. One slice. Off with your head. It reminded me of a miniseries I did, playing a French revolutionary."

"*The Affairs of Madame Baudin*," I said, nodding. "I still think you're evil incarnate, but I've seen that miniseries, like, eight times. *So* good."

"Thank you." She then swept her gaze over Jack's torso. "Your marks have faded to nearly nothing. You have no magic left within you. Do you think you have any chance to defeat me?"

"That I still exist is enough to defeat a thief and a murderer like you." He straightened his back, standing tall, his chin raised. "Do it, Sarah. Send me back."

Did he realize what he was asking for? "Jack, no . . ."

"My magic will leave her and fully return to me once I go back to my prison. It's the only way we can fix this."

Wild guess here—he finally had his memories back, if not all his magic. He knew what he was asking for. It was the exact opposite of what he'd wanted.

He was willing to sacrifice himself to stop Tasha. To save all of us.

Tasha gasped with surprise as I pulled the amulet out of the handy pocket of my dress.

"Oh, did I forget to mention I found it earlier?" I swung it from its chain. "Sorry about that."

"Where was it?" she demanded.

"Let's just say . . ." I paused for emphasis. "The butler hid it."

"Thierry, take it away from her," Tasha snarled. "Now."

Thierry took a step toward me, but not another one. His entire frame shook with the effort it took to resist her spell.

"Thierry!" she shouted. "Do as I say!"

"To quote a favorite phrase of my beautiful wife, who believed in me when no one else would," he growled, "bite me."

"Fine. You're dead, too. You will all die"—she looked at the clock—"in twenty seconds . . ."

"Sarah." Jack's tone held both pain and courage. "Do it now. There's no time to waste."

He drew closer to me and his eyes turned green to match the amulet.

Proximity seemed to make all the difference. The closer he was to it, the more it controlled him.

Everything in life came down to control. Who controls what. And who. And why.

But control was a fleeting thing. You might have it one moment, but lose it the next. While you had it, you had to use it.

Or choose not to.

I took a step back from Jack.

"Not yet," I said, shaking my head. I had to wait just a little longer and hope another solution would present itself. It always did, right? I couldn't put Jack back in that prison; I couldn't do it. There had to be another answer.

Tasha could be wrong about what she believed would happen.

Theme of the night. What we believe in and what we're willing to sacrifice to defend those beliefs. Our lives, our freedom . . . but not someone else's.

"Sarah, what are you doing?" Jack demanded. "It's now or—"

"Three, two, one." Tasha counted down and sighed with relief. "It's dawn."

"—never," Jack finished.

Her tattoos darkened and solidified before my eyes as the remainder of Jack's faded away to nothing.

"The power is mine. All the magic of the Jacquerra Amulet belongs to me. Thank you all for your help." Tasha sounded like she was giving another rehearsed Oscar speech.

She'd won and we'd lost.

I'd made the wrong choice. Instead of damning Jack by putting him back into the amulet, I'd just put everyone at risk—here in the mansion and beyond. I'd failed because I'd clung to my beliefs. Whatever happened now was entirely my fault, and I had no idea what to do next . . .

A glass of water appeared out of thin air in my hand. I looked at it, frowning.

"Sarah, your dress . . ." Thierry said.

I glanced down at myself. My previously red dress was now a lovely forest green.

"What the . . . ?"

From the ceiling, or what seemed like the ceiling, Veronique's book fell and landed hard on the floor right in front of Tasha.

"The magic was delayed," I whispered.

The wishes I'd made earlier had just been granted. One for water, one for the color of my dress.

Two out of three.

I exchanged a tense look with Thierry.

"What is going on?" Tasha demanded.

I was the owner of the amulet. I hadn't meant to win it in the auction, but it was mine in a universal sense. My wishes were finally coming true.

And I had one more to go.

"Here, catch." I tossed the amulet at Tasha. She caught it automatically.

"Giving up?" She clutched it, smiling, as if she'd just won a valuable prize at the state fair. "I think that's a very good idea."

I shook my head. "Obviously, you don't know me very well. I don't give up. Not even when I probably should."

"Too bad for you, then."

"Too bad for me. Too bad for you."

Tasha didn't realize her eyes had turned a bright emerald green. She was full of djinn magic, therefore she reacted to the amulet the same way a real djinn would.

I hoped like hell this worked. "I wish for Jack to be free of the Jacquerra Amulet and for Tasha Evans to take his place, since she obviously wants to be a djinn so much she'd try to steal its magic."

She gasped and dropped the amulet, scrambling back from it as if it had suddenly burst into flame. "You can't wish for that!"

"I think I can. I get three wishes and that was number three." I stepped back from her until I felt Thierry behind me. "Be careful what you wish for, Tasha. You just might get it."

Already, her feet clad in the open-toed silver stilettos had turned to swirling green smoke. "No! Sebastien, do something. Help me!"

"Help you?" Sebastien repeated. "Why? Isn't this what you wanted? All the magic you can handle and true immortality? Got to say, it won't be as much fun as you thought it would be, trapped inside a tiny place for all of eternity. I should know."

She stared down at herself with horror, now smoke from the waist down. "No, I don't want this. Take it back! Take the wish back!"

There wasn't fear or sadness on her face, something that might have tweaked my sympathy a little, despite all the horrible things she was responsible for. There was only rage. Blame. Hate.

Proof that she wasn't that great of an actress after all.

"I'll be back and I will destroy you!" It was the last thing she screamed before turning fully to swirling green smoke. A moment later, all the smoke disappeared into the amulet.

Thierry moved toward the amulet, snatched it up from the floor, and slipped it into his inner jacket pocket. "No, Tasha, you won't be back."

I wasn't quite ready to celebrate yet. "Thierry, you're feeling . . . ?"

He met my eyes. "Much better now, thank you."

My heart lifted. "So glad to hear that."

I grabbed his face and kissed him hard. He pulled me closer and kissed me back, and I felt him smile against my lips.

"What would I do without you?" he asked.

"Let's find out the answer to that . . . never."

"A truly brilliant plan."

Veronique cleared her throat. I glanced at her over my shoulder and she gave me a pointed look. A "please stop kissing and untie us now" look.

So we did just that. Using Frederic's enchanted dagger that Thierry retrieved from his other pocket, but trying very hard not to cut anyone with it, he sliced through the bindings to free Veronique, Marcellus, and Melanie. They rubbed their raw wrists as the silver-infused ropes dropped away.

Sebastien and Jack stayed off to the side, giving us space to move.

"You all right?" I asked Melanie.

She nodded, looking at Thierry with trepidation. "He grabbed me and tied me up. You sure he's okay now?"

I studied Thierry for a moment. "Still a five-point-five?"

He considered this for a moment. "I'm down to a four. So, back at my normal level."

I cringed. "Your normal level is a four?"

"A very manageable four, believe me."

I glanced at Melanie. "He's fine."

"She wanted me to kill you," Thierry told the three of them. "But she didn't make it an order. I believe she wanted to do it herself once she came fully into her djinn powers. Let's be grateful she's now safely contained."

"You fooled her well," Marcellus said to Thierry. "I'm very impressed."

"Don't be. The spell worked. It was nearly impossible to resist her command."

"Then how did you manage it?"

He gave me a sidelong look. "Someone convinced me tonight that I needed to believe in myself as fully as she did. And she was right. I assumed I had no true control over my thirst at its worst, but I always have. And to harm someone I care about was not acceptable to me on any level. Once I realized that and fought past the first part of the spell, it was possible to resist the second part."

"In other words"—I looked up at Thierry with pride—"she didn't know who she was dealing with. A total badass master vampire."

He raised an eyebrow. "Badass?"

I nodded enthusiastically. "Yes, absolutely. The badassiest."

Sebastien had taken a seat on the unstained sofa and put his head in his hands.

"That was a dangerous move," Jack said to me as I met his gaze. "Did you know what you were doing?"

"Honestly?" I grimaced. "No, not even slightly."

"She stole all of the Jacquerra Amulet's magic from me." He looked down at his arms, now bare of any tattoos. "It's all gone."

My chest clenched at the thought that, in a weird way, Tasha had won. "I'm so sorry."

A grin spread over his face. "Don't be. That magic was a curse from a vengeful coven of witches that's been a heavy burden for well over a thousand years. I'm finally free, thanks to you."

Then it was good news. Hooray, magic-stealing evil actress! "So what are you now? Mortal?"

"Well, no." His grin widened. "I've always been more than that."

"Remember, Sarah, djinn are a form of demon," Thierry explained. "A group of troublemakers imprisoned by that original coven of witches."

Jack nodded. "You know what they say—Hell hath no fury like a coven of witches scorned. But that was a long time ago."

"I hope so." I poked him in his bare chest. "You better behave yourself, mister. And here's a question for you. What exactly does 'a form of demon' mean?"

"Nothing worth worrying about. I mean, unless you're a witch. We don't get along with witches."

"You're not going to turn evil, are you?"

"I was never evil. Just misunderstood, kind of like a vampire." Jack grabbed me and gave me a tight hug. "Thank you. Thank you so much for saving me. I won't forget it."

"You're very welcome." He released me and I looked at him quizzically. "By the way, what's your real name?"

He waved his hand. "It's kind of long and complicated. I think 'Jack' works for the next phase of my existence. I like it."

"It suits you." I glanced toward Sebastien, who looked up at me sheepishly through his fingers.

"I don't know what to do now," he said. "It was my fault. Everything. Everybody nearly died because . . . because . . ."

I sat down next to him. "Because you trusted someone who didn't deserve your trust. That doesn't make you the bad guy, Sebastien. It makes you someone who has hope in his heart, even after everything you've been through."

He let out a long, shaky sigh. "I thought she loved me."

"Tasha only loved herself."

"I'm such a fool." He stood up, raking his hands through his hair. Thierry drew closer and Sebastien flinched away from him. "And I don't even know what to say to you."

Thierry shook his head. "You don't have to say anything."

"I'm sorry. I'm so, so sorry I—"

"No. Don't. Let's put the past behind us. The future lies ahead and it's a clean slate for us both." Thierry extended his hand.

Sebastien looked at Thierry's hand for a long moment before he finally clasped it in his. He nodded. "That sounds good to me."

"This is so wonderful." Veronique came up to them, smiling broadly. "How it always should have been between you. We're a family again."

Marcellus stood by, watching Veronique very carefully. "I still don't understand my place in any of this."

That made two of us. And by the looks on Thierry's and Sebastien's faces, four of us.

"Who am I?" Marcellus continued. "I believed I was Marcellus Rousseau, as I have been all of my life, but this strange place makes no sense to me. The way you are all dressed is very odd. And I can't figure it out."

Veronique's expression was pinched. "Oh, darling . . ."

I heard a loud noise. Someone was yelling and banging on something. Hard.

"What the hell is that?" Melanie exclaimed.

"Some sort of warning signal that all Hell is about to break loose?" Sebastien said.

I grimaced. "Um, no. Actually, that would be Atticus."

Time to face the most powerful vampire on the vampire council.

Maybe Jack wouldn't be the only one to lose his head tonight.

Chapter 25

Both Thierry and Veronique accompanied me to the room in which Atticus was trapped. I fished the key out of my bra and inserted it into the lock of the chest.

"Atticus, you need to stay calm," I told him.

"And you need to let me out of here," he snarled. "Immediately!"

"Since you asked so nicely, okay." I turned the key.

He shoved the lid of the chest up and sprang out like a jack-in-the-box. His black hair was matted and sweaty, his face red, and his eyes wild.

"You!" He wheeled around to face me. "I warned you what I'd do to you when I got out."

The man who'd threatened my life to get Thierry to work for the Ring again was an intimidating creep at the best of times. At the moment, I would allow it since I myself would have hated to be locked in a tiny chest for a couple of hours. "Yeah, well, you'll feel better in a minute. I hope."

"De Bennicoeur, this woman is a detriment to your position with the Ring. She cannot continue to travel with you."

"Wrong." Thierry stood solidly next to me, his arms crossed over his chest. "She most certainly will."

"She is a troublemaker and a liability."

"She is an asset and my wife, today and always. And you will speak to her with respect. I swear, Atticus, if you ever, ever threaten her in any way again or even look at her with anything less than respect, you will regret it."

"Is that a threat?"

"You can take it however you like. You may have had me sign your contract, and I will hold true to that promise, but Sarah is now a part of that deal. A nonnegotiable part."

Atticus continued to look outraged. "She trapped me in a chest!"

"She saved your life."

Atticus blustered for a while longer, but finally calmed down enough to see logic. All this time he'd believed it was Thierry who'd killed the other elders. But earlier he'd heard Tasha's confession with his own ears and couldn't deny it.

She was deceitful, wily, and completely sociopathic. And now she'd been magically contained within the Jacquerra Amulet.

Thierry pulled the amulet out of his jacket pocket. "Take it."

He quickly explained what had happened with Tasha.

Atticus eyed it skeptically. "You're giving it to me without my having to take it."

"If you'd tried to take it, you would have failed," Thierry said simply. "However, I acquired it on behalf of the Ring. Despite any personal issues with you, I've come to believe that you are fully committed to the goals of the council, even if your methods have often been questionable. I'm giving you this as an act of faith."

"You have faith in me?"

"I didn't. But Sarah believes in you."

Atticus looked at me with shock. "You do?"

Believe in might be a bit of an overstatement, but I didn't correct him. "I believe down deep that you want to help people, not hurt them. But you need to stop being a bully. Asking for what you want instead of making threats and intimidating people works much better and makes fewer enemies. Just a friendly observation."

Frowning deeply, he fell silent before he finally took the amulet from Thierry.

"Very good. Well done, de Bennicoeur. And . . . Sarah. I will store Tasha somewhere she won't be able to cause trouble again." He glanced at Veronique as if noticing her standing there for the first time. "Do you have anything to add?"

She shook her head. "Not really."

"Then what are you doing here?"

"I was here to offer additional protection in case you chose the wrong path, Atticus."

"Additional protection? You would have, what, killed me?"

That earned him the edge of a smile on her beautiful face. "Oh, darling, no. Violence has never been my style. But I would have helped to get you back into that rather uncomfortable-looking chest."

"Mmm." Atticus pursed his lips. "That won't be necessary. But now I must make some phone calls and figure out how best to go about explaining the disappearance of Tasha Evans to the world, as well as

Jacob Nelson. They were two very high-profile people. Not to mention the other casualties tonight."

"It's been an eventful night," I said. "Thanks for handling the paperwork."

He swept his gaze over me, as if appraising my current worth. "Perhaps I was wrong about you. Tasha wanted me dead and your actions may have thwarted that."

"You're welcome."

That reply got me another studious look. It wasn't with the interest of earlier in the evening; this one held much more distaste. Which was all right with me. Just because I didn't think he was totally evil didn't mean I wanted to invite him out to a celebratory dinner.

"So you two are happy together," Atticus said after a moment, still with disbelief coating his words. "What you told me earlier was only a lie, Thierry."

Thierry and I shared a glance. "Yes, that's right," he replied.

"*Happy.*" He frowned as if the concept of this escaped him. "With a *fledgling*. Who would have guessed it?"

Leaving us with that canny observation, he pulled his cell phone out of his pocket and began making calls now that there was reception again.

"I can't believe you gave him the amulet," Veronique said with disapproval as we moved away from Atticus's presence.

"I don't want it anywhere near me," Thierry replied. "And I know Atticus won't risk summoning Tasha out of it for fear she'll escape. I have faith that he will put it somewhere very safe for the indefinite future."

"And what about Frederic's dagger?" I asked.

"That is a more delicate matter. We saw for ourselves that it can bestow true immortality. That is a dangerous goal that many might want to achieve. I will have it destroyed."

His words surprised me. "Dangerous? But wouldn't that be a good thing? Living forever and not fearing death?"

"We already live forever, darling, if we're very careful," Veronique said. "But true immortality is a curse. Not just hundreds or thousands of years, but millions. Trillions. Forever is far too much to contemplate, even for someone like me."

She had an excellent point. The idea of forever was kind of mind-blowing. I think I'll stick with the indefinite ending of a normal, run-of-the-mill vampire, thanks.

Suddenly I felt rather sorry for Tasha.

Be careful what you wish for, indeed.

We headed back downstairs and found Melanie consoling Sebastien. He seemed open to her attention, and she'd even coaxed a smile back to his face.

Maybe they wouldn't need my matchmaking skills at all.

Jack gave me another hug. "It's time for me to leave."

"Where are you going?" I asked.

"I have absolutely no idea." But he grinned as if that wasn't a bad thing. I noticed that the red line around his throat had disappeared. He was whole again, the damage Tasha had done now healed. "But I figure Los Angeles is a great place to start. Remember, though, I owe you one. You saved me when I didn't think it was possible to be saved."

"You were worth it. Have fun—but not too much fun, okay? I still don't totally understand the 'a sort of demon' thing."

I watched as he departed through the front doors. He didn't ask for any money or any help, but he practically glowed with hope as he waved good-bye to us.

Actually . . . yeah, I think he *was* glowing a little bit in the early-morning light. Definitely not just a mortal, that was for sure.

When I returned to the parlor, the first thing I saw was Veronique standing at the doorway with her hand over her mouth, her eyes wide. I followed her line of sight to Marcellus, who'd sat down on a large chair and was currently reading her memoir, quickly flicking through the pages.

"What is he doing?" She closed the distance between them and snatched the book away from him.

Marcellus looked up at her, his face a mask of confusion. "Is this all true?"

"Oh, darling, you shouldn't be reading that."

"Did I die like it says? But—if I died, how am I here? How is this possible?"

She wrung her hands. "I didn't want to have to tell you. I've been waiting all this time, not sure what would happen next. I thought you might disappear, but you haven't. You're still here. You're different from what you once were, but you're also completely the same. You are my Marcellus from that book brought to life."

"From this book?" He frowned. "What you're saying . . . how is this possible?"

"Magic made it possible."

Marcellus shook his head. "I'm not even real, then. I'm a figment of your imagination given breath."

He pushed the book aside and stormed out of the room.

She didn't chase after him. I exchanged a worried look with Thierry and he turned to follow after Marcellus. I drew Veronique into a corner of the large parlor.

Her expression remained calm, her chin raised. She didn't look upset at all; she looked resigned.

"It's expected," she said with a nod. "I'm sure it's quite a shock to him."

I had no idea what to say to help, but I had to try. "Of course. I mean, it's not every day you realize you're nothing but a fictional character."

"He is different from the Marcellus I knew in real life, of course. I took certain liberties with his less savory characteristics." She sighed. "For example, I deleted the part where he was constantly unfaithful to me."

"The delete key does wonders," I agreed.

"This Marcellus is wholly devoted to me and only me. He'd never even want to look at another woman."

"It's a perfectly respectable edit."

She met my eyes and reached down to clutch my hand in hers. "I have no time for a relationship, especially one with an updated version of someone I loved a long time ago. I have far too much else to do." She nodded as if she'd managed to convince herself that this was the right response. "But, Sarah, I did want to tell you that I am so very happy for you."

"For me?"

"All this time, I'll admit, I belittled your relationship with my hus—" She paused as if to correct herself. "With Thierry. But to see you together, to see how you believe in him no matter what happens. You love him so much—as much as he loves you." She smiled, and her eyes had become shiny. "It warms my heart. I'm glad he found you. He deserves to be happy after all these years."

I swear, I'd never have thought I'd see the day that Veronique admitted that she believed in Thierry and me like this.

"I appreciate that more than you know." I hugged her, my own heart warm from her words. Veronique didn't lie about stuff like this. She saw the truth.

Although, perhaps not her own truth.

"Your own soul mate just walked back into your life," I told her. "And he's a damn miracle looking you directly in the face. Do not even try to tell me you're going to let him walk away."

"Soul mate?" She shook her head. "I don't believe in such nonsense. Marcellus was my first love, but that was a long time ago. This—this manifestation isn't even him."

"I don't think you really believe that. Look, I know you're jaded. At your age, no offense, it would be hard not to be. You're a survivor and you don't believe in love anymore. Well, get over it. A little while after I first met Thierry you told me that when the world's gone mad and you're feeling really lost, that's when you have to trust your heart to lead you where you need to go."

Her brows went up. "I said that?"

"Yes. And at the time, I thought it was kind of lame. But you know what? It's also completely true. Trust your heart, Veronique. Take it from me—it never lies."

She stared at me as if I was speaking a different language. And then a smile touched her lips. She grabbed me and planted a kiss on both of my cheeks.

"Thank you, my darling. You are not nearly as silly and naive as I always thought you were."

She ran out of the parlor.

"Gee . . . thanks?" I laughed and followed her.

Marcellus stood at the open door next to Thierry, who was talking to him. Marcellus had his arms crossed over his chest, his face a mask of despair. He looked up as Veronique appeared.

"I may not be the man you once fell in love with," he said, his voice hollow. "But I stand before you with my heart on my sleeve. If I'm not real, then what I feel can't be possible, because *it* is real. I love you, Veronique. You are my other half. Please give me a chance to show you that we were destined to be together again."

Tears now streamed down her cheeks. Had I ever seen Veronique cry before? I honestly didn't think so.

"You're real, my darling. I didn't want to believe it, but you are. And I love you, too."

They embraced and he kissed her. Seriously, it was like something out of a movie.

"Where shall we go, my love?" Veronique asked him.

"It doesn't matter," he told her, "as long as you're by my side."

"You know . . ." Thierry drew up next to me and took my hand in his. "I couldn't have said it better myself."

I looked up at him, so relieved that we'd made it through this night even stronger than we'd been when we arrived. Funny how a few hours can change so much. "You and me, what do we have . . . forty-nine years and eleven months of servitude to the Ring left? And I have a funny feeling Atticus isn't going to be in the mood to promote you anytime soon."

"You never know what the future will hold."

"No, you really don't. Except I know one thing yours will hold, if I can make a wild guess."

"What's that?"

"Me." I grinned.

He smiled and drew me closer to him. "Even if that future will have more vampires, witches, were-wolves, ghosts, and other sundry creatures giving us a difficult time whenever possible?"

"Things like that keep an immortal life interesting, Mr. de Bennicoeur."

"Indeed, they do, Mrs. de Bennicoeur."

I didn't know where life would take us next, or what adventures lay ahead, but I wasn't lying about where I wanted to be. Wherever I went I'd be perfectly happy, as long as we were together.

Call me a hopeless romantic, but I considered that the best ending, ever.

Read on for a look back at
the first Immortality Bites Mystery,

Blood Bath & Beyond

Available now from Obsidian!

The fangs don't get nearly as much attention as you'd think.

Your average, everyday person doesn't notice that they're sharper than normal human canines. If they did, they'd have to deal with the possibility that vampires really exist. It's a survival instinct on their part, culminating from centuries of living side by side with something they'd prefer to think of as a fictional predatory monster. Or, more recently, as an eternally sparkling teenager.

Real vampires make up approximately 0.001 percent of the population—that's one in a thousand. So, worldwide, there are about six million vampires.

Humans just don't see us. It does help that, despite what you might have heard, we can go outside into the sunshine on a lovely early June day like today without turning into a pile of ashes. We blend in with regular human society just fine and dandy.

It's kind of like we're invisible.

Someone bashed into me when I glanced down at the screen of my phone as I walked down the busy sidewalk.

"Hey!" the woman snarled. "Watch where you're going, you dumb bitch!"

"Bite me," I replied sweetly, then added under my breath, "or I might bite you."

She gave me the finger, stabbing it violently in my direction as if it were a tiny, flesh-colored sword.

Okay, maybe we're not *totally* invisible.

I couldn't help that I had a natural-born talent to rub people the wrong way. It had very little to do with me being a vampire and more to do with me just being . . . me. I liked to think it was simply part of my charm.

I looked bleakly at the phone again. No messages. No calls. It felt like everyone I knew had recently deserted me. It wasn't far from the truth, actually. Last month, my parents had moved to Florida to a retirement community. Two weeks ago, my best male friend, George, had headed for Hawaii to open a surf shop after he won a small fortune in a local lottery. And now, my best girlfriend and her husband were in the process of moving to British Columbia so she could take a job in cosmetics management.

"We'll totally stay in touch," Amy said to me at the airport before she got on her flight an hour ago. I'd met her there to say a last good-bye.

I hugged her fiercely. "Of course we will."

Her husband stood nearby, giving me the evil eye like he usually did. We'd never really gotten along all that well. You win some, you lose some. "Are you finished yet? We're going to miss our flight."

I forced a smile. "I'm even going to miss *you*, Barry."

He just looked at his wristwatch.

Amy smiled brightly. "This is a new beginning, Sarah. For both of us. We have to embrace change."

I hated change.

I did hope to see her again soon, not too far into the future.

The future was something I thought about a lot these days. After all, as a fledgling vampire, sired less than seven months ago, I had a lot of future to look forward to. I just hoped it wouldn't suck too much.

Yes, that was me. Sarah Dearly, immortal pessimist. I had to turn my frown upside down. Right now, I was so far down in the dumps that the raccoons had arrived and were starting to sniff around. Metaphorically speaking, of course.

It seemed as if new opportunities and new adventures had been presented to everyone but me, like they'd won the lottery—*literally* in one case—and I'd mistakenly put my ticket in the wash and now couldn't even read the numbers.

"You look sad," someone said.

I glanced over my shoulder, surprised to see a clown standing at the side of the street holding a bunch of balloons.

White makeup, poufy costume covered in colorful polka dots. Red hair. A hat with a fake flower springing out of it. Big red nose. The works.

It was like a bad omen. Clowns scared the crap out of me.

"Sad? Who, me?" I said warily, slipping my phone back in my shoulder bag. "Nah, I'm just melancholy today. There's a difference, you know. Please don't murder me."

"Somebody needs a happy happy balloon to make her happy happy." He handed me a yellow ribbon tied to a shiny red balloon. I looked up at it.

"Yes," I said. "This will make all the difference in

the world. Thank you so much. Now life is happy happy for me again."

The clown glared at me. "No reason to be sarcastic, lady."

"I don't need a reason."

"The balloon's five bucks."

"Three."

"Four."

"Sold." I grinned, then fished into my purse and pulled out the money. "Thanks so much, Bozo."

"It's Mr. Chuckles."

"Whatever."

The balloon did cheer me up more than I would have guessed. It reminded me of going to the National Exhibition with my mother every fall when I was a kid. Popcorn, cotton candy, hot dogs, and balloons. High-calorie memories with a little bit of helium and latex thrown in for good measure. Those were good times.

I'd needed the walk to clear my head. My head was officially cleared, so I returned to the huge luxury townhome I shared with my fiancé and let myself in.

Immediately, I sensed there was something different there. A big clue to this was the large black suitcase placed by the front door.

I heard Thierry on the phone, speaking French to someone. He was fluent, since he was originally from France centuries ago.

Yes, my fiancé was significantly older than me—by about six hundred years or so.

Some of the words I understood:

"Aujourd'hui," which I knew meant "today."

"Seul," which meant "alone."

"D'accord," which meant "alrighty."

"*Importante*" . . . well, that one didn't really need a translator.

Thierry entered the front foyer with his phone pressed to his left ear. He stopped when he saw me standing there gaping at him.

"*À bientôt*, Bernard." He slipped the phone into the inside pocket of his black suit jacket. "Sarah, I was about to call you. I'm glad you've returned."

He didn't have an accent. His English was flawless, since he'd spoken it for at least five hundred years.

Thierry de Bennicoeur appeared to be in his mid-thirties. He was six feet tall, had black hair that was usually brushed back from his handsome face, and piercing gray eyes that felt like they could see straight through you clear to the other side. He always dressed in black Hugo Boss suits, which wasn't the most imaginative wardrobe choice, but looked consistently perfect on him anyway. He was, in a word, a total fox. Even after all the time we'd spent together, there was no doubt in my mind about that.

Some people perceived him to be cold and unemotional, but I knew the truth. That facade was for protection only. Down deep, Thierry was fire and passion. Only . . . it was *really* down deep. Most people would never see that side of him and I was okay with that. I had the rock on my finger that proved I *had* seen the fire and hadn't been burned yet.

However, I had to admit, that suitcase was causing a few painful sparks to fly up in my general direction.

"What's going on?" I asked cautiously. "What's with the luggage?"

"I have to go somewhere."

"Where? And . . . when?"

The line of his jaw tightened. "I've been called

upon to meet with someone about important Ring business in Las Vegas."

The Ring was the vampire council. Thierry was the original founder of the organization that tracked any potential vampiric issues worldwide and did what they could to neutralize them. He'd left a century ago after dealing with some personal issues and he hadn't looked back since. The Ring had carried on without his input or influence.

"What business?" I asked.

"I've been offered a job with them. One I can't decline."

My eyes widened. "What kind of job?"

"Consultant."

"What do you mean, you can't decline it?"

He hesitated. "They made me an offer I couldn't refuse."

"Who were you just talking to, Don Corleone?"

He raised a dark eyebrow. "His name is Bernard DuShaw. He was the most recent of several people I've spoken with over the last couple of hours. It's his position I would be taking over now that he's retiring."

I thought of my parents settling in to Florida's sand and sunshine now that they'd reached their retirement years. "He's immortal, isn't he? He doesn't ever have to retire."

"After a contracted term with the Ring, one is permitted to leave to pursue other interests if one wishes to. He wishes to."

I tried to breathe normally. Contrary to one of many popular myths about vampires, we needed to do that regularly. "Okay. Well, the universe does work in mysterious ways. I guess this isn't a bad thing. I think you'd be a great asset for them. Keep them from making any mistakes or judging anyone too harshly without a proper assessment. So . . . you're going today to meet with Bernard about this job?"

"Yes."

"And when will you be back?"

"Perhaps you should sit down, Sarah."

"I don't want to sit down." My anxiety spiked. "You are coming back, aren't you?"

His expression tensed. "I'm sorry, but I don't believe I'll be returning to Toronto. The position calls for constant travel. I won't be able to stay in one place for very long during my term as consultant."

I tried to absorb all of this, but it was too much all at once. "How long is a term?"

He didn't speak for a moment. "Fifty years."

I just looked at him, momentarily rendered speechless by this unexpected news. Silence stretched between us.

His gaze moved to my balloon. "What's this?"

My mouth had gone dry. "My happy happy balloon. I got it from a clown named Mr. Chuckles."

His lips curved at the edges. "I thought you were going to the airport."

"I did."

"You stopped by a circus on the way home?"

"Thierry," I said sharply. "What is going on? How can you just leave? Fifty years? It sounds like a prison sentence, not a new job. Are you saying . . . Are you saying that—" I didn't want to speak my thoughts aloud. After everyone else I loved put thousands of miles between me and them, perhaps I should have expected this. But I hadn't. This was a complete and total shock.

Everyone was leaving me. And now Thierry was joining the list.

"Sarah—"

"I heard you on the phone. You said *seul*, which means you're going alone."

"That's what they want. This job requires focus and twenty-four/seven availability. I assumed you wouldn't want to travel so much, never knowing where you're going next. There's a great deal of uncertainty involved with this job."

"This job that you can't say no to for some mysterious reason. A job that you're going to be doing for half a century all by yourself, with no prior warning." I crossed my arms tightly. Everything about this made me ill. "You know, maybe this job came at just the right time for you to change your mind about being with—"

"Please don't finish that sentence." He took me by my shoulders, gazing fiercely into my eyes. "All I want is for you to be happy—don't you know that by now?"

I swallowed hard. "The clown thought a balloon would make me happy."

"And did it?"

"For a couple minutes."

He looked up at it. "It is a nice balloon."

"Screw the balloon." My throat felt so tight it was difficult to speak.

Thierry's and my path hadn't been an easy one, not since the very first moment we met. It wasn't every day a twenty-eight-year-old fledgling hooked up with a six-hundred-year-old master vampire—we were so completely different in temperament and personality it was frequently glaring and often problematic. But we had and it felt right, yet somehow I knew, down deep, that it might not last forever. Forever was a very long time when you're a vampire.

Just because I knew it, didn't mean my heart didn't break into a million pieces at the thought of losing him.

I tried to compose myself as much as possible after realizing that someone else I cared about would be moving away from me. This, though . . . *this* stung even more than saying good-bye to Amy. This felt permanent. Forever.

I wanted to be cool about getting dumped for a "job he couldn't refuse," but I wasn't sure if I had it in me.

"I get it, Thierry. You don't want to be distracted by someone who has a tendency to get into trouble at the drop of a hat. I can take a hint. I'm a liability. You want me to stay here."

He let out a small, humorless laugh. "What I want is irrelevant. Can you honestly say you'd leave behind your life here in Toronto, everything you've ever known and most of your possessions, in order to accompany me on a job that will be frequently boring for you; one that will mean you'll never know where your true home is?"

I stared up at him. "Are those rhetorical questions?"

"No, they're real questions." His brows drew together. "Would you come with me if I asked you to?"

I let go of the balloon, which floated up to the high ceiling of the front foyer before catching on a sharp crystal from the chandelier. It popped on contact.

I grabbed the lapels of his black jacket. "In a heartbeat."

Something I rarely saw slid behind his gray eyes then, something warm and utterly vulnerable. "Then I suggest you pack a bag. Our flight leaves in three hours."

I looked at him, stunned. *"Our* flight?"

"I wasn't sure you'd be open to this abrupt change, but I did purchase you a ticket just in case."

My heart lifted. "You're so prepared. Just like a Boy Scout."

"I try." A smile played at his lips. "I just hope that this trip doesn't make you change your mind about me."

"Don't be ridiculous." My smile only grew wider before faltering just a little. "But I thought they wanted you to come alone. Won't they give you a hard time about this?"

"If they want me for this job, then they will get my fiancée as well. They'll just have to deal with it." He took my face between his hands. "I love you, Sarah. Never doubt it."

He kissed me and I couldn't think of any happy happy balloon that could make me this happy happy.

Change was good. I liked change.